MW01235040

*This book is dedicated to Angie
who kept wondering what
Louise would do next.*

Special Thanks

I would like to thank my editor and publisher, Anne Kaylor, for her support, encouragement, and sharp eye for the passive verb. Also Phil Arnold, Pat Chatman, and Mary Jane Gisiano, who read advance copies of this novel and provided their thoughts and insights, and Jim Saunders, who helped guide me through the stock market crash of 1929.

As always, continuing love and affection to my wonderful wife, Vicki, my First Reader, Favorite Muse, and Greatest Cheerleader. May my best plots always be hatched while sitting with you and a glass of wine in the front porch swing.

CONTENTS

Although certain characters within this novel are based on real-life members of the author's family, this work is a fictionalized account of their lives. The views and opinions expressed are those of the fictional characters only and do not necessarily reflect or represent the views and opinions held by individuals on which those characters are based.

PART ONE

THE ROARING TWENTIES

CHAPTER 1

L ouise stood dispassionately in front of her father's coffin, lacking even a sense of relief at his passing. Will had seen 1921 arrive while confined to his bed. Subdued, almost repentant, he'd been so unlike the uncaring, abusive father she'd always known. Even now, he looked out of character surrounded by the white satin fabric, his hands crossed over his chest as if praying. *You'd better be praying, Daddy, praying for anything that'll cut down on your burning time in Hell.*

As if captured in a sepia photograph, the lighting in the funeral home cast a sickly yellow glow. The flowers—what few there were—filled her nose with a sweetly cloying fragrance that reminded her of dime-store perfume. She had provided the family flowers, a blanket of red roses. The city clerk's office sent a potted lily, and, as Louise stood there, another arrangement arrived, carried in by one of the funeral home staff. She walked over and bent to read the accompanying card: *From your loving stepdaughters, Sylvia, Edith, and Kaye.*

Louise could hardly believe what she read. As she straightened, she felt eyes boring holes into her back. Turning away from the flowers and her dead father, she spied her three stepsisters standing at the rear of the funeral home's "reposing room."

They wore dark dresses, as did Louise, in keeping with the expected image of a mourning family, though in Louise's mind, she'd be hard pressed to name anyone genuinely distressed by her father's death. It wasn't notable. If anything, it was meaningful for only a few, most of whom were probably relieved.

Sylvia, the dark-haired, oldest stepsister, glared at her, joined by Edith, the pudgy middle child. Only Kaye—fifteen, close to Henry's age—wore a faint smile. Louise had not seen any of the girls since the trial but remembered well the hatred in the oldest girl's eyes as she implicated Louise in the death of her mother. The charges had been dropped after Jesse, the maid and house-keeper, confessed to the crime, but ill feelings apparently still existed—at least with Sylvia and Edith. *Not surprising.* Sylvia had always done all the talking for the girls, and most of the thinking, too. Louise steeled herself and walked to where the trio waited.

She stopped a few feet from them, trying her best to shield the discomfort she felt. "Hello, Sylvia. Hello, Edith." For Kaye, who still wore that faint smile, Louise managed one of her own. "Hello, Kaye. It's so nice of you to come." The two older girls exchanged a glance and strode past Louise toward the coffin. Kaye held out her hand, and, although surprised at the young girl's openness, Louise grasped it warmly.

Kaye, still petite and blond, seemed to possess poise beyond her years. "I'm so sorry about your father. He and I were never close, but I think, in his own way, he respected you."

Louise wasn't sure how true that was but appreciated the kind words. "Thank you for being here today, Kaye, and speaking with me. I'm sorry we were never able to talk before."

Louise watched as Kaye's gaze wandered to where her sisters stood staring into the coffin. "I'm sorry, too. Mother and Sylvia, they didn't…" Color rose in the young girl's cheeks as she looked down at her shoes. "I guess what I really want to say, what I've felt inside for so long, is that I'm ashamed of the way you and your family were treated. I loved my mother but didn't always agree with her. Unfortunately, I never spoke up about what I felt. I was a coward."

So was my father. "Don't feel bad about that. Adults seldom listen to their children."

The smile on Kaye's face widened. "I don't know about that. From what I've heard, I think *your* mother does."

Maybe, Louise thought, *but not so much as you might think.* "I heard you and your sisters were staying with an aunt in East Ridge. Are you all doing well?"

"I'm still there, at least until I finish school. Sylvia and Edith have jobs now and live in a small house near the hosiery factory." Kaye again glanced at her sisters. "I suppose I should join them." She grasped Louise's hand once more. "I apologize for my sisters' rudeness. They feel they've been cheated out of what they imagined to be my mother's inheritance."

Louise opened her mouth to speak, but before she could, Kaye continued. "I don't feel that way at all. If anyone was cheated, it was you and your brother, Henry, and your mother. You deserve anything you've gotten and more." She leaned forward and planted a brief kiss on Louise's cheek. "I'm not sure when I might see you again, Louise, but I wish you and your family all the best." She left Louise standing in the rear of the room and joined her sisters at the coffin.

Louise touched the place where Kaye had kissed her and marveled at how things sometimes worked out. She couldn't help wondering how everything might have been different if her stepmother Maude and her father hadn't died. She'd be pretty much the same, she figured, though not so well off financially—but Kaye—how might she have turned out living under the same roof with what Jesse had sometimes referred to as the nest of vipers. Maybe Kaye—possibly all the girls—were luckier than they knew.

As the organ music started, Louise looked around the room. *Not many mourners.* Her husband, Murray, and son, Bobby, sat in the front pew on the left. A few men from the city offices sat together—holdovers, Louise guessed, from Will's high-roller city council days. In the back, near the door, See-Boy's father, Lawrence, sat by himself. Why he had come she wasn't sure—there was certainly no love lost between him and Will—perhaps out of some sort of allegiance to the family. See-Boy and Pearl, whom she enjoyed seeing under any circumstances, had not shown. Fannie had not come, either. Louise wouldn't allow it, for fear her mother might disrupt the meager service by breaking into laughter.

Oddly, that thought almost caused her to laugh, but she disguised it as a cough. She felt in her pocket for the money she'd brought to pay the minister, one recommended by the funeral home to say a few vague words about a man he never set eyes on alive. *A sad testament to anyone's life,* she thought, remembering the short time she'd spent with her father after he'd been diagnosed with cancer and she'd brought him into her home. She'd tried to find a reason to forgive him for all the cruelties he had heaped upon her and her mother and brother.

But she couldn't. *You could patch up whatever might be broken,* she reasoned, *but if you were there when it happened, you'd always know in your heart where the fault lines lay.*

She took a deep breath then found her way to the family pew, where she sat beside her husband and son.

CHAPTER 2

After being confined to bed rest, Louise's father had required a fair amount of her time. Fannie refused to tend to him and Murray still had the Chattanooga to Cincinnati Railway Express run that kept him out of town four nights a week. That left only her and Henry, and Louise would never subject her brother to the possibility of verbal abuse from her father, even as the old man lay dying.

Now fourteen, Henry had begun seeing a psychiatrist twice a month and seemed to be doing better. There'd been no trouble at school, and Henry had lately become interested in music. Louise hoped that interest continued. To encourage him, she'd purchased a gramophone and taken him to Miller Brothers' Department Store so he could choose a few favorite recordings. Henry's preferences ran to jazz, and especially music featuring the drummer, Gene Krupa. She couldn't tell if it was the music or his father's death that brightened Henry's outlook. It mattered only that her brother seemed genuinely happy for the first time in years.

At any rate, Will's passing left Louise with time on her hands. Schmidt Enterprises, which her father had signed over to her, consisted solely of rental houses, twelve at present, and, while providing a modest income, really didn't require much in the way of daily business dealings. See-Boy and Lawrence handled maintenance, and See-Boy's wife, Pearl, kept the books.

Louise lit a Lucky Strike, shook the match out, and dropped it into an ashtray. It was a warm morning for April, and she'd opened the window over the sink to let in a little air. Fannie walked into the kitchen wearing a green plaid flannel housecoat and stifling a yawn. She went directly to the cabinet, then to the stove-top percolator, where she poured a cup of coffee.

"Good morning, Mother. I was just sitting here thinking how little I have to do since Daddy died. The house rental business practically runs itself."

Fannie snorted and sat down beside Louise at the table. "It's a good thing for us it's like that. Any business requiring hard work your father would have run into the ground long ago. Thank goodness we had Lawrence and See-Boy maintaining those houses. They would have fallen in on themselves if left up to Will."

She reached across the table and pulled a cigarette from Louise's pack, then lit it and released a plume of gray smoke into the air. "What would you want to do, anyway?"

Louise sighed. "I don't know. It's just that Bobby will be starting school this fall. He'll be gone much of the day. I feel like I should be doing *something*."

"You've been caring for somebody most of your life, Louise. Before Will, me and Henry, and now Bobby. The only difference is money coming in. You don't have to slave away to keep us happy." She smiled. "Enjoy life. Lord knows, you deserve to."

Louise stubbed out her cigarette in the ashtray. *There's a certain irony here,* she thought. *Mother chose both my father and my husband. I suppose I should be indebted to her in a way. What is it they say? All's well that ends well?* "I guess you're right. I have a wonderful husband, a wonderful son, and a business that makes money." *So why do I feel like I need to do more?*

A warm breeze stirred the white chintz curtains hanging from the open window, and Louise's gaze drifted in that direction. From outside, the voices of Bobby and a number of his neighborhood friends reached her ears. Happy sounds. She rose, walked over to the sink, and looked out at the red and blue painted metal swing set Will purchased for Bobby a few months ago. Bobby, dressed in denim overalls, watched as four, five, and six-year-olds queued up to take turns on either of the two swings or the trapeze.

"Come look, Mother. Bobby's sharing his swing set with the other children. Isn't that sweet?"

Fannie joined her at the window. "Yes, he's a sweet one, that boy, and smart as a whip. He'll shine in school this fall, too, and likely be reading before that."

"Already is," Louise said. "We just finished *The Adventures of Tom Sawyer* a few nights back, and he often read along with me." Louise turned away from the window and leaned with her hips against the counter. "I remember when Murray and I named him. I'd found a list of boys' names and their meanings. His means 'bright fame.'"

Fannie turned on the cold tap and extinguished her cigarette in the water, then tossed the butt into the trash. "He's definitely bright; maybe he'll be famous, too. Maybe get his picture on the cover of *Life* magazine."

"I don't care about that," Louise said, "as long as he's safe and happy."

Murray returned home that evening, and, as they readied themselves for bed, Louise recounted what she and her mother had discussed that morning about Bobby's intelligence and potential.

"There's something…" Murray stepped out of their bedroom and returned a moment later with a leather-bound book in his hand. "If I can just find it." He flipped page after page and finally stopped. "Here it is—a Chinese proverb from long ago. It says, 'A child is not a vase to be filled, but a fire to be kindled.'" He closed the book. "I'm not sure, but I think that means we need to be the kindling for whatever fire he has in his heart. He could be the next Warren G. Harding or Andrew Carnegie, and who knows what else."

Louise nodded. "He just needs our help."

Murray smiled and held out his hand in a sweeping gesture toward Louise. "Think about it. One day you might be introduced as the mother of the president."

Louise laughed. "Wouldn't that just be something?"

CHAPTER 3

The early morning sun shone brightly through the kitchen window as Bobby wolfed down eggs and grits. He planned to spend his day, most of it anyway, in the backyard with the neighborhood children, parceling out playtime on the swing set. The idea came to him after he and his mother read the book about Tom Sawyer. Tom tricked his friends into painting a fence by telling them what fun it was. Bobby's idea wasn't quite the same—the swing set was truly fun—but the payoff proved even better.

He felt the lump of pennies in his trouser pocket. He'd only started the business yesterday morning and already he had nearly a dime's worth of copper coins. He wondered idly as he chewed his last bite of food just how much money it would take to build—or have one built for him; he was only six, after all—the one thing he wanted most in the world.

The steady drone of an approaching airplane interrupted his thoughts. He tore his napkin from where it was tucked into his collar, pushed back from the table, and nearly spilled the glass of milk beside his plate.

"Where on earth are you off to, young man?" His grandmother asked as he ran for the back door.

"I'll be right back. I just want to—"

The rest of his words forgotten, he bounded down the steps, shielded his eyes from the sun, and scanned the sky. His search rewarded, he spotted the aircraft's approach on a line almost dead center over the two large trees in the backyard. It flew lower than he first thought, and he began to jump up and down, waving frantically to get the pilot's attention. As he watched, the pilot saluted from the open cockpit and waggled the plane's double-decker wings. Bobby kept waving as the aircraft roared directly over his head and disappeared behind the roof of his house.

Fannie's voice called out, "Bobby, you need to come back and finish your milk."

He turned and strode back to the porch steps. "I'd like to fly in an airplane one day."

"God help us," his grandmother said. "You'd most likely crash and burn to death. I pray you never leave the ground."

As he climbed the steps, Bobby grinned. Grownups always fretted over their kids. When his grandfather bought him the swing set, his mother and grandmother worried he'd fall and break an arm or leg. As yet, he had not broken a single bone, and, since he had the only swing set in the neighborhood, he also made money.

He didn't bother to sit down at the table, but drained his milk standing at the sink. His friends would finish breakfast soon. He needed to get ready for the day's business.

A t supper, Bobby struggled with his pork chop, knocking food from his plate as he tried to cut the meat. Henry laughed until Bobby's grandmother looked sharply in his uncle's direction.

"Do I have to eat this?" Bobby asked. "I'm messing up the rest of my food."

"Yes," his mother said. "You need meat as well as vegetables. It will help you build muscles and grow tall."

His father said, "I'll cut it for you if you want me to."

"No thank you, Daddy." Bobby rested his hands in his lap for a moment, staring at the chop. "If I eat it, can I go down to Miss Pearl and See-Boy's house after supper?" He'd thought about it earlier and figured if anybody would know how much his idea might cost, See-Boy would.

His mother and father looked at each other for a few seconds, then his father shrugged. "It's only a few blocks, and it'll be light outside for another hour or two."

"I suppose it'll be all right," his mother said. "I know how much See-Boy enjoys seeing you. But stay on the sidewalks and don't be gone long."

"I won't." Bobby picked up his chop with two hands and bit off a piece. He glanced around the table, enjoying the feeling of the pork grease on his lips. "I'm eating it," he said, smiling broadly.

Henry laughed again, but this time Fannie didn't reprimand him. Bobby's mother grinned as his father turned away and shook his head. Bobby thought he might be grinning, too.

CHAPTER 4

S ee-Boy nailed the last sheet of tar paper into place and worked his way back to the ladder. Tomorrow, if he had the time, he'd start on the shingles. Within a week, the maintenance shed should be finished. An unremarkable wooden structure, each side wall ran roughly twenty feet long and eight feet high.

Until Miss Louise had agreed to fund the shed, he and his father, Lawrence, had worked on sawhorses in their backyard. Now, not only would they have a place to work out of the weather, they'd also have a facility to store tools and supplies.

And whatever else needed to be stored. The beginning of the decade had brought the Volstead Act and Prohibition. Problem being, folks who were going to drink could always find a way to get their alcohol. It was the law of supply and demand, and he was well acquainted with the demand—most he knew liked to have a little snort now and then—and he felt pretty sure he could supply it.

Leery of the idea at first, his daddy came around after See-Boy put forth a pretty convincing argument. Pearl being pregnant hadn't hurt either. Raising a child took more money than they brought in between them, regardless of their good fortune and Miss Louise's generosity. *Best thing that happened to them was when old Mister Will placed his business interests in Miss Louise's hands.* He was a hateful man and a bigot if ever there was one. Probably best he'd died before Prohibition came along else he might have ended up one of See-Boy's best customers. *Probably want a house discount, though.*

A tiny voice drifted up to the roof as See-Boy checked to make sure he hadn't forgotten any of his tools.

"Hey, See-Boy, what you doing up there?"

He looked down to where Bobby stood at the foot of the ladder. "Well, hey there, little man. Your momma know you're here?"

"Yep, Daddy does, too. They let me come because I finished my pork chop."

See-Boy gathered up his hammer and his pouch of roofing nails and began to back down the ladder. "You'd best back off a bit, Bobby. I don't want to drop anything on your head." As he stepped off the last rung, he said, "So you got to come 'cause you ate your pork chop, huh? Well, that makes sense to me if not to anybody else. Come on inside here, and let's have ourselves a conversation."

He pulled open the single door to the shed and yanked the pull-chain on a bare lightbulb hanging from the ceiling.

Bobby followed on his heels and turned in a slow circle, looking all around the shed's interior. "Gosh, See-Boy, this is nice."

"Uh-huh, me and Daddy will have a decent place to work now." He placed a hand on Bobby's shoulder and walked him over to a workbench outfitted with metal vises at both ends and backed by a wall with hooks for various tools. "This is where we'll do the measuring and sawing and nailing." He pointed toward one wall where rectangular frames were stacked next to each other and a roll of screen wire stood. "That's what we use to make screens for the windows of the rental houses. Lord knows, we could spend half our time replacing screens." Next to the roll of screening, a hodgepodge pile of lumber laid flat on the poured cement floor. "And that's for repairing porches and steps and railings."

Bobby looked up at See-Boy. "You ever just build something? I mean, not just fix it but really build it?"

See-Boy laughed. "Sure enough I have. Me and Daddy built this whole building." He strode over to a closed wooden cabinet with two doors that opened out like wings. Then he pointed to a row of maroon-colored, leather-bound books. He took one down and showed it to Bobby. "See this here? It's called *Modern Shop Practices.* Your great granddaddy lent them to my daddy once upon a time. I guess, if you wanted to, you could use these books to build just about anything."

Bobby took the book and riffled through the pages. "Do you think they could show you how to build an airplane?"

See-Boy hid his grin and pinched his bottom lip between his thumb and forefinger. "Hmm, I don't know about that. That might take a mite more knowledge than I have available. Tools and lots of money, too. Besides, it'll be a while before you're grown enough to fly one, don't you think?"

Bobby sighed and looked down at his shoes. See-Boy thought he saw tears welling up in the boy's eyes. "Of course, we wouldn't have to build one big enough to fly right now. We could maybe build one that's just your size."

The boy looked up. "You think so, See-Boy, you really think so?"

"Uh-huh, I might be able to find time for that. But you'd have to help me."

"Oh, I'd help you all right. I can even give you money." He dug into the pocket of his trousers and pulled out a handful of pennies. "Is this enough?"

See-Boy took the coins and jingled them in his palm. "Good enough to start, Bobby. Good enough to start."

CHAPTER 5

F annie sat at the kitchen table as Louise walked into the room. The aroma of fresh coffee filled the air and Louise saw biscuits covered with a dishcloth waiting on top of the stove. She smiled at her mother. "You've been industrious this morning."

"I've been washing clothes, too," Fannie said, "and I found some treasure."

"You found treasure?"

"Well, I suppose it depends on what you think of as treasure." She reached into her housecoat pocket and pulled out a handful of pennies. "Bobby probably thinks so. These were in his trousers' pocket." Fannie went to the stove and poured coffee for herself and Louise then came back to the table. "I figured he must have picked them up somewhere."

"Let's ask him when he gets up for breakfast." Louise blew on her coffee to cool it and tried a tiny sip. "I hear someone. Maybe that's him now."

Instead, Henry bounded into the kitchen. He wore gray cotton slacks and a darker gray open-collar shirt with a green cotton sweater tied loosely around his shoulders. "Morning, Momma, Louise." He grabbed a biscuit and started back out.

"Where're you in such a rush to go?" Fannie asked.

"Jimmy Farr and me are going downtown and listen to records. You can listen to them for free at Miller's."

"Not all day," Louise said. "Unless you buy, sooner or later they'll throw you out."

Henry grinned. "There's another department store just down a block or so."

"Wait just a minute," Louise said. She left the kitchen and returned a moment later with fifty cents in change. "Don't you and Jimmy be trying to catch a ride downtown. Use this for streetcar fare. If you've got money left over, you can buy a record. Maybe they won't be as apt to toss the two of you out."

Henry took the money and hugged Louise. "Thanks, Sis. You're the best." Then he hurried out of the house.

Fannie shook her head. "You know they'll hitch a ride or walk, and use the money to buy two records, don't you?"

"Probably so, but I'm just happy he's making friends."

More sounds emanated from the hall, then Bobby appeared, his black hair still tousled from sleep. He yawned and stretched as Fannie got up and brought over the plate of biscuits and a jar of apple butter. "Would you like milk?"

Bobby nodded. "Yes, ma'am."

After he'd taken a couple of bites, Louise asked, "Where'd you get all these pennies, Bobby?"

"Ma'am?"

Louise pointed to the small stack of pennies by her mother's coffee cup. "Those were in your pocket. Your grandmother found them while washing clothes. We just wondered where they came from. Did you find them?"

Bobby stared at the coins for a moment. "Yes, ma'am … kind of."

"Kind of?"

Bobby stopped eating his biscuit. He sat with his head lowered and hands in his lap. "My friends gave them to me," he finally said.

"Why did they do that?"

"Because I let them have turns on the swing set."

Louise frowned, but a smile played at the corners of her mouth. "You *sold* turns on the swing?"

"Yes, ma'am, I did, and the trapeze, too." He remained quiet for a few seconds before adding, "It's the only swing set in the neighborhood."

Louise looked over at Fannie and let the smile all the way out. "If they're your friends, shouldn't they be allowed to play on the swings without paying for it?"

"Yes, Momma. I'm sorry. Do I have to give the money back?"

"Do you have more?"

"Not anymore," Bobby said. "I gave it all to See-Boy."

Louise and Fannie exchanged another glance. "Go ahead and finish your biscuit, Bobby. Then we'll talk more."

L ouise knocked on the shed's wooden door. "It's me, Louise. Pearl said you were working out here."

The door opened, and See-Boy's face peered down at her. He had become even more handsome as he entered his late twenties, she noted. She saw his wife, Pearl, regularly as they collaborated on the business records and finances, but she might go weeks or even months sometimes without seeing See-Boy or Lawrence.

He showed her a huge grin. "Well, Miss Louise, you are a sight for sore eyes. C'mon in and check out the shed. You paid for it, so you oughta take a look."

Louise stepped inside and put her arms around the man and hugged him. He had always been special to her, particularly as a child, and she was apt to show her affection even when he seemed nervous about what others might think. But here, inside the shed, he hugged her back.

"I do believe, Miss Louise, that you get prettier all the time."

She sighed. "Must you always call me Miss Louise? Pearl calls me Louise."

"It's just a habit, I guess. But I'll try to do better." He showed her around the shed's interior as he had Bobby the night before.

When he'd finished the tour, Louise brought up the arrangement with Bobby. "He says you're going to build an airplane."

"Not one that flies." See-Boy chuckled. "But I do think he'd try to fly it if he could."

"He said he gave you money for materials. I found out this morning he's been charging his friends to play on the swing set his grandfather bought him."

"Yes," See-Boy said. "He told me about his business. In fact, I've got the proceeds here in this Mason jar." He reached into the cabinet and pulled out the jar.

Louise guessed there might be twenty or so pennies inside. "I told him he'd done a bad thing, charging his friends to play. I've asked him to return all of it."

See-boy shook the jar, jingling the coins as he held it up to the light. Then he placed the jar in her palm. "Money's not bad or good, Miss Louise, it's just money. But I suspect you're right. And I feel pretty sure I can get by using scraps and things. You can tell Bobby we've worked it out between us."

He accompanied her to the door and took her hand briefly. "I always enjoy seeing you, Louise"—he winked at her—"now and again."

He finally called me Louise, she thought, walking away. *Were we flirting?* She decided absolutely not. That would be silly.

CHAPTER 6

Murray came home from his Cincinnati run on Friday evening as usual. After supper, as they prepared for bed, Louise told him about the pennies and her conversation with See-Boy.

"On the bright side," Murray said, "it shows Bobby has a mind for business."

"I suppose you're right. In any case, though, I still think it wrong for him to charge his friends for swinging."

"Absolutely, but I can't help but be impressed he thought of the idea." Murray stood on his side of the bed and helped Louise turn back the covers. "I didn't know he had an interest in airplanes."

"You're not usually here to watch him race outside every time he hears one flying over." She slid under the covers and, when Murray joined her, she nestled against his shoulder. "I can't imagine what kind of airplane they'll build."

Murray chuckled. "We'll ask Bobby to tip his wings as he flies over our house."

Louise snuggled closer and ran her hand over Murray's chest, wishing his job didn't keep him away as much as it did. "I'm so glad you're here. You help me keep things in perspective."

"I'm glad I'm here, too." He reached across Louise and turned off the light. Then he turned her face to his and kissed her on the lips. "In fact, I'm very glad."

Later, as they lay in each other's arms, Murray said, "I've got a surprise for Bobby tomorrow. Really, I guess it's for everyone in the house, but I think it will be a great resource for Bobby, especially when he starts school this fall."

"What is it?"

"A surprise. You'll see tomorrow along with everyone else."

Louise let her mind wander for a while then turned onto her side. She remembered when Murray came to her Grandmother Cornelius' house in North Chattanooga—before she realized he wanted to marry her. He had brought her a book by Zane Grey, her favorite author. He seemed to have a way of knowing what other people wanted or needed. Her mind still speculating, she fell asleep.

Though downcast at having to face childhood poverty once more, Bobby spent Saturday morning returning the last of the pennies to his friends. Louise remained torn between wanting to comfort him and staying resolute about her decision. Murray sat beside her on the couch in the living room ostensibly reading the newspaper, but she saw him check his pocket watch every few minutes and peer out the window. Bobby lay sprawled on the floor nearby drawing on a sheet of scrap paper.

Murray tossed the paper aside when a black delivery truck stopped at the curb in front. "This is it," he whispered to Louise. Together, they watched the driver remove two cardboard boxes from the rear of the truck and place them on a handcart, then start up the sidewalk toward their front door.

She whispered back, "Shouldn't we go to the door?"

He shook his head and held a finger to his lips. When the doorbell rang, Murray said, "Bobby, would you see who's at the front door, please?"

Bobby glanced up. "Me?"

"Yes, please, if you don't mind."

The boy got up and walked into the hallway and to the front door. Murray grasped Louise's hand as they followed silently.

Bobby opened the door and looked up. "Hello."

Dropping to one knee, the deliveryman consulted his clipboard. "I have a delivery for a Mister Bobby Carlyon. Is Mister Carlyon home?"

Bobby turned and saw Louise and Murray standing behind him. He wore a confused expression on his round little face, his mouth slightly open.

"That's you, Bobby," Murray said.

Bobby turned back to the man, grinning. "That's me."

The deliveryman arched his eyebrows and held out the clipboard. "Well then, son, just sign here and it's all yours."

Bobby turned again, a worried expression this time. "I can't write yet."

"Don't worry," Murray took the clipboard, and the man stacked the boxes just inside the doorway.

As the driver left, Murray asked, "Would you like to see what's inside?"

Bobby nodded, face beaming now, and Murray ripped the top flaps off one of the boxes. Inside were tan, leather-covered books, each one bearing a letter of the alphabet and the title *The Children's Encyclopedia.*

Murray read the crestfallen look on his son's face and quickly pulled out the volume marked "A" and flipped through the pages, stopping on one and showing it to his son.

Bobby's eyes brightened. "It's an airplane! Thank you, Daddy!"

Louise looked over her son's shoulder at the delicate renderings of several different types of aircraft, accompanied, apparently, by a wealth of pertinent information.

"You know I can't read yet, Momma, not really."

"We'll read to you—your father and I—and before long you'll be reading, too."

Murray tousled Bobby's hair. "And, hopefully, you'll want to read about more than just airplanes." Louise walked over and slid her arm around Murray's waist. "It's a good place to start," she said, and gave her husband a squeeze.

CHAPTER 7

S ee-Boy pulled the truck—a six-year-old 1915 Ford pickup— next to the front door of the maintenance shed. Shortly after Miss Louise took over running the business, they'd acquired several new rental houses, not all as close by as the original clusters. She bought the vehicle from Johnson's Dairy when the firm went through a fleet update, and, though it had considerable mileage on it, the truck still ran good and came in handy servicing the new rentals, as well as for purchasing and hauling maintenance-related items.

See-Boy tapped the horn once and alighted from the cab.

A moment later, Lawrence appeared at the screen door then came outside and walked over to the truck. He took a quick look at the well-used chairs loaded in the truck bed. "They don't look like much."

"They don't have to, Daddy. They're mismatched, and nicked and scraped a little, but they're sturdy. Nobody'll care what they look like, anyway. Not as long as they're sippin' a glass of whiskey."

"I don't know, son, I still have a real uneasy feeling about what you're planning."

See-Boy placed a hand on his father's shoulder. "Don't worry. It won't be much more than a social club, just a few friends and neighbors getting together in the evening for conversation."

"While they sip on bootleg whiskey," Lawrence added. "What if the police raid your social club and put you and your friends and neighbors in the jailhouse?"

"That's not likely, Daddy. First off, it's not bootleg whiskey, it's 'shine. Second, the police are so busy running after the white bootleggers, they don't have time to worry about some colored fella entertaining a few buddies." See-Boy grabbed a couple of chairs and lifted them from the truck bed. "Anyway, from what I hear, except for a few of the overly righteous ones, most of the coppers like to take a little drink every so often."

Lawrence sighed and slid a couple of chairs closer to the truck's tailgate. "You're likely to drive *me* to drink before this is all over with."

See-Boy laughed as he entered the shed. "I remember finding your stashes of whiskey around the house as a teenager. Had a little nip for myself sometimes, too."

"You were as bad as your momma, God rest her soul. Only difference being, she'd be as like to pour it down the sink when she ran across one."

"Well, think of it this way, Daddy. Pretty soon, you won't have to drink alone."

Three nights later, the shed welcomed its first customers. Only four, but See-Boy wasn't worried. The word would get around soon enough. The secondhand chairs were arranged away from the shed's work area in a rough semi-circle around a kerosene heater. Though still cool, the spring evenings weren't cold enough to fire up the heater. Once the weather turned colder, though, visitors to the un-insulated building would be grateful for the warmth it provided.

In the cabinet, behind the leather-bound books, sat a number of pint and quart-size Mason jars, each filled with clear liquid. They could be purchased by those who preferred to drink at home and placed in a paper grocery sack or snugged into a coat pocket for travel. For those who liked company with their imbibing, the cabinet held several old-but-clean jelly glasses.

Roosevelt Foster, who lived just around the corner from where Schmidt's Meat Market used to be, held his glass up to the shed's single bare light bulb and studied its contents closely.

"Are you sure this stuff ain't gonna blind me? I heard about a bunch of folks got blinded or dead after they drank it."

"Naw," See-Boy replied. "I got this from my wife's cousin lives up on Sand Mountain. He's been making moonshine years before Prohibition even started. He's got a clean operation. Besides, he wouldn't sell bad whiskey to his kin."

Roosevelt tilted his glass to his lips, took a drink, then grinned at See-Boy. "Well, I hope you right, because I sure do like the way it taste."

The other three men laughed, adding, "Amen."

Roosevelt ambled over to the work table and set his glass to the side as he examined the item there. "What you doin' here, See-Boy?"

See-Boy joined him, and the others followed. "That's for Miss Louise's boy, Bobby. He's all caught up on airplanes, wants to fly one someday. He asked if I could build him one, so I'm working on it when I have the time." He pointed to the model's metal fuselage. "This right here is a child's pedal car. Found it down at the dump." He leaned in and pointed to the interior. "See the pedals down there." Then he gestured to the long slender metal pieces bolted to the sides and extending up over the cabin area. These are the struts that'll hold the wings. I'm still thinking about what material I'll use for that, and also how to do the tail assembly."

Marcus Baggett spoke up. "My brother-in-law's kind of a shade tree mechanic. He got a welding kit, and for a taste of this moonshine, I bet he'd whup you up somethin' real nice."

"Ask him to come see me," See-Boy said. "Or better yet, bring him with you next time. We'll work something out."

Roosevelt laughed. "I can see it now, boys. Pretty soon we be saying to each other, let's go down to the hanger and get us a drink."

"It's as good a name as any, I reckon," said See-Boy.

CHAPTER 8

A week and a half later, Louise and Bobby walked the short distance to See-Boy and Pearl's home. Although she'd visited on several occasions, it still felt strange to walk up the steps and ring the doorbell of the house where she, her mother, and Henry had once lived.

Pearl answered in a brown cotton dress, her hair down around her shoulders, pretty as always even with the few extra pounds she'd put on in the last few months. She held the door for them to enter. "Hello, Louise, and hello to you, too, Bobby." She put her hands on his shoulders and gave him an assessing look. "I believe you're growing faster than summer corn."

Bobby grinned and glanced up at Louise, who smiled back. "It's true. He'll be tall like Murray, I think."

See-Boy stepped in from the hallway off the kitchen, hugging Louise then shaking hands with Bobby. "You ready to see it?"

Bobby nodded vigorously. "I sure am."

"It's all he can talk about," Louise said. "He's wanted to come see the work in progress, but I told him you wanted to surprise him."

"Then let's not wait any longer." See-Boy led them through the kitchen, down the back porch steps, and out to the shed. Inside, on the poured-concrete floor, a gray canvas tarp covered the finished product. See-Boy strode over and whisked it off.

"Wow!" Bobby said, his mouth forming a small oval.

Silver paint covered the plane's pedal car fuselage, and the double wings, made from hammered tin, sat just in front of the cabin area. The tail assembly, also tin, had been welded to the rear of the fuselage, and a varnished, wooden propeller protruded from the front of the craft.

Bobby walked slowly around the plane, stopping to twirl the prop and run his hand over the wing.

See-Boy appeared as delighted with Bobby's reaction as the boy was with the airplane. "It's kind of like one of the barnstormers, except this one is a little fatter in the fuselage."

"It's great," Bobby said.

Louise smiled, impressed. She'd always figured See-Boy could do just about anything he set his mind to, but this went well beyond what she'd expected.

"Can I try it?" Bobby asked.

"Sure you can." See-boy turned the steering wheel and pushed the car out into the yard. "You'll probably do better on the sidewalk. Help me push it out there."

Once outside, See-Boy helped Bobby into the cab and showed him how the pedals worked. Then he went to stand by Pearl and Louise. "I hope it's not too heavy for him to move. I tried to keep it as light as I could."

Louise squeezed See-Boy's arm. "I know he'll love it whether he can pedal it or not. You did a wonderful job making it."

"I had a little help from friends."

Bobby struggled with the pedals as the craft inched forward reluctantly then gradually picked up speed.

"Did you have to pay them?" Louise asked. "I'll be glad to reimburse you."

See-Boy gave her a shy grin. "No, ma'am, we just bartered a bit."

Down the block, Bobby looked back over his shoulder. "It's moving, Momma, it's moving."

"Watch where you're going," Louise and Pearl called in unison.

The three watched as Bobby made it to the end of the block, turned in a tight circle, and headed back. When he reached them, he coasted to a stop and said, "I wasn't able to take off, but this is still fun. Maybe I can take it up on a hill."

Louise frowned, knowing pedal cars had no brakes. "We'll see about that. For now, you can practice on the sidewalk."

"Okay." Bobby cranked the steering wheel to start down the block again.

Louise turned to See-Boy. "Do you think he realizes it won't really fly?"

"I expect so, Miss Louise, he's a smart boy, but it probably won't keep him from imagining it can."

"I guess if anybody can get it to leave the ground," Louise said, "it'll be him."

CHAPTER 9

L ouise sat at her kitchen table with Pearl, the file folders and journals Pearl used to keep track of the rental houses and related financial records scattered between them. Once a month, the two women met and discussed needed house repairs and maintenance, which tenants were paid up, and those who needed a reminder.

Louise appreciated Pearl's competence and, more so, enjoyed her company. And it pleased Louise that not only did she and See-boy seem happy in their marriage, they also took care of Lawrence, who had lived with them since Jesse died. Aside from her late grandfather Schmidt and Murray, See-Boy and his father were the closest male friends she'd ever had. Though she didn't see them as often, they were still family—would always be.

The late spring heat didn't yet call for the electric fans, but Louise couldn't help noticing sweat on Pearl's face as she bent over the accounting files. "Are you too warm, Pearl? I can get you ice water or tea, or even pull out one of the fans."

"Oh no, ma'am, I'm fine."

"Are you sure? Your face is absolutely *glowing*."

Pearl put down her pencil and folded her hands together on the table top. Her dark eyes danced and her generous lips curled up into a smile as bright as the outside sunshine. "I'm going to have a baby, Louise."

"That's wonderful, Pearl." She reached over and hugged the other woman tightly. "I had a feeling, but I, uh—"

"Uh-huh, you thought I was getting fat, didn't you?"

"No, no, I didn't. I just—well, maybe just a little. But it looks good on you."

"I'm due in September," Pearl said, "but my mamma says I'll be late, told me she carried me for a full ten months."

"Good lord," Louise said, thinking of how proud Jesse would have been to have a grandchild. "I so wish Jesse could be here to be a part of this."

Pearl nodded. "I do, too, Louise. We all do." A tear appeared in Pearl's eye and she blinked it away. "I could see it on See-Boy's face when I told him, and again when we told his father. Lawrence actually cried."

Louise shook her head, picturing the scene. She wondered why most every good thing in life seemed to carry a speck of sadness. Rising from the table, she started for the ice box. "I think we should have tea at least, to celebrate the news. See-Boy might enjoy some as well. It's getting warmer every day."

Almost as soon as his name was spoken, See-Boy appeared at the back door. "Did I hear iced tea mentioned?"

"Yes," Louise said as she gave See-Boy a hug. "So, you're going to be a daddy. I'm so happy for you, for both of you."

"Thank you, Miss Louise."

See-Boy sat down as Louise gathered glasses and the tea. "I should have your storage building ready by the end of the week. All that's left is finishing the roofing and painting."

At Louise's request, See-Boy had constructed a scaled-down version of his maintenance shed in her back yard. It would house most of the lawn and garden tools and the lawn mower, but she mostly wanted it to provide a place for Bobby's airplane, which had turned out to be too big and heavy to store on the porch.

"Wonderful," Louise said. "Bobby can hardly wait. He's wanted to go to your house almost every day to ride in his plane. Now he can have it here, and you don't have to take up space in your shed."

"It's not been a problem," Pearl said. "Everybody's started calling the shed 'the hanger.'"

Louise caught See-Boy frowning but couldn't imagine why. She thought the name sort of cute. "Well anyway, it'll be nice to have a place to put our tools and lawnmower."

"Yes, ma'am," See-Boy said, finishing his tea and slipping outside quickly.

Louise took their glasses and placed them in the sink then returned to the table. "I suppose we should get back to going over the books."

Pearl gathered papers. "All right, but before we do, may I ask you a question, Louise? It's kind of personal."

"I believe you can ask me almost anything."

"Do you ever think about having another child?"

Louise's gaze shifted to the window, where sunlight splashed through the paned glass and filled the room with a golden glow. From outside, she heard the rhythm of See-Boy's roofing hammer, along with the joyful shouts of Bobby and his friends taking turns on the swing set.

"No, I guess not. I think Murray might like to have more, but he hasn't made an issue of it. My mother's birth was difficult when she had Henry, and if it hadn't been for Jesse, I think Bobby would never have taken his first breath. I suppose I just couldn't bear to think about that happening." Louise stood and walked to the window, crossed her arms over her chest, and watched the children playing. "I know it sounds like superstition, but I feel like Bobby's so perfect it just couldn't happen again."

CHAPTER 10

See-Boy and Pearl walked hand in hand down the sidewalk as they headed for home. They'd left the Carlyon's together, and See-Boy carried the cardboard box filled with Schmidt Enterprises' business papers under one arm. The May afternoon was warm, promising hot.

"Are you upset I told Louise about the baby?" Pearl asked.

See-Boy shook his head. "She'd figure it out soon enough anyway. Your tummy is beginning to round out."

"But you're upset I told her about the shed being called the hanger."

"Not really upset. I just thought she might ask who calls it that."

"What would you tell her if she did?"

"I don't rightly know. I been thinking on it, though."

As they rounded the last corner and their house came into view, See-Boy sighed. If ever a place felt like home to him, this was it. He'd loved it as far back as he could remember, had spent a lot of time *around* it, if not inside. Between it and Mr. William's house across the street, where his momma had worked, he'd almost felt like part of the family—a white family at that. And Miss Louise had become his favorite since she stood knee-high to him. Her selling her former home to him and Pearl—giving it to them, really—set them up better than he could have hoped for.

A frown crossed his face as he thought about the shed's side business causing her or her family trouble. But the money he made seemed just too good to pass on.

Pearl stopped and looked up at him. "One way or another, sooner or later, Louise will find out what you're doing. If she finds out from you first, whatever she says about it, it'll be better than if she found out on her own. Like having the police come by and say 'Mrs. Carlyon, we've got your man down at the jail for selling bootleg whiskey.'"

"It's not bootleg whiskey; it's moonshine, your *cousin's*."

Pearl walked on, leaving him to catch up. A fine distinction, he realized—what you called the alcohol—but it probably didn't matter either way to Pearl. She'd had her say, and nothing he did or said would change that. He figured he'd best be thinking harder on how to inform Miss Louise.

The following Friday morning, See-Boy eased the truck to the curb and shut off the engine. Bobby's pedal car airplane rested in the truck bed, tied down snugly with lengths of sturdy twine. After he put the finishing touches on the Carlyon's storage shed this morning, he'd talk with Miss Louise about his own shed business. Today seemed the best day, in his estimation, to bring the subject up. Murray would be home this evening, and See-Boy wanted it settled, if at all possible, before then. It wasn't that he didn't like or trust the man; Murray had proven to be one of the kindest men See-Boy had ever met. But he'd known Miss Louise much longer and felt more comfortable with her. Besides, it was her business involved here.

Bobby raced down the front porch steps and climbed into the truck bed before See-Boy could get out of the cab.

"Slow down, Bobby. I'll undo the twine and set your plane down on the sidewalk for you."

As he did, Bobby wrapped both arms around one of See-Boy's legs. "Thank you, See-Boy. I love you."

See-Boy tousled the boy's hair, dark like his mother's. "I love you, too, little man. I sure do."

As Bobby pedaled down the sidewalk, See-Boy saw Miss Louise at the screened front door. She waved and he waved back, then she disappeared back into the house. See-Boy retrieved his tool box from the truck cab and headed for the back yard.

A little before eleven, See-Boy knocked on the back door, more nervous than he'd ever been around Miss Louise. But Pearl was right that she needed to know—after all, it was her shed, really—and if he didn't tell her about it soon, Pearl just might.

"Come in, See-Boy," Louise said from the table where she sat stringing green beans. "Have you finished?"

"Yes, ma'am, I have. Care to take a look?"

"Of course I do." She wiped her hands on her apron and followed him out to the shed.

See-Boy walked her around the building's board and batten exterior, painted in a pale yellow to match the main house. Though less than half the size of his shed, he'd built it big enough to easily accommodate the airplane and miscellaneous tools and equipment. He'd provided a double door to accommodate the wingspread of the plane, and a couple of small windows for light.

Louise breathed in the fragrance of raw wood and fresh paint. "You've thought of everything, it seems, See-Boy. I love it, and I'm sure Murray will as well. And Bobby can ride his airplane every day now."

"Thank you, Miss Louise. Uh … before you go back inside, I need to talk to you about something. If you have time, that is."

"I'm just getting a mess of beans ready to cook for supper. They can wait. Anyway"—she touched his arm and smiled up at him— "I always have time for you."

CHAPTER 11

See-Boy wished he had a couple of the chairs so he and Miss Louise could sit down while they talked. They could sit in the kitchen, of course, but what if Miss Fannie or the boys came in? He took a deep breath and began to speak—wishing all the while he'd practiced his words instead of just letting it all gush out like water from a wide-open faucet.

"It's about the shed, Miss Louise."

"It's truly lovely, See-Boy. I even like the way it smells."

"No, ma'am, not this shed, the one I built so me and Daddy would have a place to work out of the weather."

"Oh, okay, what about it?"

"I've been inviting a few neighborhood friends over after work, and we've been using the shed to sit around and talk for a while. I bought chairs from a second-hand store, so we'd have a place to sit."

"That sounds nice," Miss Louise said. "I know more colored folks have begun moving into the neighborhood behind where we used to live, and I think that's a good thing. I'm glad you and Pearl are able to make new friends, Lawrence, too, I hope."

See-Boy nodded absently, his anxiety rising. *Help me, Jesus. This is not going well.* Then he took another deep breath and said, "I'm using the shed for a speakeasy at night."

"What?"

"It's not really a speakeasy—not like the ones you read about in the newspapers that the police raid and arrest everybody—it's just some friends and neighbors come around and sip a little moonshine one of Pearl's cousins makes." *There. He'd said it; now what would happen?*

Miss Louise remained quiet. Stunned, he figured. He watched her face as she walked over to the double doors, stared out at the yard, and then turned back to him. "How is it not like one of those speakeasies?"

See-Boy thought. He wasn't a criminal. He didn't wear flashy clothes or drive a fancy car. He was just trying to take advantage of a business opportunity to make life a little easier for his family and the baby on the way.

"It just don't seem that way to me, I guess. It's a real small-time operation. Most I've had so far is six people and me."

Miss Louise tilted her head forward the way a school teacher might, locks of black hair framing her face as she studied him. "So it's just a *little* illegal, I suppose. What does Pearl think about this, and Lawrence, what's he think?"

"Daddy's not too keen on it, but he's coming around. Came out yesterday evening and had a little nip with his buddies. Pearl, she knows I'm doing it for us, for the baby. Mostly, she's worried about you finding out before I told you myself." He crossed his arms over his chest and stared down at the floor. "On account of us doing it in the shed you paid for."

Miss Louise stepped over to him and grabbed his upper arms. "Oh, See-Boy, I just don't want you to get into trouble. I'm worried you might get arrested and have to go to jail. What would Pearl and that new baby do then?"

At least she wasn't angry with him. A feeling of relief flooded through his body. "Ah, Miss Louise, nothing like that's gonna happen. We just a few colored folks sitting around having a drink. Nobody cares about us."

"I care," she said, and gave his arms a shake before releasing him from her grasp.

"I know you do. That's not what I mean."

"Well, thank you for telling me about this. I can't say I approve. In fact, I'm not quite sure how I feel about what you're doing. Murray's coming in tonight. I believe I'll discuss it with him."

"Yes, ma'am, if that's what you want to do, I understand. Pearl and me, we sure don't want to do anything that might affect you and your family in a bad way."

His stomach tightened as she stared at him again, the school teacher look. But then she smiled and turned toward the doors.

"Come on," she said over her shoulder. "Let's see if we can find Bobby and get him to hanger his plane for a while."

After supper, Louise and Murray sat on the front porch drinking iced tea while Fannie and the boys busied themselves inside getting ready for bed. The air, still warm and breezy, set the oak leaves rustling softly, and the tree whispered in their ears.

"I really don't know quite how I feel about it," Louise said. "On the one hand, it seems like nothing to fret about, but, on the other, what if See-Boy gets arrested and goes to jail? He won't be able to work for who knows how long, and Lawrence is getting too old to handle the heavy work by himself. Then there's Pearl and the baby. What would they do without See-Boy?"

"It's his decision," Murray said. "We can't live their lives for them. And from what you've told me, all three at least condone what's going on."

"I know. I just worry." She reached over and grasped Murray's hand. "After having a drunkard for a father, I was glad when the Volstead Act passed. I hoped no one else would have to experience what my family went through. But now, it seems nothing has changed, really. People still drink. They just do it more discretely." She turned and looked at her husband. "What about you, Murray? Do you think drinking is a sin?"

"I was taught so, but I've learned to live well enough with a number of things I originally thought were sinful."

"Things like dancing?" Louise asked, smiling.

Murray squeezed her hand. "Yes, like dancing."

"And what about drinking, do you think it's a sin?"

"I had a taste of French brandy in France during the war. The other guys teased me until I finally gave in." He winked at her in the scant light bleeding out from the parlor window. "I only did it once. I liked it, so I thought I'd better not do it again."

She rose from her chair and held out her hand. "I hope that doesn't apply to everything you like."

"Indeed not." Murray took her hand in his and followed her inside.

CHAPTER 12

Next morning, the sun hung well above the horizon when Fannie joined Louise and Murray at the kitchen table. Her auburn hair, streaked now with gray, was piled loosely on top of her head and held in place with an ivory pin.

"Morning, everyone," she said, then found a coffee cup and helped herself to the pot on the stove. "The boys are sleeping in, it appears."

Louise glanced at Murray, who raised an eyebrow, shrugging. Then she blew out a breath of air and said, "That's good. There's something I should tell you about See-Boy. He's using the maintenance shed in back of his house to sell moonshine to his friends. They sit around on secondhand chairs and talk and sip their drinks."

"He's not making it there, is he?" Fannie asked.

"No, he gets it from one of Pearl's cousins up on Sand Mountain. He says it's just a small operation, that only a few of his friends and neighbors are aware of it."

Fannie removed a pack of Lucky Strikes from her bathrobe pocket and used a kitchen match to light one. "He's not afraid of the law catching him?"

"It doesn't appear so," Murray said. "My only concern would be if and how we might be affected legally if he were caught. The business did finance construction of the shed, and he is Louise's employee."

Fannie nodded. "And now you know he's doing it. It might've been better if he hadn't told you. If you know and do nothing about it, wouldn't that be like consenting to it?"

Louise raked her fingers through her hair and closed her eyes. "Lord, I don't know what to do. He says he's just trying to bring in a little extra money for the family, especially with the baby coming. I understand that, really I do, but if he gets into trouble—"

Louise paused when she heard footsteps on the front porch followed by the sound of the mailbox being opened and closed.

"I'll get the mail." Murray stood and left the kitchen.

Louise shook a cigarette from her mother's pack. "What do you think, Mother?"

"I'm really not sure. That family has stood by us for years."

Murray returned with a handful of envelopes. "It's mostly bills, but here's one addressed to you from a law firm, Hodges and Arnold. Are you doing any business with them?"

Louise shook her head. "Open it and see what it says."

Murray ripped off the edge of the envelope and removed the folded sheet of paper. He read silently for a moment then glanced down at Louise, frowning. "It says you're being asked to show cause why your inheritance from Will shouldn't be divided equally among all his heirs ... and the plaintiffs are shown as your stepsisters, Sylvia and Edith Reason. You're directed to appear in probate court two weeks from Monday." He handed the letter to Louise.

"But—" Louise paused as the words sank in. "They're not his children. They never were. My father left no will. He signed over all his business interests to me. He never even mentioned those women after he moved in with us."

Fannie stubbed out her cigarette in the ashtray. "Maude was a devil, and those girls are the devil's spawn. Damn it all, she and Will have found a way to plague us from the grave."

Louise read the letter herself. A deep tendril of ache started in her bowels and wound its way around her chest and neck, making her short of breath. Feeling sick to her stomach, she looked up at Murray and felt her eyes tear. "What should I do?"

He came around and stood behind her chair, resting his palms on her shoulders. "We'll call an attorney and tell him about the letter. He'll know what to do."

Louise, seeking any avenue to lessen her anxiety, seized on Murray's suggestion. She remembered Harrison Evers from when she'd been tried for Maude's murder. He'd impressed her with his knowledge and professionalism. "Yes, let's call Mr. Evers. He'll know what to do."

Murray sat back down across from Louise, shaking his head. "Mr. Evers is strictly a criminal attorney. But I feel sure he can recommend someone who deals with civil matters."

Fannie lit another Lucky and stuck it between her lips. Then she left the table and walked over to a drawer under the kitchen counter where she found the telephone directory. "Let's call him now," she said, blowing a thick cloud of smoke toward the ceiling. "I'm mad as a wet hen about this."

Murray made the call. Evers' office was closed for the weekend, but the directory also listed his home telephone number, which he answered on the third ring. Murray spoke briefly with the attorney, reading from the letter Louise had received. The kitchen stayed quiet for several minutes while Murray listened, then he thanked Evers and replaced the receiver.

"Mr. Evers recommends John Adamson. He has an office downtown on Cherry Street. Evers seems to feel he is highly competent and will do a good job for us, whatever it is."

"All right," Louise said. "Will you make the call again?"

"Of course." Murray flipped through the directory and found Adamson's office number. This time, he reached the attorney's secretary and arranged an appointment.

"His assistant said he has court the first part of this week but will see you Thursday at two. In the meantime, she asked that you collect all the paperwork from the business transfer and bring it with you." He walked over and took Louise's hand. "I wish I could be here to go with you."

"It's all right, Murray. I know you have to work. I'll be okay." She really wasn't sure of that at all, and waiting four long days to see the attorney would be torture. "I'm sure it will work out fine."

"You won't have to go alone, Louise," Fannie said, her eyes still ablaze. "I'll be there with you all the way."

Like it or not, Louise thought, but secretly she appreciated the moral support. Then she had a thought that, ironically, almost made her smile. She'd hoped for something to distract her from her concerns about See-Boy. Well, she had it now.

CHAPTER 13

S quire Adamson's office, located in a brick building just a few doors down from the corner of Cherry and Chestnut Streets sat across from the courthouse, a shingle identifying the entrance. Two brass lantern lights hung on each side of the ornately arched doorway.

Louise and her mother stood at the base of the steps leading up from the sidewalk and took in the décor.

"Looks expensive," Fannie said.

"Not if it saves the business. It's all relative if you think of it that way."

Fannie nodded and started up the steps. "Well, if it gives you peace of mind, it'll be worth it. Let's go on in."

The entrance foyer led into a modest but tasteful reception area attended by an attractive woman who looked to be close to Louise's age. She stood when they entered, greeted Louise by name, and ushered them into Squire Adamson's office. He also stood, introduced himself, shook each of their hands, then gestured toward two leather wingback chairs facing his desk.

"Please have a seat and make yourselves comfortable. Would either of you like something to drink?"

Wearing rimless spectacles and with just a hint of gray at the temples, the attorney, rather handsome, looked to be nearing fifty, Louise thought as she said, "No thank you."

Adamson turned to Fannie. "And you, Ms. Meyers?" His brilliant smile showed even, white teeth.

"No thank you, Squire Adamson, but you're very generous to offer."

"Please, just call me John."

Fannie returned the smile and actually blushed. "Then you shall call me Fannie."

Are they flirting? Louise wondered. She almost laughed, then remembered the purpose of her visit. "Well, I suppose we should get down to business, shouldn't we? I'm sure you have a very busy schedule."

Adamson leaned forward and picked up an onyx fountain pen. "You ladies have my attention for as long as you need, but yes, why don't you tell me about your problem."

Louise began by handing the attorney the letter she'd received and, after he perused the document, she detailed the circumstances surrounding her father's death and the transfer of the business assets.

Adamson took notes on a legal pad and, when Louise had finished, he capped the pen and leaned back in his chair. "I see little chance for this action against you proceeding, Ms. Carlyon. However, since your father died intestate, the probate court does routinely consider cases of this type." He glanced at Fannie, smiled for the briefest of moments, then turned back to Louise. "Unfortunately for you, at least—it keeps us lawyers from the poorhouse— anyone can bring legal action against anyone else, assuming they have the money to do so."

"Where do we go from here?" Louise asked.

"I'll speak to Squire Arnold, and we'll discuss the merits of the case. I suspect he sees the same flaws as I do but, here again, a lawyer's time and advice are his stock in trade. Relax and try not to worry. I'll want to meet with you again after I make inquiries and prior to your scheduled appointment with the court. If I need further information, I'll be in touch."

Squire Adamson rose and came around to shake the women's hands again before seeing them out.

Fannie stepped to the sidewalk and turned. "He seems competent. I feel we're in good hands."

Louise paused on the middle step and smiled down at her mother. "Were you *flirting* with him in there, Mother?"

Fannie dismissed the notion with a wave of her hand. "I most certainly was not. He *was* rather good-looking, and I think he might have appreciated my appearance as well."

As the two women walked to the streetcar stop, Fannie added, "Besides, he's married; I noticed the wedding band on his left ring finger."

"Funny," Louise said. "It never occurred to me to look."

CHAPTER 14

L ouise and Fannie arrived home and prepared an early supper for themselves and the children then retired to the porch to catch the welcome evening breeze. Louise shifted her rocker to mostly face her mother.

"I feel better now that we have Squire Adamson on the job, but I still don't know what—if anything—to do about See-Boy."

Fannie paused in her rocking. "You know, we should have asked about that while we were in his office."

"Oh, Mother, I think you're right. Truly we should have. Perhaps I'll give him a call tomorrow and ask him what he thinks."

Fannie stared off into the settling dusk, a slight crease forming between her eyebrows. "He might charge extra for something like that. He's going to call you soon anyway. I believe I'd wait until we meet with him again, and kind of *slip* the question in. Remember what he said about a lawyer's time and advice."

"I do, and maybe you're right. I just hate all the uncertainty about the matter."

"Could be we need to check it out. Perhaps we should see firsthand what's going on over there. The more information we have, the easier it will be to figure out what to do."

"Mother, surely you aren't serious. Do you really think we should just show up at the door and expect to go inside?"

"See-Boy might be a little surprised," Fannie said, "but you must know he'd do pretty much anything you asked him to."

Louise took a turn staring off into the distance, pondering her mother's idea. If only a few customers dropped by for a drink, that would hardly be worth worrying about. No one could get in trouble for that. Certainly, she would feel better if that were the case. "When were you thinking of going?"

"Murray's coming in tomorrow, so if we're going, it'll have to be tonight or next week."

Most likely, Murray wouldn't think it a good idea, Louise noted mentally, and her mother apparently agreed. She didn't like going behind his back, but really all they would do is visit See-Boy and his family. *No harm in that, right?*

"I suppose Henry could watch Bobby for an hour or two." Louise said, rising from her seat. "Let's go pay a visit to See-Boy's family and see the shed."

L ouise and Fannie walked shoulder to shoulder in the darkness as they made their way to their former home, Louise already regretting her decision. Still, she was glad her mother came, too.

"I understand," Fannie said, "that the Ridgedale community is gradually attracting more coloreds."

"I heard that, too, and See-Boy agreed. He says it's mostly across Dodds Avenue, over behind the elementary school. I think it's nice, and he and Pearl have more opportunity to make new friends."

"If nothing else, it should be good for his side business."

They rounded the corner at Baily and Bennett and saw the house half a block down on the right. "Pearl has put in several beautiful flowers and shrubs since they moved in," Louise said. "She and See-Boy seem so happy. I know they'll be wonderful parents."

"I wish Jesse could be here to see her grandchild," Fannie said.

"We all do."

They stopped in front of the house and glanced briefly at each other before Louise stepped onto the porch and rang the bell.

Pearl opened the door seconds later and smiled. "Why, Louise, hello, and you, too, Ms. Meyers. What a surprise. Please come in." She called over her shoulder, "Daddy Lawrence, come see who's here."

Lawrence ambled into the room and a smile broke the lined contours of his face as well. "Miss Louise and Ms. Fannie, how good to see you both. I guess we were at the funeral the last time I saw you."

Louise stepped into Lawrence's outstretched arms.

"Well, what brings you ladies out this time of night? Something we can do for you?"

Fannie lifted her chin. "We've come to see the shed."

Lawrence and Pearl looked at each other. "The shed?"

Louise grinned and felt her neck begin to color. "What she means is we've come to see how See-Boy's business venture is progressing."

Lawrence glanced at Pearl, who raised her eyebrows. "Daddy, why don't you escort Louise and Ms. Meyers out to the shed?" Pearl's grin matched Louise's. "Won't See-Boy be surprised?"

Louise and Fannie followed Lawrence out the back door and across the yard. See-Boy had included two windows, one on either side of the shed, and a soft warm glow issued through the panes of glass.

When Lawrence stopped in front of the door, Fannie asked, "Do you have a secret knock or one of those peep holes in the door?"

He chuckled. "No, Ms. Fannie, we got nothing like that. We just drift on in." He opened the door to the sound of muffled conversation and laughter. "Hello, boys, we have a couple of visitors here tonight." The big man stood to the side and made way for the two women to enter.

Louise counted five seated men, including See-Boy, with their mouths agape and eyes wide. "I hope it's all right we came by, See-Boy. We wanted to see your, uh, operation."

See-Boy regained his composure, but a nervous smile played across his coffee-with-cream face. "Why Miss Louise and Ms. Fannie, you know you're always welcome." He stood and found two more chairs, pulling them toward the informal semi-circle near the kerosene heater. "Won't you sit down?"

The other men stared in silence. Not sure what to do, Louise offered her hand to the man on her left. "I'm Louise Carlyon, and this is my mother, Fannie Meyers. We've known See-Boy and Lawrence as long as I can remember."

The man stood quickly, looked at Louise's hand, and finally took it. "I'm Seymour Hasty, ma'am, and pleased to meet you." Louise approached each in turn until she got to See-Boy, whom she hugged while Lawrence stood off to the side and chuckled.

Fannie looked at See-Boy after Louise had released him. "Now that we all know each other, why don't we have a drink?"

The women sat as See-Boy got fresh jelly glasses from the cabinet and poured a shot of clear liquor in each. Again, the others stared silently as first Fannie and then Louise took a swallow.

Louise felt the burn in her throat and blinked back tears, barely managing not to cough. She let her breath out slowly and looked around the room. "Good."

Fannie held her glass out to See-Boy and nodded. "I believe I'd like another." She glanced at the men. "How about it, fellows, can I buy a round for the house?"

Seymour held his glass up in a small salute. "Ms. Fannie and Miss Louise, you ladies are all right. I can surely see why See-Boy and Lawrence talk so highly of you."

Murmured agreement filled the space as Lawrence added, "Boys, these ladies could charm the cream off milk."

Louise took another small sip of her moonshine. She didn't know any more what to do now than she had before. Or what, if anything, she'd tell Murray.

CHAPTER 15

The receptionist greeted Louise and Fannie warmly and led them directly to Squire Adamson's office. Resplendent in a gray, pinstriped three-piece suit, white shirt, and mauve necktie knotted snugly over a gold collar pin, the attorney shook their hands, holding her mother's a fraction longer than necessary, Louise noted with amusement.

As she took in his two-tone wingtips, white over black, Louise couldn't help but wonder if he'd dressed for Fannie's benefit. The only thing missing was a carnation boutonniere on his lapel and a bouquet of flowers for her mother.

"Ladies, it's so good to see you both again." He gestured toward the leather wingbacks. "Please have a seat."

Louise and Fannie sat and waited as the attorney shuffled through documents on his desk.

"I have discussed the nature of the action taken against you with Squire Arnold. Apparently, the plaintiffs argue that your father squandered the money their mother received following the death of her first husband—a portion of which they feel should rightly be theirs as their mother's heirs. Further, they allege that you"—he glanced at Louise— "duped your father into signing over all his assets to you."

Color rushed to her face as Louise's heart skipped. "Duped? How? I let him live with us in our home after he learned he was dying from cancer. We—I suppose I should say I—cared for him. That was all."

Adamson raised his palms in a calming gesture. "These are only allegations, and ones I believe to be unsupportable in the court." He lowered his hands and picked up a piece of paper. "I've examined the documents related to the transfer of assets, and they appear completely in order." His gaze drifted from Louise to Fannie, and he smiled. "In my opinion, you ladies have nothing to worry about."

Fannie leaned forward in her chair, eyes blazing with anger. "I certainly respect your opinion, but may I say you don't know these women. I knew their mother and her deceptions all too well, and I fear these bad apples have not fallen far from the tree."

"You make an excellent point. I do *not* know either woman, and I feel sure you are quite right in your assessment. Trust me. I will keep your advice in mind throughout our dealings."

Fannie sank back into her chair. "Thank you."

"It is my pleasure, believe me." He looked at Louise. "Our court date is next Wednesday, and by this time that afternoon, all this will be behind you. Now, if there's anything else I can do for you between now and then, please let me know."

He started to rise when Louise spoke. "There is one thing. Not related to this case. I wonder if I might ask your opinion about something."

"By all means."

She went through the details of her concerns regarding See-Boy's use of the maintenance shed for his after-hours business. The attorney listened attentively, interrupting her occasionally with a question.

"As I see it," he said when Louise had finished, "your only real liability—and it's not much of one—is that the business paid for the materials used in the construction. The shed is on property owned by your employee, so it's likely to be considered his, even though you financed it through the business. If he chooses to operate an illegal enterprise after hours *without your knowledge and consent,* he is the only person accountable for his actions."

"But we do know about it," Louise said. "He told me because he didn't want to do it without our knowing, for fear it might somehow cause trouble for my family."

"Yes, of course you do," Adamson said. "But that knowledge is protected by attorney-client privilege. I suggest you tell no one else and advise your husband not to as well. There is also one other thing I can do to help ease your minds further. I'll have the shed added as an improvement to the existing property. It would happen anyway, sooner or later, when the property is re-assessed. This will simply remove any question as to who owns the building. You, Mrs. Carlyon, as the business owner, employ your friend and his family. They, in turn, use the maintenance shed to assist them in carrying out their work-related activities."

Louise felt the weight release from her shoulders. "You make it sound so simple."

"In this case, it is. And my role is likewise simple. I'll not charge you for our discussion or my work with the assessor's office."

Fannie rose and thrust her hand across the desk. "I knew the first time we met you'd be the best attorney in Chattanooga. And that is certainly true."

Adamson accepted her hand. "Ma'am, you're too kind." He glanced at Louise and grinned. "Perhaps the best *civil* attorney?"

They all laughed as Adamson walked them to the outer office. "I'll leave you ladies with one further bit of free advice—I believe your first trip to the shed after hours should remain your last."

CHAPTER 16

L ouise and Fannie arrived at the courthouse an hour before the scheduled hearing. Notwithstanding what Squire Adamson had told them, Louise remained nervous about the outcome and—though she hated to admit it—about seeing her two older stepsisters.

They sat on a slatted wooden bench just outside the double doors leading into the courtroom where they could watch as people entered and subsequently departed, footsteps echoing under the high, domed ceiling. A few appeared happy, others angry or disappointed. The latter didn't help Louise's mood. "I wish this were already over and done with."

"Try not to worry," Fannie said. "The worst that can happen isn't nearly as bad as the last time we were in court."

That's certainly true, Louise thought. *At least I'm not on trial for murder.* She wished Squire Adamson would hurry and meet them, his presence reassuring. To keep from dwelling on the worst, she thought about Bobby, currently home with Pearl. Sometimes, Pearl showed Bobby the accounting books and how they kept track of the business. Far from appearing bored, he seemed fascinated by the columns of numbers. *Who knows, maybe he'll become an accountant someday*—an occupation much more comforting to her than his wild ideas about flying a plane.

A skinny, middle-aged woman walking hurriedly down the marbled hallway interrupted her reverie. Clutching a hatbox to her bosom, she stopped in front of the courtroom doors and peeked inside. Snippets of conversation reached Louise's ears as the woman opened the door further and nodded. Then she turned toward Louise and Fannie, gave them a conspiratorial wink, and barged inside the courtroom.

A few seconds later, Louise heard a commotion and several people shouting from inside the room. Squire Adamson chose that moment to arrive, carrying a leather briefcase and wearing a gray Homburg that matched his suit perfectly.

"My goodness," he said. "What's going on in there?"

"A woman carrying a hatbox just barged into the courtroom," Fannie said. "She seemed suspicious to me."

Just then the doors opened and a uniformed bailiff emerged, dragging the woman along by her left arm. In her other arm the hatbox dangled by a lace ribbon. As they turned toward the exit, Louise noted the bailiff also carried a live chicken under his left arm. The woman's protestations and the chicken's squawks echoed down the hallway. "I told them this was a chicken-shit case," she shouted. "Now they goddamn know for certain!"

Adamson exchanged raised eyebrows with Louise and Fannie. "We still have a few minutes before our case is called, but I think it may be quieter inside. Shall we go in?"

Louise entered last, happy to at least not have to meet Sylvia and Edith face to face in the hallway.

They took seats on the left behind the rail separating the main part of the courtroom from the pews available for visitors, reporters, and others awaiting their turn before the bench. It looked much the same as when Louise had been on trial, but without jurors.

In her peripheral vision, Louise saw movement to her right. Glancing quickly in that direction, she spied her two stepsisters accompanied by another stylishly clothed man she assumed was Squire Arnold. The trio took seats on the right. Louise looked straight ahead but still felt the hardened stares of Sylvia and Edith boring into her.

Minutes later, Louise's case was called, and she followed Squire Adamson through the gate in the railing. Instead of heading toward the defendant's table where she'd spent agonizing hours during the previous trial, Squire Adamson took her arm and ushered her up to stand before the judge's bench. Sylvia and Edith, with their attorney, stood on her right, Sylvia stone-faced and grim.

"Counselors," said the judge, a heavyset, balding man with owlish eyeglasses. "I have reviewed the briefs you've presented." He turned to Squire Arnold. "Do you have anything further to provide to the court in support of your clients' claims?"

"No, your honor," the man said.

To Squire Adamson, he said, "And you, counselor?"

"No, your honor," Adamson answered. "We believe our case to be fully outlined in the documents you have reviewed."

"Very well. I can find no evidence in support of the plaintiffs' assertions or accusations, and therefore no basis for any further legal action regarding this matter. I find for the defendant and order the plaintiffs to assume all court costs." He banged his gavel once and added, "Bailiff, please call the next case."

Stunned, Louise stared at the judge. All the worry, all the sleepless nights she'd spent imagining the worst—all of it gone like a leaf in the wind. She turned to her attorney open-mouthed, but he simply smiled, took her elbow, and escorted her to the hall. Fannie exited right on their heels.

"Sir," Fannie said, "we owe you a debt of gratitude. You are a brilliant attorney, and we thank you."

The courtroom doors opened again, and Sylvia and Edith stormed out. Sylvia planted herself in front of Louise. "You may have won this time, Louise, but you know that I know what you did. Our stepfather loved us and would have wanted us to share in his assets if you hadn't kept him so doped up he didn't know better. Keep your money and your houses and enjoy your ill-gotten gains now, because they'll do you no good at all while you're rotting in Hell."

Fannie gave Sylvia an icy stare. "If anyone here knows anything about keeping someone doped up, it's you, Sylvia. I'm quite sure you learned at your mother's knee. And don't act as though you don't know what I'm referring to. You and she—" Fannie pointed at Edith "—were both old enough to understand what was happening to my mother-in-law, Mary Alice. You two go on and spread your venom somewhere else. You're done with us."

Oh, Mother, Louise thought, *thank you for being my voice.* She wanted to hug Fannie, but her mother stood toe-to-toe glaring at Sylvia.

Sylvia and Edith's attorney came out through the courtroom doors in time to register the stare-off. He took Sylvia by the arm and started toward the exit, but she shook him off, stomping down the hallway with her sister hurrying along behind her, shoes clacking across the floor like runaway horses.

Squire Arnold smiled grimly. "I'm sorry for that."

Squire Adamson returned the smile. "No need to be sorry. We won, after all."

Arnold shrugged. "Money is money, win or lose. Maybe next time, I'll have a better case. But not with you fine folks, I hope."

Louise, Fannie, and Adamson watched as the other attorney disappeared down the corridor.

"Well, ladies, all's well that ends well," Adamson said, doffing his Homburg.

"Good thing it went the way it did," Fannie said. "I'd hate to have had to go out and find myself a hatbox and a live chicken."

CHAPTER 17

S quire Adamson dabbed at his lips with a white linen napkin. "Ladies, this is quite possibly the finest beef roast I have ever eaten."

Fannie, the reason the attorney graced their table, smiled demurely. "My late father-in-law operated the best meat market in Chattanooga. All his ladies knew their meat and how to prepare it."

Louise smiled, too, and glanced at Murray, whose expression told her he found both the setting and conversation as amusing as she did. Against Louise's advice and better judgment, Fannie had invited the attorney to share supper with them. He'd declined that invitation. *Most likely,* Louise figured, *his wife might have had something to do with that.* But he had accepted lunch on Saturday.

Fannie laid out the best china and silverware, and even ironed the linen napkins. Louise thought her mother ridiculous—not to say downright obvious—but decided to let Fannie have her day, and hoped that would be the end of it.

Grateful for Murray and the boys' presence, Louise felt sure her mother's overt flirting would be kept to a minimum.

"I want to thank you, sir," Murray said, "for addressing our problem so quickly and competently. I know how worried Louise was, and I hated I couldn't be here with her."

"My pleasure, Mr. Carlyon. I assure you few of my dealings or clients are as pleasant as your wife and mother-in-law." He cut another piece of roast and pierced it with a fork. "And none whom I can recall have rewarded me with such wonderful food."

Bobby spoke up for the first time since sitting down to eat. "Wait until you see what Grandma fixed for dessert—strawberry shortcake and whipped cream. We don't usually have dessert with lunch, so maybe you could come next week, too."

The room went quiet until Squire Adamson leaned toward Bobby and whispered, "You may have something there, young man. You know, I seldom get dessert with lunch, either."

Louise laughed and the others joined in. She patted Bobby's shoulder. "Squire Adamson has lots of people he helps, Bobby. I doubt he has time for indulging every Saturday in lunches with former clients."

"Well," Bobby said in absolute sincerity, "if I ever need help, I'll be sure to find you. Then you can help me and come to lunch again."

The attorney grinned, offering the boy his hand. "That sounds like a deal to me. Let's shake on it."

As they shook hands, Bobby said, apropos of nothing, "I'm going to be a pilot when I grow up."

"Really? A noble profession, for certain," Adamson said. "I have a daughter about your age. I hope she sets such great goals for herself." He turned to Henry, who had been quiet throughout the meal. "How about you, young man? Do you have a profession in mind?"

Henry's green eyes danced. "I'm going to be a drummer in a band, and I'm going to play the drums in places where people come to dance."

Adamson's eyebrows rose. "My goodness, we have a pilot and a drummer." He glanced around the table. "I'm afraid it makes the practice of law seem a bit mundane."

Louise shook her head. "Not true at all, Squire Adamson. Believe me, I speak from experience. Next to having a wonderful husband—" she grinned at Murray "—a good attorney is sometimes the only thing that will set your mind at ease."

Fannie nodded and beamed an adoring smile at their guest. "Yes, I've always admired attorneys."

See-Boy looked around the interior of the maintenance shed. Though it didn't look any different, somehow it *felt* different, knowing a piece of paper now existed somewhere downtown declaring him the owner. Not that Miss Louise had ever suggested otherwise, but now it was official.

According to the attorney, that paper placed a layer of protection between him and Schmidt Enterprises, so, if he got caught selling moonshine, he'd be the only one affected, and that's the way he wanted it.

And the fair amount of cash that side business brought in would come in handy, what with the baby coming soon. Pearl literally glowed with her pregnancy—eyes bright and cheery, tummy growing more and more every week, it seemed. *I'm rich*, he thought, *and not with money, though there's enough.* He, Pearl, and his father, they were family—all in good health, all working—and now the baby. *Boy or girl, it doesn't matter. Just that we're all together.*

He closed his eyes and sniffed the air, smelled the rough-cut wood of the shed, the concrete floor, and, through one of the open windows, pork chops frying in the kitchen. He hoped life would always be so good.

CHAPTER 18

Though breezy outside, mid-summer's heat baked the confines of the kitchen. Louise opened the back door and the window over the sink to create a cross-draft, then retrieved her cup of coffee and the *Chattanooga Times* before settling down at the table. The headlines lately focused on the famous—or infamous, to her thinking—Scopes "Monkey Trial" taking place just a few miles' northeast in Dayton, Tennessee. She had never been particularly religious, but neither did she discount the presence of a divine power, especially since she respected and admired Murray's faith.

She continued thumbing through the paper. Sworn into office after President Harding died in '23, President Coolidge, now five months into his second term, extolled the country's rapid economic growth, often referring to the decade as the "Roaring Twenties."

Louise didn't necessarily agree with the "roaring" part, but she had to admit the past few years had been good for her family—and for See-Boy's, too. Their baby, Franklin—whom Pearl insisted on calling Frankie—had turned five last December and spent so much time in the Carlyon household when his mother worked there, he'd become another member of her family.

"Momma," Bobby said, leaning on the doorjamb separating the kitchen from the hallway, "I'm heading downtown now."

Louise looked up from her newspaper and smiled. Dressed in dungarees, a muted-red plaid shirt, and gray flat cap—what the mail-order catalogues now called the "newsboy" cap—her eleven-year-old now surpassed her height and stood nearly as tall as Murray. During the summer, Bobby rode the streetcar downtown twice a day, morning and late afternoon, to sell copies of the *Times* on the street corner.

Well, he certainly looks the part, Louise thought with amusement. "All right," she said, "but you should eat before you go."

Bobby spotted the plate of biscuits left over from breakfast, now covered and still warm on the stove. "I'll just grab a biscuit and eat it while I'm walking to the streetcar stop. Can't miss the car or somebody else might get my corner."

"Well, at least take a couple."

Bobby grabbed two and kissed Louise hurriedly on her cheek. "Bye," he called over his shoulder as he disappeared.

Seconds later, she heard the front door close. Sometimes, she found it hard to believe he was actually hers. *So tall and slender and handsome, he could be in the movies,* she thought. *And garrulous— he could talk with adults as well as anyone.* A natural-born salesman, he charmed passersby as though they were long-time friends. And though he didn't need to work selling newspapers, he liked having money of his own. *That, and he simply likes dealing with people.*

Unlike Henry, who completed high school but still shied away from anyone he didn't know well. The counseling sessions, which Louise paid dearly for, helped—his eccentricities now fewer and general health better. But his only real passion was for music.

Henry had been ecstatic when, for his nineteenth birthday, Louise presented him with a set of drums—the only thing on his wish list. Never had Louise seen him so happy. Fannie and Murray were less so. Even though the drums were set up in the backyard shed—Bobby's pedal airplane now long gone—Henry's practice sessions could be heard in every room in the house. As a compromise, she confined his drumming to weekdays between the hours of ten in the morning and five in the afternoon.

Fortunately for all, especially Henry, his friend Jimmy Farr and another couple of boys had started a band and included Henry. They'd named it "Farr and Away." Jimmy's father had a garage separate from their house and allowed the boys to practice there. Louise had gotten See-Boy to move Henry's drums to the Farr's garage.

It wasn't much of a band, Henry told her—just a trumpet, trombone, clarinet, and the drums—but it might as well have been Duke Ellington's orchestra in Henry's eyes. The group had actually played for a couple of high school functions before the end of spring classes, and the boys were doing their best to line up performances for the coming fall.

Henry might not be the entrepreneur Bobby appeared to be, but he did better than Louise had ever allowed herself to hope.

Fannie strolled into the kitchen smoking a cigarette. "Have the boys gone?"

Louise nodded. "Bobby's on his way downtown and Henry left earlier for Jimmy's."

Fannie gestured toward the newspaper. "How're the monkeys coming along?"

Louise folded the *Times* and passed it to her mother. "I suppose it depends on who you ask. If I were in John Scopes' shoes, I'd have to say not so well."

CHAPTER 19

L ouise and Pearl sat in the parlor in their makeshift office when Bobby swept past them later that morning and went straight to his room.

Pearl raised an eyebrow. "That's strange. Bobby always says hello."

"I know. He's early, too. He usually waits until after all the office workers—even the ones running late—are off the street before he turns in his unsold papers and catches the streetcar home."

Pearl handed another piece of scrap paper to Frankie, who leaned intently over the coffee table drawing and coloring circus animals. "I want Bobby to see my elephant."

Louise stood and stretched. "Perhaps in a minute, Frankie." Then to Pearl, "I'm just going to check on him. I'll be right back." She walked down the hallway and knocked on the door to Bobby's room. "May I come in?"

"I guess so," Bobby mumbled.

She closed the door behind her and stepped over to Bobby, who sat on the far side of his bed staring out the window.

"You're home early this morning. Is something wrong?"

When he turned to face her, she saw his swollen right eye, turning dark around its edges, and his cheek showed signs of a scrape. She sat down beside him. "What happened? Were you in a fight?"

Bobby hung his head. "It wasn't really a fight. I didn't even get a lick in."

She put an arm around his shoulder. "Tell me about it."

"I was selling newspapers at my usual corner at Cherry and Chestnut when a couple of older boys came up and told me it was *their* corner now and I needed to find somewhere else. I told them I'd been selling there for months."

"What happened when you said that?"

"One of them grabbed my papers and the other pushed me down. I got up and swung at him, but he punched me and I fell again, scraped my cheek on the sidewalk."

Bobby hung his head. "After that, I just left. I felt too afraid to fight them."

Louise squeezed Bobby's shoulder. "It's all right. I'm glad you didn't fight. There are other ways to settle things."

"But what do I do?"

"Nothing today. Don't go back there this afternoon. I'll telephone the *Times* and see if they can help."

"They won't do anything," he said. "They told us to find our own corners."

Louise rose from the bed and started toward the hall telephone. "We'll see about that. I feel sure there's something they can do."

The switchboard operator at the *Times* routed her to the circulation manager, who told her he appreciated her problem but didn't get involved in such disputes. "If I did that, ma'am, I'd be running all over Chattanooga. Even then, it wouldn't help. A few of those boys play pretty rough when it comes to getting a high-volume corner."

Louise replaced the receiver and sighed. *Oh, Murray, I know the railroad job pays well, but I wonder sometimes if it's worth your being away all week. If you were here, you'd know what to do.* Twelve years ago, she would have gone after the ruffians with a sawed-off broomstick, a solution she couldn't undertake as an adult.

Then again, her mother didn't mind undertaking less-than-adult measures when it called for it. Maybe she'd talk to her after she and Pearl were through for the day. She walked softly back to Bobby's room and peeked in to find him still sitting on the bed staring out the window. She decided to leave him be until she had something worth telling him.

Louise and Pearl worked until late that afternoon, stopping only when Louise smelled fried chicken cooking. She bid Pearl and Frankie goodbye and joined Fannie in the kitchen.

Fannie looked up from the stove. "You two were still pouring over the books, so I thought I'd start supper. I like to have it ready as soon as Bobby gets back from downtown."

"He didn't go back downtown this afternoon. In fact, that's what I wanted to speak to you about. He got into—"

Fannie interrupted her. "Sure he did; he left mid-afternoon. You were so busy you probably didn't notice."

"Oh, Mother," Louise said. "He got into a fight this morning with a couple of older boys who wanted his corner. I told him not to go back today."

Fannie turned off the stove and slipped out of her apron. "You call See-Boy. See if he'll give us a ride downtown. We'll find him."

Louise had just picked up the telephone when she heard a knock on the front door. When she opened the door, she saw a shiny silver automobile parked at the curb and Bobby waiting on the porch beside a very nicely dressed man. Both smiled.

"Good day, Ms. Carlyon," Squire Adamson said.

Flustered, Louise smoothed back her hair. "Why, Squire, this is quite a surprise. Please come in."

"Thank you very much." The attorney followed Bobby inside. "In fact, it's been a day for surprises."

Fannie peeked around the corner, fluffing her auburn curls. "John, how nice it is to see you again. Do come in and have a seat in the parlor." She hurried ahead and moved the business ledgers to make room.

"Thank you, ladies, but I cannot stay. I will, at least, explain why I've shown up on your doorstep with my latest client."

Louise and Fannie exchanged glances.

"Bobby here came to see me this afternoon and explained his problem. After a brief discussion—" Adamson retrieved a dollar bill from his vest pocket— "he put me on retainer for legal services. I then tracked down Officer McCrory, whose walking beat includes not only my office but the corner of Cherry and Chestnut."

"I remembered Squire Adamson from when he came for lunch, and I knew his office sat just up the hill across from the courthouse," Bobby added.

"Yes," Adamson continued, "and the three of us confronted the older boys who stole Bobby's corner and threatened them with serious legal problems if they did not cease and desist immediately."

Bobby grinned. "Officer McCrory's thumping his nightstick into his palm probably also helped a little."

"Indeed so. In any event, he promised to keep his eye on the corner during morning and late afternoon rush hours to ensure there's no repeat of this incident." The attorney placed his hand on Bobby's shoulder and patted him. "I knew this was a smart boy as soon as I met him. He knows how to handle a situation."

"I really don't know how to thank you," Louise said, relief flooding her.

"I certainly do," Fannie responded. "You'll have to stay and have supper with us. I happen to make the best fried chicken in the city, and there's mashed potatoes, butterbeans, and coleslaw." She tilted her head and arched her eyebrows. "You will stay, won't you?"

Adamson pulled out his pocket watch and checked the time, then smiled at Fannie. "Well, all things considered, I think I'd be a fool not to."

CHAPTER 20

A week passed without any further trouble, and Louise silently celebrated with a meal of baked pork chops and fresh squash. The telephone rang just as Louise, Fannie, and the boys sat down for supper.

"Go ahead, Louise," her mother said. "I'll answer the phone."

Louise served while Henry and Bobby buttered fresh, hot biscuits. She couldn't hear the telephone conversation, but it seemed to be taking a while. The thought of Murray being hurt on the job whispered fleetingly through her head but vanished just as quickly. It was Wednesday, right in the middle of his layover. By this time of day, he'd be eating supper with the other railroad men who patronized the same Cincinnati hotel—that or playing canasta, their every-night pastime.

Fannie returned and took a chair at the table, her expression pensive. Her hands lay folded, one atop the other in her lap.

"Who called?" Louise asked.

Fannie turned slowly, speaking quietly. "The minister from my mother's church. It seems your grandmother Cornelius passed away."

Louise looked at Bobby and Henry. Bobby had never seen his great grandmother; she had never taken an interest in him. Henry, of course, would remember her. She had frightened and intimidated him so much he'd refused to be alone in the house without Louise or his mother. Still, his face showed nothing.

She rose from her seat. "I'll call Cincinnati long distance and let Murray know."

Fannie shook her head. "No, let's finish our supper first. I know these boys are hungry, and Mother Cornelius surely isn't going anywhere."

They all attended the funeral, held Saturday in the same church where Louise's mother first met Murray. It brought back so many memories of hardships they'd faced that Louise wondered if they'd suffered just so they'd appreciate the better life they now had. Or perhaps Fannie's perseverance and determination, coupled with Murray's availability, had just won out. She thought of her husband as a godsend, so maybe it was both.

Mama Cornelius looked no happier in death than she had in life. She may be rejoicing in heaven, but her mortal coil didn't let on. The fragrance from lilies and carnations situated around the coffin reminded Louise of her father's funeral. Only Will's face had looked different in death—almost pleasant. Not so with Mama Cornelius. She appeared ready to snap open those stern, watchful eyes and direct her glare on any unsuspecting mourner.

And, unlike her father's bleak event, plenty populated the rows of polished wooden pews—members of the church, Louise assumed, since her grandmother had no other friends or acquaintances to her knowledge.

It didn't surprise Louise to see Murray circulating among members of the congregation, shaking hands and conversing prior to the funeral's start. He had known many of these people when he regularly attended this church. She stole a glance at Bobby, sitting on the other side of her husband. He possessed those same qualities. With luck, or—remembering her present setting—perhaps through the grace of God, he would go far in life.

The same minister who Louise had half-listened to that Easter Sunday when she first met Murray performed this funeral. He spoke with a smile on his face and, according to him, a happy heart, knowing for certain Mrs. Cornelius walked hand-in-hand with Jesus on streets paved with pure gold.

Louise snuck a look at Henry, sitting on the far side of his mother. Henry chose that same moment, no doubt in reaction to the minister's vision of Mama Cornelius, to glance in Louise's direction. He rolled his eyes and grinned. She turned away as her own grin threatened to spread.

The five of them rode together in the funeral home family car to the cemetery at Forest Hills, where Mama Cornelius would spend eternity lying next to her husband, Fannie's father. After the brief graveside service, as their car started for the exit, Louise asked the driver to turn right and go up a slight rise to where the Schmidt family plot lay.

As Louise viewed the headstones and let her mind wander back to the happy days when her other grandparents were alive, the others stood by the car, waiting solemnly. "I wish you could have met them, Murray, and you, too, Bobby. You would have loved them."

Fannie spoke for the first time since leaving the church. "They would have loved you, too—both of you."

After a supper prepared and left at the house by several of the church members, Louise and Fannie sat together on the back steps watching lightening bugs do their lazy, early evening dance.

Busy on Friday when Mama Cornelius' attorney called and talked with Fannie, the two had not, until now, had a chance to discuss the conversation.

"I'm the sole heir to the estate, such as it is. Other than the house itself, I believe a few assets remain—a burial policy signed over to the funeral home, probably a few dollars in savings and checking accounts. I'll know more after I meet with Mother's attorney next week."

"I'll be glad to go with you if you like. I appreciated having you there when I had that trouble with Sylvia and Edith."

"That's kind of you, dear, but you've enough to do without shepherding me around town. Actually, I believe I'll ask John to come along and advise me on these matters." Fannie turned and looked at Louise. "What do you think about that?"

Louise didn't know what to think but dared not say so. "Whatever you think. I'm sure he'll have your best interests at heart."

"Good then," Fannie said. "That's exactly what I'll do."

CHAPTER 21

S quire Leonard Bates' reception area wasn't nearly as nice as Squire Adamson's. Fannie imagined the attorney's interior office would also pale in comparison. She had arrived early for the meeting and now wondered what time John would be there. Not that she worried. She just felt more comfortable in his presence.

When she explained her situation over the telephone, he'd said she would not likely need his services, that the proceedings appeared uncomplicated. "Just the same," she'd replied, "I'd feel so much better with you present." And with that, he graciously agreed to meet her at Bates' law office.

Fannie stood to ask the receptionist the time when the outer door opened and Squire Adamson swept into the reception area. She took a deep breath at the sight of him, and his beaming smile as he saw her almost took her breath away.

He walked to her and took her hand in both of his. "Fannie, always a pleasure."

Such a simple thing, yet it made Fannie's heart thump inside her chest like one of Henry's drums. She exerted only the slightest pressure on his hand as they sat down. "I'm so glad you agreed to be here, John." She loved saying his name aloud. "I feel so protected when I'm around you."

The receptionist interrupted. "Now that you're both here, Squire Bates will see you in his office." She stood, stepped to the inner office, and opened the door.

Adamson followed Fannie inside, shook hands with Bates, and introduced them. A short and portly man with brown hair mostly gone to gray, Bates blinked behind the thick eyeglasses perched low on his nose.

"Well, John," he said, smiling to show he meant no ill will, "I hope your presence here won't mean a protracted fight through the court system."

"Not at all, Leonard, I'm merely here in the capacity as a friend of the family."

Bates gestured to seats and winked at Fannie. "It's handy to have an attorney as a friend of the family, eh, Ms. Meyers?"

"Indeed it is." Fannie glanced around Bates' office. Just as she had imagined, the office didn't compare with John's.

The discussion was, as Squire Adamson predicted and Fannie expected, a simple matter. Mrs. Cornelius had few assets. She left the house and its contents to Fannie. The remainder of her holdings—a small amount of money in a savings account and a Liberty Bond she had purchased during the war—she bequeathed to her church. Bates gave Fannie the deed and keys to her mother's house, they all shook hands, and the meeting terminated—all too soon for Fannie's purposes.

Outside on the sidewalk, Fannie again thanked Adamson for coming, and again he told her it had been his pleasure.

"I'm not sure what I will do with Mother's house," Fannie said, looking at the keys in her hand. "I haven't been there in such a long time. I suppose I really should go and take a look at it." She turned her face up to his. "Do you know where I might catch the bus to North Chattanooga?"

The attorney hesitated only a few seconds before he pointed to the silver Chrysler Imperial parked at the curb. "I have a bit of time today. Why don't I drive you?"

"Oh, John, I don't want to inconvenience you any more than I already have. Really, I can take a bus."

"Nonsense, I'm curious anyway. I dabble in real estate now and then. Perhaps I can give you an idea of the house's worth on the market."

Fannie placed her hand on his arm. "Oh, John, that would be lovely."

They pulled up next to the modest frame bungalow and got out, pausing to inspect the front. The old house still looked the same as when Fannie, Louise, and Henry all shared it with Mama Cornelius. The grass needed cutting and the shrubbery could stand pruning, but the paint, the porch, and walkway all seemed in good condition.

"Shall we go inside?" Fannie asked, jangling the keys.

"Let's do."

The house smelled faintly of lavender, and Fannie tried to remember if her mother ever wore perfume. It wouldn't have fit with Fannie's image of her—*an unnecessary extravagance when it took all she had just to keep groceries on the table.*

Together, they walked through the quiet house: the kitchen, where it occurred to Fannie she'd have to clean out the ice box and do something with the non-perishables; the parlor, where her mother had died of a heart attack while reading the Bible; and her mother's bedroom, the bed fully made—one of many daily rituals her mother had insisted on. The other bedroom she and the children had used.

"This is where Louise and Henry and I slept when we stayed here. Louise used a rollaway bed over there by the wall." Fannie ran a hand over the wallpaper—repeating roses ran vertically, encircled by green, thorny vines. "Louise never cared for this pattern."

As they stood in the doorway, Fannie allowed herself to lean back against Adamson's chest. He tensed slightly, then relaxed and leaned into her back. They said nothing. Then his hand moved to her shoulder and slid down her right arm. She felt the gentle pressure of his hand on her other arm and turned, lifting her face to his. They kissed, softly at first then more urgently.

"We shouldn't be doing this," he said, breathing heavily.

"But we are," Fannie said against his throat. "I want you, John. I have since the first time we met." She loosened his tie, pulled it from his neck and unbuttoned the first two buttons of his shirt. Then she kissed his chest.

"And I, you," he said. "God help me. I've thought of this many, many times."

She took his hand and led him to the bed where she'd spent so many nights worrying about her future. But she wasn't thinking of the future right now, only the present.

L ouise happened past the parlor window just as the big silver car rolled up to the curb. Squire Adamson got out and came around to open the door for Fannie. They shook hands on the sidewalk then the attorney got back in the car and drove away.

Fannie's auburn hair fell loosely, just brushing her shoulders. *Unusual,* Louise thought. *She tends to wear it up.* Fannie's face, always pretty, fairly glowed as she stepped through the front door.

"How did it go? I began to worry, you took so long."

"Oh, it went fine, dear. John and I stopped by Mother's house for a few minutes. He promised to work up an estimate for me on its worth."

"So you're thinking of selling it?" Earlier, Louise had allowed herself the idea of a home with only Murray, Bobby, and herself. Now, she felt that pleasant notion slip away.

"Obviously, Henry and I couldn't live there. I'd have no way to afford the monthly utilities. But I may hang onto the property for a while. John thinks the value will increase over time." She smiled and smoothed a stray lock of hair from her forehead. "I'll need to go over there occasionally to keep the house and yard in order—for whenever we do decide to sell."

"Who is 'we'?" Louise asked.

"Squire Adamson and I. John agreed to advise me on the financial aspects of the situation—free of charge, of course. It's just friendly advice, not professional services." She smiled again and flounced down the hallway to her room.

We? Louise thought. Now that gave her pause.

CHAPTER 22

Herbert Hoover made his inaugural speech on March 4, 1929, just two weeks before Bobby's sixteenth birthday. Louise listened on the radio as the president spoke of the nation's prosperity. "I have no fears for the future of our country," he told the large crowd gathered outside the East Portico of the U.S. Capitol. "It is bright with hope."

In a family predisposed to vote Democratic, the Carlyon household had gone with the Republican candidate in the '28 election. And why not? With unemployment down and the economy going great, the future did, indeed, look rosy. So much so, in fact, Louise invested part of the business's profits in sound stocks.

Fannie still had occasional contact with Squire Adamson, whom Louise had learned invested heavily in the stock market. When she first discussed the idea of investing with her mother, Fannie assured her the squire would be glad to advise her. And, through his guidance, Louise compiled a modest-sized-but-profitable portfolio.

It made her feel good, not only about the growth in her earnings but also because she'd invested in her country. America had truly become the land of opportunity.

When President Hoover's speech ended, Louise rose from her chair in the parlor, stretched, and walked into the kitchen. One of the more immediate investments Louise made stood tall and proud in the corner of the room—a shiny, white Frigidaire. Prior to her purchase, she'd never realized how onerous it had been dealing with the old icebox. This, by comparison, felt like heaven.

She removed loaf bread from the bread box and sliced ham and mayonnaise from the Frigidaire. Bobby would be home from school soon, ravenous as always—and, like as not, he'd have his buddy, Harry West, following on his heels. The two had become inseparable over the last year. Harry's father, who owned an automobile dealership, had provided his son a well-used Ford sedan. Harry had his license already, and Bobby would, too, after his birthday. Though they had no car, she and Murray agreed he'd need it since he planned to work with See-Boy over the summer, and it would come in handy if he needed to drive the business truck.

It seemed almost no time at all since Bobby switched from building model airplanes from balsa wood—consumed by everything flight-related, including Charles Lindberg's solo flight across the Atlantic Ocean—to a passion for cars and girls.

Even as she pondered this, Harry's auto horn blared outside, and he pulled in next to the curb. Stepping into the hallway, Louise watched the two boys clamber from the vehicle. Both handsome, tall, and slim, Bobby's hair, dark and straight like Louise's own, contrasted sharply with Harry's golden-blond and wavy locks—either quite a catch for any young girl someday.

As she held the screen door for the boys, she caught sight of something printed in white paint on the car's black exterior—*Harry "Ace" West and Bobby "The Flash" Carlyon*.

"What in the world have you two done to that automobile?"

Bobby grinned and pecked her on the cheek. "Pretty catchy, don't you think, Momma?"

"We gave ourselves nicknames," Harry added.

Louise frowned at Harry. "Won't your father be upset you did that to your car?"

"No, ma'am, he's got plenty more."

Bobby swept past Louise and headed for the kitchen. "Can you make us sandwiches, Momma? We're hungry."

She took another look at the car and shook her head. "I've no doubt of that."

See-Boy took a long look around the space and wondered what Mr. William would have said about the newly planned use of the former meat market. He thought it ironic his father had worked here so long for Mr. William, learning the butcher business, only to be let go after Miss Louise's father sold the market. The man who had bought the facility had little knowledge of marketing and even less of butchering. The business closed less than a year later and stood empty until See-Boy purchased it for back taxes. In a way, it was back in the family now.

After-hours business at the maintenance shed had grown slowly but steadily since See-Boy started selling moonshine and offering a place for colored folk in the neighborhood to hang out in the evening. So much so he'd begun to worry a little about the pedestrian traffic coming and going in his backyard. Nice for the business, but he didn't want to attract attention.

That's why the former meat market offered the perfect opportunity for expansion. Though musty and still harboring the faintest scent of meat, it needed only a bit of airing out. Easily twice the size of the shed, the back door opened onto an alley, offering a discrete entrance.

He'd done most of the remodeling himself, knocking down a couple of interior walls and painting over the windows that faced the sidewalk. His father helped, and Pearl added touches to make the place look more elegant.

The new setting seemed ideal, given its location closer to the predominately colored neighborhood behind the elementary school and the fact surrounding businesses shut down around five, so noise shouldn't become a problem. He might even get one of those coin-operated phonographs he'd heard about. That made him smile—music and dancing in his own club. *Lord, whoever would have thought.*

Now, the club just needed a name. Wouldn't be no signs out front advertising what went on inside. But maybe a small hand-lettered one over the rear entrance. He'd always kind of favored "the hanger" like they used to call the shed. But there'd been no airplanes in there for years. He guessed he'd just have to think on it a while longer. He still had a couple of weeks before he opened, plenty of time.

CHAPTER 23

During the summer of '29, the Carlyon and Meyers/Schmidt families fared well enough. The rental houses remained occupied, and the work needed to keep them in good repair justified Bobby helping See-Boy and Lawrence.

On the occasions when Louise interacted with See-Boy, he told her Bobby worked hard and carried his weight. Pearl agreed, from what she had observed, and said Daddy Lawrence really enjoyed having him around. Bobby had gotten his driver's license in the spring and learned how to handle the truck as well as See-Boy, according to Pearl.

Working mostly outdoors rewarded Bobby with a healthy tan—something the girls noticed, too. Weather permitting, he and Harry loaded up the Ford with snacks, beverages, and a varying bevy of young girls, driving over to Chickamauga Lake for a picnic and swim.

Louise wondered if the girls' parents knew and approved of the dates—if you could call them that—or if the truth might have been somewhat circumvented. She'd asked Bobby that question and he'd said, "Everything's okay, Momma. It's not really dating when there's a bunch of us." Maybe so, but she still wondered.

Then, around the middle of June, Bobby and Harry honed in on two girls in particular. Since the two boys started hanging around together, Louise had overheard them talking about so many different girls she couldn't keep all the names in her head. Lately, however, Reba and Helen dominated their discourse.

Louise even had a chance to meet the girls one Saturday in late June. She stood on the front porch, sweeping, when the *Ace and Flash* Ford eased to the curb and Bobby climbed from the back seat.

He blew by her. "I forgot my bathing suit."

When he reappeared half a minute later carrying his swimsuit and a rolled towel, Louise said, "I'd like to meet your new friends, if that's all right."

"Sure, Momma, come on."

Louise followed him to the car, where he opened the passenger-side door and moved back so she could get a better look at the girls. "Momma, this is Helen."

The girl in the back seat leaned forward. "Hello, Mrs. Carlyon." Helen had blue eyes and a pretty, heart-shaped face framed by a blond bob-cut.

Bobby then introduced the girl sitting next to Harry as Reba. "Pleased to meet you, Mrs. Carlyon," she said and got out of the car so Bobby could climb into the rear seat. She wore a yellow sundress that made her dark eyes stand out, and she sported a hairdo of brown cropped curls. Her tan legs flashed as she slid back onto the front seat.

"We won't be back for supper," Bobby said. "We're going to pick up food for a picnic at the lake."

"Well," Louise said, "just don't be too late. I'm sure these girls' parents will want them home at a reasonable hour."

Harry cranked the car's engine, gave Louise a wave, and pulled away from the curb. She watched as the car rounded the corner and disappeared from sight. The girls seemed nice enough, she thought. But this wasn't a bunch of kids going to the lake together— this was dating. She thought once more about making sure Helen's and Reba's parents—especially their fathers—knew of the situation. She'd mention it again when Bobby came home.

Bobby came in a little after seven-thirty, his cheeks and nose reddened from the sun and his hair hanging in dark threads that grazed his eyebrows. Though not full dark out, twilight hosted dozens of lightening bugs sparking the dusky evening shadows.

Louise and Fannie stood by the kitchen sink finishing the supper dishes while Murray sat in the parlor scanning the previous week's newspapers for local items he missed during his Cincinnati layover.

He followed Bobby into the kitchen "How was your picnic?"

"Really swell, Dad. We roasted wieners over a little fire, and the girls brought lemonade."

Laying her dry cloth on the counter, Louise walked over to her son and brushed the hair from his forehead. "You're sunburned. I can put cold cream on it, if you want."

Bobby shook his head. "No thanks, Momma. I'll be fine."

He turned to leave the kitchen when Louise asked, "Do Helen's mother and father know she's dating you? I hope you and Harry don't get those young ladies in trouble with their parents."

Bobby turned and smiled. "Momma, you don't have to worry. I spoke to Helen's parents a couple weeks ago when Harry and I picked her up. Actually, I've known her father for years. He thinks it's great we're seeing each other."

"Really?" Louise said. "Where did you meet her father?"

"Here. He had lunch with all of us. Then later, I put him on retainer to help with my newspaper sales." Bobby's grin grew wider. "It's Squire Adamson."

Louise felt a wave of relief. She remembered the attorney saying he had a daughter about Bobby's age.

"Well, Louise," Murray said, matching Bobby's grin. "What do you think of that? Our son dating Squire Adamson's daughter." He reached out and gave Bobby a hug.

"What a surprise," Louise said.

Bobby nodded and slipped out of the kitchen, retreating to his bedroom.

Louise glanced at Fannie. "It's funny, isn't it, Mother, how we keep crossing paths with Squire Adamson? Who knows, perhaps we'll have him and his wife as in-laws someday."

Fannie turned back to the supper dishes. "Yes, that would be quite something, wouldn't it?"

CHAPTER 24

Bobby continued seeing Helen Adamson throughout the summer, usually double-dating with Harry and Reba, but Helen also joined them for supper. On those occasions, Bobby borrowed See-Boy's truck, returning it the next morning.

Late one evening three weeks into Bobby and Helen's last year of high school, Bobby knocked on Louise's bedroom door.

"Come in." Louise sat before her dresser mirror rubbing cold cream on her face.

Bobby perched on the edge of his parents' bed but said nothing. Louise turned and smiled—then registered his expression. He'd seemed distracted at supper. Now, he appeared distraught, head hanging, hands clasped between his knees, staring at his feet.

"What's wrong?"

He said nothing for a moment but looked up at her, his eyes moist. A flash of pain ran through her own body to see her son obviously hurting.

"Helen is going to have a baby," he finally whispered.

Louise closed her eyes, lifted her head, and took a deep breath. When she opened her eyes, Bobby stared at the floor again. "Oh, Bobby." She waited, hoped for words to come, but they didn't.

"I don't know what to do, Momma."

Louise grabbed a tissue from the dresser top and swiped at the cold cream on her face. Then she stepped over to the bed, sat down beside her son, and put her arm around his shoulder. They sat for a full minute not talking. Finally, Louise asked, "Is she absolutely sure?"

Bobby nodded.

"How far along is she?"

Bobby shrugged. "She told me she's missed two periods."

Louise's mind raced. She had a thousand questions, but she tried to focus on the ones immediately relevant. "Do her parents know?" *Surely not, or Squire Adamson would be here even as we speak, pounding on our front door.*

He shook his head. "Momma, she's found someone who can get rid of the baby. I've heard stories about girls who do that, and sometimes they die afterward." His eyes grew moist again. "I don't want Helen to die."

"Do you love Helen?" *He's too young to know what love really is. How can anyone sixteen know love?* She hadn't known when she married Murray at fifteen. He'd loved her and been her lover long before she really fell in love with him. Many weren't so lucky.

"I … I don't know, Momma. I think I do. I might. I like her a lot. I'd even marry her if I had to."

There's a 'but' there somewhere, Louise thought. The idea of Bobby and Helen marrying before graduating high school seemed bad enough. *But to do so for the wrong reasons?* She'd married so the family would survive—but for her son to travel down that same path? He had so much potential. Would it all go to waste?

"What do you want to do?"

"I don't want her to die. I don't want to get married. And I don't want a baby. I just want everything to be like it was."

Louise sighed, thinking, *If only that could happen.* But she knew, no matter whatever else happened, it would never, could never be the same as before.

"What should I do? Just tell me and I'll do it."

Louise got up and went back to the dresser. After retrieving a Lucky Strike, she paced the room, blue-gray smoke trailing after her like thin, low-level clouds.

She stopped pacing. "How did Helen find someone to end her pregnancy?"

He shrugged once more. "A girl at school had an abortion last year from a woman in East Lake. A few of her friends knew about it, I guess, and she got the woman's name and telephone number from them. But she'll need money. She can't ask Squire Adamson for any, so she asked me."

Louise crushed out the cigarette in an ashtray. "How much does it cost?"

Bobby rose from the bed and walked over to the window. Darkness painted the windowpane black, except for a faint reflection from a moon on the wane. He spoke with his back to Louise. "She said fifty dollars. Is that too much? I can use my saved wages from this summer."

Louise remembered her Grandmother Schmidt with only the fondest memories, but she knew, from her own mother's stories, how the woman had developed a discrete reputation as an abortionist for the daughters of more affluent families in Chattanooga. If anything, she felt sure the cost—at least from someone who knew what they were doing—would have climbed significantly by now.

"No, Bobby," Louise said. "It's not nearly enough."

CHAPTER 25

As Louise and Bobby talked, she learned that, once he had the money, he and Helen planned to borrow Harry's car and drive to East Lake. They would leave for school as usual and meet Harry in the school's parking lot. They hoped the procedure would be done by the time school let out, so no one would ever know.

"Tell Helen you'll have the money soon," Louise said, "but not for a day or two. I need time to think. Find out where this woman lives and her name if you can."

"All right, Momma."

"Try not to worry." She gave him a hug. *I'll worry enough for both of us.*

Bobby paused at the bedroom door. "Do we have to tell Daddy and Grandma about this?"

"I don't know the answer to that right now."

Bobby nodded silently and disappeared.

Louise took a deep breath and let it out. Then she sat down at the dresser and rested her head on her forearms. *Dear God, what to do?* Once again, she wished Murray home. She didn't know if he would handle the situation like she would—in fact, she didn't have any idea at the moment how she *would* handle it—but he would handle it, one way or another. And that would be enough.

After a while, she finished removing her makeup, then took off her bathrobe and crawled into the empty bed. Through the window, she could just see the curved, pale yellow slice of moon. Sleepless hours later, she saw it overtaken by the sun.

Within a day, with the abortionist's name and address scrawled on a piece of lined notebook paper, Louise picked up the telephone and dialed See-Boy's number. Still early, she caught him before he started work.

Before he even said hello, Louise asked, "Can you do something with me today?"

See-Boy laughed. "Miss Louise, I can always do something with you. Besides that, you're the boss lady. I got to do what you want me to do, right?"

Louise smiled in spite of herself. "It's not like that. You're a friend and I need a favor, a big favor."

"All right, friend," See-Boy said. "Consider myself at your disposal."

The drive to East Lake took only half an hour. On the way, Louise told See-Boy everything she'd learned from Bobby the night before last. He listened quietly and nodded occasionally. "I'm sorry for your trouble. Sorry for Bobby, too, and the young lady."

They found the address on a block of hunkered, stoop-shoul-dered houses that looked as though age and squalor had sapped the strength from the wooden frames. See-Boy pulled to the curb a few houses down from the one where the woman lived.

"What you going to do now?" See-Boy asked. "It don't look like much of anything good can come out of this neighborhood."

"I'm not really sure. But I've got to have a better sense of things than I do at the moment."

She got out of the truck and walked back to the house. A rusted, chain-link fence enclosed a yard of mostly dirt with a few clumps of grass spaced out unevenly. The gate hung open. Louise steeled herself and started up the crumbling concrete walkway. She knocked on the door, saw a curtain twitch in what must have been the parlor or living room, and waited. A few seconds later, the door opened a crack.

"What do you want?" A disembodied voice came from behind the crack.

"I have a daughter," Louise said. "She's in … trouble. I understand you might be able to help."

"Help you with what?" The voice sounded less brusque now, maybe interested but still suspicious.

"Making it go away." She remembered what Bobby had said on the night of his confession. "Making everything like it was before." She paused for a second, then added, "I have money."

The door opened further, and Louise caught a glimpse of the voice's owner. Short, with straight, mousy-brown hair that fell to her shoulders, the woman wore a stained chenille housecoat around her ample body. Her eyes were bright, like bird eyes, predatory.

Louise said again, "I have money. Fifty dollars, right?" She patted the purse slung over her shoulder. "I just wanted to see your operation. Make sure everything looks all right."

The woman looked Louise up and down, making up her mind.

"I'll pay you in advance." Louise opened her purse to show the cash. "I'll bring my daughter later today."

The woman grunted, opening the door just far enough for Louise to step inside. The dark, dingy room smelled of cooked onions. A threadbare sofa slumped against one wall, and an equally tattered chair and floor-model radio made up the rest of the furniture.

"You said you'd pay in advance."

Louise nodded and produced two twenties and a ten. When the woman reached for it, Louise held the money back. "I want to see where you do the procedure."

Grunting again, the woman led Louise down a short hallway and into a small room probably once designed to be a sewing room or office. Illuminated by a bare, yellow bulb hanging from the ceiling, the room housed a single bed, a stained mattress, and a metal cabinet.

"All right, you've seen it. Give me the money now, bring your daughter anytime today, but be prepared to wait while I do the procedure. And bring pads. She'll probably bleed for a while."

Louise handed over the bills and followed the woman back to the front door. The sun felt warm on her shoulders when she stepped outside, but she shuddered anyway. *Out fifty dollars,* she thought, *but at least I know.*

After she told See-Boy what she'd found, he waited a minute before responding. "Pearl got another cousin—not the one makes moonshine—who's a doctor. He lives over near Red Bank. If you want, I'll see whether she thinks he might do what's needed. If you decide to do that, I mean."

Louise studied See-Boy's face and wondered where she'd be if she hadn't had him in her life. "I don't know what I'll decide to do. I don't even know if it's my decision to make. But yes, please ask Pearl and let me know as soon as you can. The more information I have the better."

CHAPTER 26

O nce again, Louise entered Squire Adamson's office. She'd telephoned earlier and made an appointment. As she waited in reception, her heart thumped even more quickly than her first time. After a few minutes, the inner office door opened and Adamson bade her come inside.

"It's nice to see you again, Mrs. Carlyon." They shook hands, and Louise seated herself in front of his polished oak desk. The attorney settled in his chair. "Now, how can I be of help today?"

Louise had practiced what to say—how to break the news to him—but words failed her now. Finally, she said, "I received some troubling information a few nights ago. It has to do with my son and your daughter."

The attorney frowned. "What do you mean?"

Louise nodded. "There's only one way to say this, Squire Adamson. Your daughter is going to have a child. Bobby is the father."

Adamson said nothing for a few seconds, staring at Louise as though she had spoken in tongues. Then his face hardened. "Tell me more, Mrs. Carlyon."

What more? It was out there in plain daylight. She struggled with words again. "A few nights ago, Bobby came to me and told me of his concern for Helen. He told me about the baby and that Helen planned to see a woman who would abort the child."

Adamson leaned forward on his desk and placed his face into his hands. "My God, my God. When is she going? Who is this woman?"

"She hasn't gone yet, but I have, and this is not a person who should ever touch your daughter."

"Unlike your son, I suppose," Adamson snapped.

Louise waited for the pulse in her neck to abate before answering. "My son is partly to blame for this—but only partly. I think we should both be glad he came to me when he did. He felt afraid for Helen, afraid she might die from a botched abortion. Girls do, you know."

Adamson stared at her, his expression angry, but gradually, it softened. "Yes, I know these things happen. Young girls make mistakes then often make greater mistakes. But please, Mrs. Carlyon, don't deny me the right to be angry."

"I understand. I'm angry, too, believe me, but I'm more concerned for both our children. This could destroy them. I believe our best course of action is to decide how we'll proceed. And do so as quickly as possible."

The attorney leaned back in his chair and folded his hands in his lap. "You're right, of course. What do you suggest?"

"Bobby told me he is willing to marry Helen. I'm not sure if Helen is equally willing, but that's one option. Helen could have the baby, possibly with relatives living outside Chattanooga, and give it up for adoption. Or, we could go through with the abortion, except it would take place in a safe environment with a medically trained physician."

"Helen's having a child at this point in her life—or having this pregnancy become known to others—would ruin her, her education. We'd planned on her going to college. *She'd* planned on college." He pinched the bridge of his nose and sighed. "And my wife … even knowing about this situation would devastate her."

"That leaves only one solution," Louise said.

Adamson shook his head. "I am acquainted with a great many people in this city, many of them physicians, but I wouldn't have any idea about how I would approach one with this."

"Fortunately for all of us, Squire, I do. Will your schedule let you take time this afternoon to pick up your daughter from school?"

"I have an appointment out of the office, but … under the circumstances, yes, this certainly takes precedence."

They spent another half hour discussing what Louise had in mind. They planned to meet at Louise's house after school. Fannie had made plans to take care of a few chores at Mama Cornelius's house, and Henry had band practice.

When Bobby arrived home after school, Louise gave him an abbreviated explanation of what she and the squire had discussed. They'd barely finished when the big silver car pulled up in front of the house.

As soon as Helen and her father entered, Louise could tell the girl had been crying. Louise retrieved tissues from her bedroom, noticing that Helen and Bobby seemed unable to meet the other's eyes, and only in fleeting glances did they meet Louise's or Squire Adamson's.

"Why don't we all go into the parlor and sit down?" Louise suggested.

Louise and Adamson did most of the talking for a while. Once the shock of having their problem known to both parents wore off, Helen and Bobby relaxed a bit.

Louise and Adamson agreed beforehand they would not bring up the subject of marriage—unless Bobby or Helen did. Neither did, and each seemed eager to follow their parents' suggested plan of action.

"We believe this is the best thing for both of you," Louise said. "You're young and smart and have the rest of your lives before you."

"You made a mistake," Adamson said. "But we all make mistakes. The key is to not let that mistake mark you for life."

Helen and Bobby nodded often and listened intently. Louise watched them closely, noting how the shared doomed expressions gradually faded from their young faces. Life no longer folded in on them, the consequences of their actions not as devastating as they'd imagined.

A cross town, in the house she had inherited from her mother, Fannie paced the living room floor, stopping every few minutes to look out the front window for John's car. Never late, she knew it must be something truly important to keep him away.

CHAPTER 27

L ouise watched Pearl closely, admiring how well she handled the truck. *Someday,* she thought, *I'll have to learn to drive.* They sat three abreast in the cab, Helen in the middle, holding fast to Louise's hand.

The drive to Red Bank took less than an hour, most of it spent in silence. Helen's eyes had grown moist at times, but she didn't cry, and Louise thought it best to keep hold of that hand.

The clinic was located in a mostly colored part of town, but if Helen felt any unease riding with Pearl or knowing she would see a colored doctor, she kept it to herself. Louise admired that. Bobby could easily have done worse in picking a spouse, but the timing simply wasn't right.

As Pearl brought the truck to a stop in the clinic parking area, Louise squeezed Helen's hand. "It will all be over soon. You don't have to worry about anything."

The girl nodded and whispered, "Thank you."

The reception area, clean and bright, sat empty except for a middle-aged woman who reminded Louise of Jesse. She took the three of them down a hallway and into the doctor's office. "He'll be with you in just a minute," she said and let herself out.

Louise looked around at the stacks of files arranged neatly on the doctor's desk and framed diplomas on the walls, along with photos of a tall man dressed in an Army uniform. The air held a faintly antiseptic scent.

"My cousin served in the Army during the war," Pearl said, "as a medic, then, after his discharge, he completed medical school."

"You must be proud," Louise said.

"I'm proud of all my family."

The door opened, and the man in the photos entered. "I'm Doctor Reis." He offered Louise and Helen his hand. Pearl rose and hugged him, giving him a peck on the cheek. "Pearl, you are as beautiful as always."

He turned to Helen, hitching a hip onto the corner of his desk. "Helen, you're going to be fine. The procedure is simple. You'll be a bit sore for a while, and you should rest after, but you'll be up and around tomorrow, even back to school, if you feel like it."

Again, Helen whispered, "Thank you."

"I want to explain exactly how the procedure goes before we get started. I can do that in the procedure room, with just you and me, or I can do it out here."

"I'd like them to be here," Helen said.

The doctor smiled. "All right, then, let's get started."

A few minutes later, Doctor Reis's nurse came in and took Helen to the procedure room. When she left, Pearl said, "Jonathon, I really appreciate your help."

"We all do," Louise added.

The doctor smiled at Pearl. "I'm always glad to help out family." Then he turned to Louise. "And from what I understand, Mrs. Carlyon, you're as much family as Pearl."

He stood and opened the door. "I'll have my nurse come and get you when we're done."

Back in the truck by eleven, they arrived at Louise's house at noon. Pearl gave Louise a hug and turned to Helen. "You'll be okay now, honey. You take care of yourself."

Helen threw her arms around Pearl's neck and held her for a long moment. "Thank you so much, Pearl."

Inside, Fannie had vegetable soup on the stove and had turned back Louise's bed so Helen could rest for the afternoon. Louise had told her mother that morning, and, while Fannie expressed both surprise and concern, she quickly agreed with everything Louise intended to do.

She'd asked, "How did John react when you told him?"

"Like any father would, I suppose, but he had the good sense to think of what seemed best for both of them," Louise answered.

Helen managed to eat a little soup and drink a glass of iced tea, then walked with Louise to the bedroom. Louise helped her into bed and tucked the sheets around her.

"You just rest for a while, dear. If you need anything we're right here." Louise paused at the door. "Bobby will be home in a few hours. If you like, I'll send him back to speak with you."

"All right," Helen said. "And, Mrs. Carlyon, I..."

"Yes?"

"Thank you for everything."

"Honey, with all we've been through, you can just call me Louise."

Bobby was ashen-faced when he came in. "How's Helen, Momma?"

"She's fine. It went well. She's resting in my bedroom. Squire Adamson will pick her up on his way home from the office."

"Does she want to see me?"

"You can ask," Louise said. "Knock on the bedroom door and let her know you're here."

Louse watched as Bobby went down the hall and knocked on the door. She heard a muffled response from inside, then Bobby opened the door and stepped through.

Fannie came up beside Louise. "Does her mother know?"

"I don't think so. The squire thought to spare her the whole ordeal."

"Will you tell Murray about it?"

Louise turned to her mother. "I haven't decided. I hate to keep anything from him, but he adores Bobby so much, I think it might break his heart."

"He adores you, too, and I'd hate to have him find out by other means. Then he'd be heartbroken twice. By the way, when is John coming to pick up Helen?"

"In another hour or so, I imagine—whenever he's through at the office."

"I think I'll change out of these clothes and put up my hair before he arrives."

Louise laughed. "You're not still flirting with the squire, are you?"

"Not at all," Fannie said. "But it never hurts to look your best when guests are coming."

She left Louise standing there, thinking. *Would she tell Murray?* She decided her mother was right. She would. She just wasn't sure exactly how or when.

CHAPTER 28

There wasn't a lot of conversation during the brief time Squire Adamson spent in the house before driving his daughter home. Aside from telling him how everything went and how Helen was doing, Louise guessed it had all been said the day before.

Helen thanked Louise again on her way out while her father hovered by her side, his fingers pressed lightly against her back, as gently as one might hold a small bird. Her color had returned, and she had bled very little. Louise followed them to the curb.

With Helen safely tucked inside the car, Adamson turned to Louise and slipped a sheaf of bills into her hand. "This will be enough to cover the physician's costs, Mrs. Carlyon. I can't tell you how much I appreciate your doing all you've done."

"It seems only right, Squire Adamson. After all, my son was party to the situation."

"I know, and I suppose I should be angry at him. But if he hadn't come to you…"

"But he did. And now, hopefully everything will be fine."

With his hand on the car door handle, Adamson said, "He's a good boy at heart, I believe. I was always impressed with him."

Louise had no idea what Bobby and Helen had in mind for the future, but she noted that Helen's father already spoke of Bobby in the past tense.

As the car eased away from the curb, she turned to the house. Bobby stood behind the screened door, and her mother watched from the parlor window.

She slipped an arm around his waist when Bobby opened the door for her. He stood a few inches taller, and she marveled at how much he'd grown and yet how vulnerable he remained. "Can we talk?" Louise asked.

Bobby nodded, and they walked into his bedroom. They sat side by side on the bed, much as they had when he'd first told her about Helen's pregnancy.

"You and Helen talked for a while before her father picked her up?"

"Yes, ma'am, we did."

"I don't imagine I have any real right to know the nature of that conversation, but I'd like to. If you're comfortable telling me."

"We decided it would be best not to see each other anymore. I don't think Squire Adamson would allow it, anyway."

Louise covered Bobby's hand with hers. "He doesn't hate you, you know."

Bobby shrugged.

"You and Helen have been through a lot together. I think it's important you let her know you still care about her, even though you aren't dating anymore. She's probably feeling kind of lost right now, and what happened will stay with her for a long time."

"It'll stay with me, too, Momma."

"I know it will, and that's not necessarily a bad thing. I want you to remember. I want you to let this be a learning experience. Not something that will keep you awake at night, but something you'll keep in mind as you go forward."

Bobby stood and walked to the window. "Why does it feel like everything you learn comes too late to use it?"

Louise smiled. "It's never too late." She rose from the bed and had started for the door when Bobby asked, "Are you going to tell Daddy?"

"Yes, I am. Murray loves you so much. He has a right to know. I think it would be wrong for either of us to keep this from him. I'm sure he will hurt, but he'll be hurting for you, for your pain. Sometimes, life spares no feelings and limits no pain, but neither does it put a ceiling on happiness. And that's what we both want for you, Bobby."

She smiled again, hoping he'd return it. After a moment, he did, but the smile turned just a corner of his mouth, as if it suggested regret as much as happiness. *And maybe,* she thought, *that is as it should be.*

Murray came in as usual early Friday evening. Louise made one of Murray's favorites: thin-cut pork chops fried in a well-seasoned, cast-iron skillet, along with cinnamon apple slices and mashed potatoes. Fannie had offered to help, but Louise wanted the alone time to contemplate the words she'd use to tell him about Helen and his son.

The meal itself went well enough given that Bobby, sitting across from Fannie and Henry, had the look of someone facing the hangman's noose, while she still bounced around mentally on her approach to the coming discussion. But Murray, being Murray, talked enough for all of them. Louise thought it must come naturally to a minister's son—the ability to converse as comfortably with strangers as with family. And he seemed almost always to be in good spirits. That, she hoped, would sustain the both of them for what came next.

They sat on the back porch steps alone after he helped with the dishes. Late September had eased into early October with no discernable difference, the evening air still and warm as they sat shoulder to shoulder smoking cigarettes and watching the moon rise in the sky.

"There'll be a Harvest Moon soon," Louise said. She had become quite a devotee of the Farmer's Almanac, though the only things she planted these days were roses and bulbs.

"It's already pretty," Murray said. "Cincinnati's so big and full of light, it's almost impossible to see the stars, and the moon's not nearly as bright."

"There's something I need to talk to you about, Murray."

He looked at her in the growing dark, flicking an ash from his smoke. "Sounds serious."

"It's about Bobby … and Helen Adamson."

Murray flipped his cigarette into the yard. "Tell me."

It didn't come out as smoothly as she'd hoped. She found herself seeking the right words as she studied Murray's face to gauge his reaction. But, in the end, she managed to get it all out.

"I suppose I should have telephoned you before I did anything," she said. "It probably sounds like an excuse, but I didn't want to upset you."

Murray shook another cigarette from his pack and lit it. "I think you most likely did the same things I would have done, had I known. You deal with life as well as anyone I can think of. It's one of the reasons I love you. But I hate I wasn't here to help you. The older Bobby gets, the more I feel I'm missing out. I've given serious thought to quitting my railroad job and finding something I can do here in Chattanooga. I miss Bobby, and I miss you."

"And my mother and Henry, do you miss them, too?" She'd often wondered about Murray's motivations for being gone most of the week but kept her thoughts to herself. This past week, she realized again just how much she would have appreciated his presence.

Murray looked her in the eyes and grinned. "Less—I miss them less than you and Bobby—but yes, sometimes I guess I miss them, too."

Louise leaned into Murray and kissed him lightly on the lips. "I do love you, Murray. And I miss you. We're doing well enough financially right now. I think your idea is a wonderful one."

"I'll give it thought. Right now, I'm going to talk to Bobby." He stood and stretched, tossing the second butt into the yard.

"He's been so worried what you'd think," Louise said. "Be gentle with him."

Murray paused with the screen door open and glanced back at her. "I wouldn't know how to be anything else."

No, you wouldn't, would you? Another reason she loved him.

CHAPTER 29

Louise put down the *Chattanooga Times*, troubled by the increasingly dismal news related to the falling value of widely traded stocks. The market had undergone a similar decline back in March, and she'd worried then, too, but Squire Adamson assured her it would recover. And it had, gaining its highest value in almost a decade in early September. But now, with Halloween just a few days away, the paper seemed far scarier than any hobgoblin—the so-called experts disagreeing on almost everything and leaving her terribly unsure what to do.

In fact, she had never really understood how the stock market worked. But so many people were making so much money that Squire Adamson's urging her to invest seemed the right thing to do. While she had no real idea of his worth, he apparently did very well.

She thought of calling him, but they hadn't spoken since he'd picked up his daughter nearly a month ago. She felt sure he wouldn't mind. It was just awkward, and she didn't want to be a pest.

It *was* Friday, and Murray would be home in a few hours. Perhaps he'd have an idea what to do. From what she'd learned so far, the widely held opinion called for investors not to panic. If Murray thought it prudent, she would call Squire Adamson Monday.

It brightened her mood to think of Murray leaving the Railway Express Agency for a job in the city. He hadn't yet turned in his notice, rightfully thinking it better to have another position in hand first, but the prospect comforted her—a family together for all life's ups and downs, seeing each other through whatever came along.

Fannie came into the parlor and picked up the paper. "More doomsday speculation?"

"I'm afraid so. I'm thinking of calling Squire Adamson to see what he thinks, but I'll wait and talk to Murray first."

Fannie glanced over the front page then tossed it aside. "Yes, I imagine the squire will have good advice. He's been investing for a long time." She went to the parlor window and pulled back one of the sheer curtains. "I suppose he's still recovering from the trouble we had."

"I guess we all are, to a degree, but it's been almost a month. Except for lessons learned, I hope we can all put it behind us."

Fannie turned away from the window. One corner of her mouth caught in a half-smile, her expression wistful, Louise thought. "I think it likely we'll find out soon enough, don't you?"

Louise wasn't sure what her mother meant but let it go. Fannie held her feelings closely, sometimes given to sayings apropos of nothing except perhaps to herself. Louise had gotten used to it.

Murray read through the *Times* articles and told Louise he'd seen much the same in the Cincinnati paper. "How much do you have invested at this point?"

They had mutually agreed not to use any of Murray's salary. When she'd first started buying stock, she'd thought that decision a mistake, that they'd lose out on capital gains and dividends. Now, though, she felt glad they hadn't. Murray's salary covered nearly all household expenses, groceries, utilities, taxes, and the like.

"Except from the money set aside to maintain the rental properties and the little bit we use to augment your salary for household needs, I've invested nearly all of the Schmidt Enterprises' accrued profit to date. I've been using the squire's broker. I'd have to check with him to be sure—several thousands of dollars, certainly."

Murray removed his eyeglasses and wiped them with a handkerchief. "I've heard a lot of talk, none of it good. I think you should talk to Squire Adamson Monday morning and see what he says.

A FIRE TO BE KINDLED

If it looks really bad, perhaps we should get out of the market altogether. I'm not sure it's worth all the worry."

Fannie called them to supper, and, as they moved toward the kitchen, Louise said, "You might be right, but I'd hate to sell at a loss. I'll call Squire first and then the broker. Between the two, we should be able to make a sound decision."

Supper that night—roast chicken and dumplings with green beans and fresh corn—most likely tasted wonderful, but Louise had no appetite.

Louise telephoned Squire Adamson's office first thing Monday. His secretary answered after several rings. "I'm terribly sorry, Mrs. Carlyon. The squire is not in the office today. May I take a message? I'll make sure he gets it as soon as he's back."

"Yes, please. Ask him to call me as soon as possible. I need to talk with him about the stock market. It's very important."

The secretary's voice became sympathetic. "I know. Everyone's upset. I guess we'll all just have to pray everything turns out for the best."

Louise hung up and immediately called the broker's office but got a busy signal. She waited five minutes and tried again: still busy. She went out on the front porch and picked up the newspaper. The news proved no better. Efforts to stop the decline had stabilized the market for a brief period, but no one knew what might happen when trading started today.

Throughout the day, Louise tried with little success to distract herself. She washed the breakfast dishes and changed and washed bedding. She even pruned her roses. Nothing helped. She tried calling Squire Adamson's office again, but he had still not come in. The broker's line remained busy.

That evening, she and Fannie listened to the news on the radio. Monday's trading ended with the market falling even more and wiping out all of Friday's gains.

"I don't know what to do, Mother," she said. I can't get ahold of anyone."

BOB STROTHER   117

Fannie got up from the sofa and turned off the radio. "What's the worst that can happen?"

"I don't know," Louise said. "I guess we could lose all the money I've invested." She closed her eyes and massaged her forehead with her fingertips. "I wish I'd never invested at all."

"Murray would probably tell you it's in God's hands."

Louise wasn't at all sure what, if any role, God played in the stock market. "I'd rather be holding Murray's right now."

CHAPTER 30

B y Tuesday morning, Louise's anxiety all but consumed her. She hardly slept the night before, her mind whirling over what might happen one minute, then hoping all her worry was for naught and that everything would stabilize.

If the latter didn't happen, she'd decided to sell her stocks anyway, even at a loss—though she hoped not much of one. At least she would have most of her investment back in the bank, safe from the machinations of something so big and so hard to understand—something she'd had no business playing with in the first place.

Once again, she placed a call to Squire Adamson, and once again the secretary informed her the attorney wasn't available. "He telephoned from home this morning and had me cancel all his appointments for the day. But I did give him your message."

"Can you please give me his home number? I really, really need to talk to him."

The line went silent for a moment, and Louise waited almost without breathing.

"I'm sorry, Mrs. Carlyon. I'd like to help you, but it's against office policy, the squire's orders."

She hung up and immediately tried the broker's number. Busy again. *What is wrong?* Louise thought. *Why is no one answering?* Tempted to smash the phone against the wall, she closed her eyes and took a deep breath. If someone—anyone—tried to call, she wouldn't be able to answer.

She sat in the parlor watching the telephone.

Fannie entered from the hallway. "You can't will it to ring, you know."

"I did all the household chores yesterday. There's nothing left except to wait on one of them to get back with me."

"Catch the streetcar and go downtown," Fannie said. "Go for a walk. Get out of the house. Do something, anything but sit around here and drive yourself crazy."

"But what if they call while I'm out?"

"What if they don't and you're still sitting there with your eyes glued to that damn telephone? You're going to drive both of us crazy."

She's right, I am going crazy. "All right, maybe I will."

"Thank you." Fannie headed back to the kitchen.

Though warm enough now, Louise put on a light jacket. She didn't really want to go downtown. She wasn't in the mood for shopping—just the opposite, in fact. Until she knew about her investments, she'd hang on to every penny.

Almost without thinking, she walked down to Baily Avenue and then further east to the corner of Baily and Bennett. Less than a block from the intersection, she came to her former home, now See-Boy's. Her grandparents' home sat directly across the street. Both brought back a torrent of memories, many good and a few bad. Grandfather and Grandmother Schmidt died in that house, but when they were alive, Louise had felt nothing but loved and protected. Jesse, too, loomed large in her life back then, working in both houses.

The door to her grandparents' home opened, and a middle-aged woman came out onto the porch to check her mail. She waved and Louise waved back. One of their renters, but her name escaped Louise at the moment. Louise took a last look at See-Boy's house then headed down the block to Dodds Avenue.

Near the intersection, she passed her grandfather's former meat market. The subsequent owner couldn't make a go of it, she remembered. Then again, nobody could select meat and butcher like her grandfather. The place looked deserted now, the windows and door that once identified Schmidt's Meat Market painted over in black.

Further down the block, she passed the school she once attended, the big ash tree in the school yard still sporting leaves though it was almost November. Louise knew it would cling tenaciously to them until spring. She couldn't help but wonder where she would be come spring and what she might be clinging to. Chapman's Dry Cleaners and Laundry, where she had worked after dropping out of school, lay just beyond. She remembered the acrid fumes from the dry-cleaning solutions and how she'd smelled after spending the day there. Henry had complained about her "scent." She'd gone back to work there again after Bobby's birth while Murray served overseas during the war.

She remembered leaving work one day and running into Jesse on her way home. They'd chatted for a while, and Louise had accompanied her home. Looking back, Louise realized Jesse had shown signs of the disease that night which would eventually kill her.

Feeling aimless and exhausted, she turned around and started back. But the closer she got to home, the more her worries returned.

Neither the attorney nor broker had called. Fannie prepared supper while Louise tried unsuccessfully to nap. At exactly six pm, she turned on the radio. Sitting with her shoulders hunched and hands between her knees, she listened as the nation learned of the ever-worsening news: at the end of trading, the market had lost $14 billion.

They all sat down for supper, although Louise couldn't eat. Fannie said nothing regarding the stock market and managed to engage the boys in conversation about their day. School was fine. Bobby and Harry planned on a movie for the following weekend. Henry and his band were playing for a fall dance at City High on Saturday. Louise felt grateful for the distraction and Fannie's efforts to keep the discussion pleasant.

Midway through the meal the telephone rang.

Louise dropped her napkin on her plate and rushed to answer.

"Mrs. Carlyon," Squire Adamson said, "I apologize for not returning your call before now." His voice came through the line soft, calm and—if Louise had to try and define it in a word—resigned.

"I wanted to ask about the investments I've made," Louise said. "The news has been so frightening I didn't know what I should do. I thought you might be able to give me advice."

"Looking at what has happened over the past several days, and what may well happen tomorrow, I'm probably not the person you'd want to take advice from."

"What has caused all this?" Louise asked.

Adamson chuckled, a hollow sound in her ears. "I suspect people will be speculating on that for decades to come. Doesn't help us now, though, does it?"

"I've tried to contact the broker," Louise said. "But he hasn't returned my calls."

"Mr. Ferguson has been very busy," Adamson said. "I've been in his office a good bit over the past two days, not that it's done either of us any good."

"What's left for us to do, Squire Adamson? I just want someone to tell me something. What has happened to my investments? Can I sell them? *Should* I sell them? What?"

"Mrs. Carlyon, I doubt there's anything you—or any of us, for that matter—can do in the short run. We're the victims of something much greater than ourselves. But I will make one more call tonight to Mr. Ferguson, and I'll ask him personally to return your call. I fear that is all I can do. I do want to say I'm sorry for having involved you in this."

"It was my decision to invest, sir. Please don't blame yourself for that."

"You are a generous woman, Mrs. Carlyon. Thank you." A brief pause, then, "If it's not too much trouble, and if she is available, I wonder if I might speak to Ms. Meyers for a moment."

A bit surprised at the request, Louise said she would see, then rested the telephone on the hallway stand. Fannie still sat at the table, the boys finished and nowhere in sight.

"It's Squire Adamson. He'd like to speak with you."

Her mother seemed equally surprised, Louise thought, and wondered what they might have to discuss.

Fannie returned to the kitchen after a few minutes, her expression guarded. "Just something about the house I inherited from Mama Cornelius, nothing important."

They cleared the table in silence and were washing and drying the dishes when the telephone rang again. Louise stepped into the hallway and answered, recognizing the broker's voice immediately. They talked for less than five minutes, then Louise walked into the parlor, sat down on the sofa, and cried.

CHAPTER 31

"We've lost virtually everything," she told Murray after she finally composed herself. Murray remained silent on the other end of the line. "The broker said everyone tried to sell before the market dropped any lower, and the more people sold, the lower it became."

"I've heard much the same. Of course, it's just speculation around here. None of us knows much about the stock market. We're just railroaders."

"Mr. Ferguson told me he'd do his best, but that, in all probability, we'll recoup only pennies on the dollar."

"Try not to feel too bad, Louise. After all, we still have income from my salary and from the rental houses. It could be far worse."

"I can't help feeling bad. It's like all we accomplished these last few years is gone."

"We still have a roof over our heads," Murray said. "We're still healthy, and we have each other. I have a feeling many out there have it much, much worse. We'll get by. We always have."

"I thought you'd be disappointed in me. I had the idea to invest in the first place."

"It sounded good at the time. I'm not disappointed *in* you, only for you. And I'm sorry for all the pain and frustration I know you must be feeling."

"I love you, Murray. Thank you for loving me."

Murray chuckled. "It comes easy. Now, try not to worry about what has happened. We're not alone in it, and, like I said, there are others much worse off than we are."

Louise rang off and replaced the telephone receiver. She did feel better. Talking with Murray, knowing she wasn't alone helped. She remembered what she'd said to Bobby after he'd told her about Helen. Learn from the experience. The same applied to her. But experience had been a cruel teacher. She thought about what Bobby asked her back then—why did knowledge only come too late to make use of it? She'd told him it was never too late, but now she thought maybe he hadn't been totally wrong.

She would have to tell her mother about the stocks, of course. Fannie had been almost as fretful as she. But she'd wait until Friday to tell Henry and Bobby, after Murray came home. She felt the loss of the money already. But surely to God, the worst had to be over. She couldn't lose it twice, could she?

She caught Bobby on his way out the next morning and asked him to please speak to Helen about her father. He'd sounded so despondent when she'd talked to him the night before. Having been in the stock market for years, he'd likely lost much more money than she had. He was such a kind man. Even after all that had happened between them. It weighed more heavily on a father, Louise thought, having to deal with an unwanted, out of wedlock pregnancy. She hoped he would recover from his financial losses, just as she felt she and her family would, eventually.

After school, when Bobby arrived home, Louise asked, "Did you have an opportunity to ask Helen about Squire Adamson?"

"No, ma'am. Helen wasn't at school today."

Louise frowned. "I hope she isn't ill." She had always liked Helen, missed her even, after she and Bobby decided not to see each other anymore. "Well, try again tomorrow. If she still isn't there, I'll call her father."

Thursday morning, Louise sat with her mother at the kitchen table drinking coffee when she saw the headline in the local news section: *Prominent local attorney found dead in downtown office.* The subhead read: *Suicide suspected.*

With trembling fingers, Louise set her cup on the table and read the article. She shook a cigarette from her pack and tried to light it but gave up after breaking several matches.

"What is it?" Fannie asked. "What's wrong?"

Louise pushed the newspaper across the table. She tried to take a sip of coffee, but it sloshed out of the cup before it reached her lips. With elbows on the table, she rested her head in her hands and took deep breaths. "Dear God. Poor Helen and her mother," she said in a shaky voice. When she looked up again, her mother's cheeks were moist with tears.

Fannie shifted in her chair, turning away from Louise. Then she pushed herself up from the table and hurried from the room.

Louise watched her go, thinking, *what else can possibly happen?*

Entering the church, Louise noted the crowded pews. She, Murray, Fannie, and Bobby squeezed together just behind the section roped off for family. Henry, having no real connection to Squire Adamson other than a supper meeting, had begged off.

Louise had never met the attorney's wife, but she assumed the woman sitting beside Helen must be her. Both cried openly and dabbed at their eyes with small white handkerchiefs.

A follow-up article in the *Times* had provided few further details of the man's death. Apparently distraught from his losses in the stock market, he had shot himself Tuesday evening while sitting behind his desk—not long after Louise talked to him. Her mother had spoken with him briefly, too, Louise remembered. He'd promised he'd call the broker, and he had. In fact, it may have been the last call he'd made. She noted mentally to ask her mother again about what he'd told her that night.

Louise waited until Monday evening to talk with Fannie about the call. They sat in the parlor well away from Henry and Bobby's rooms.

Her mother, quiet for a minute, seemed to reach a decision. She huffed out a breath and said, "If you must know, John and I were having an affair. It had been going on for years off and on. Sometimes, he'd feel bad about being unfaithful to his wife. He'd worry about Helen finding out. Then, sooner or later, he'd call and we'd start up again.

"We had our liaisons at Mama Cornelius's house—well, my house—because he was so well known around town and we might run into someone anywhere. That night on the phone, he told me it had to end, that he cared deeply for me, and that he hoped I would understand. I liked the man. I might even have loved him." Fannie crossed her arms over her chest. Rather than looking sad, she appeared angry. "But I guess, as things worked out, it's no great loss."

Fannie left the parlor. Seconds later, she reappeared in the doorway. "I suppose we might as well sell that house now." Then she disappeared again.

Louise waited, trying to absorb what she had just heard, then walked softly to her mother's door. She heard Fannie crying, sobbing really. As Louise crawled into her own bed a few minutes later, she wondered if she would ever really know her mother.

PART TWO

THE
DEPRESSION
YEARS

CHAPTER 32

The family threw a small party for Louise's thirty-fifth birthday in January of '33, with just Murray, Fannie, Bobby, and Henry present—which made Louise just as happy. Fannie prepared roasted pork tenderloin with red potatoes and garden peas and made a cake. Louise received chocolate-covered cherries from Henry, a small bottle of perfume from Bobby, and Murray—bless his heart—bought her a dozen red roses. She thought the bouquet quite extravagant, considering their financial condition and times in general, and decided to do something with them even after they dried out.

They postponed the party two days, until Saturday, so Murray could be there. Hopes of him leaving the railroad and finding a job close to home dissipated with the stock market crash and the lingering high unemployment rate. With seniority on the Chattanooga to Cincinnati run, he'd so far been able to hold his job while others lost theirs.

"What will you wish for, Momma?" Bobby asked as Fannie brought the cake to the table. Louise closed her eyes and thought for a moment. When she opened them again she said, "I wish for Franklin Delano Roosevelt to end the depression."

"Oh, come on, Momma," Bobby said, grinning, "wish for something for *you*."

Louise sat back in her chair and folded her hands in her lap. "I have an even better idea. Why don't each of you make a wish, and then you can help me blow out the candles. Mother, why don't you go first?"

Fannie drummed her fingernails on the table a moment. "All right then, I wish the house in North Chattanooga would sell." They'd had Mama Cornelius's house on the market for a while but no offers thus far. They'd thought about renting it like the others, but that, too, seemed problematic. Many of their current renters were already past due, in a few cases by several months.

"What about you, Henry?"

Henry's eyes lit up. "That's easy. I'd like to play drums in Duke Ellington's band."

"Now, Henry," Fannie said, "that's an all-colored band. I don't think they'd allow a white man to play with them."

"It wouldn't matter to me," Henry said. "I'd be playing with probably the best jazz band around."

Louise reached over and patted Henry's hand. "I think it would be wonderful if it came true." Then she asked Bobby for his wish. After graduating from high school, he had been unable to find work, so he'd been helping See-Boy maintain the rental houses. Since Louise paid him, it wasn't extra income, but it kept him busy and made him feel a part of things.

"Mine's easy, too," he said. "I want to become a pilot."

"That's nothing new," Murray said. "That's what you've wanted since you were a toddler."

"That's true," Louise said. "I still remember your first airplane, the one See-Boy made for you."

Bobby rolled his eyes. "I think I'd like one a little bigger and a whole lot faster."

"Well," Louise said. "Maybe one day you'll have that wish." But she hoped not. She didn't think she could bear seeing her boy fly off into the sky.

Murray took a sip of sweet tea and wiped his mouth. "As for me, I'd like to be home more than a couple days at a time."

"I'd like that, too," Louise said. "That's my wish, and that can be our goal—something the whole family can work toward."

Fannie stood and picked up a box of matches. "I guess if we're going to help blow these candles out, someone's got to light them first. Happy birthday, Louise." They all blew until the last candle flickered and died.

As Fannie sliced and handed out pieces of cake, Louise thought perhaps the best birthday wish had already come true. They struggled to make ends meet, but they were all here right now, together.

See-Boy looked in on Frankie, who slept soundly in his room. Despite turning ten soon, he looked so innocent See-Boy remembered how he used to lie back in the bed and read to the boy. On summer nights with the warm breeze pushing the bedroom curtains in and out, Frankie would nestle in the crook of See-Boy's arm, pleading, *Read me more, Daddy* again and again until he finally fell asleep.

Sometimes, See-Boy sang to Frankie the songs his mother had crooned to him when he was a boy. "Swing Low, Sweet Chariot" or "Froggy Went a Courtin'." Frankie loved what he called the Froggy song. Other times, See-Boy might sing a more popular tune. It didn't matter to Frankie as long as he sang.

See-Boy chuckled. He kind of liked singing, thought he sounded pretty good. His momma had sung in the church choir, so maybe he got it from her. Thinking about her and looking at his child never failed to bring on the heartache he felt knowing she'd never see her grandbaby.

"What are you doing?" Pearl asked, coming up behind him.

He turned and slipped an arm around her waist. "Just looking at what we and God made."

"Uh-huh, I know what you mean."

"And thinking how much Momma would have loved him."

She leaned her head against his chest. "At least Daddy Lawrence gets to watch him grow. Maybe he'll tell your mother all about it one day."

"I like to think she's already watching him, watching *over* him. She just don't get to wrap her arms around him like we do."

He reached in and pulled the bedroom door closed.

"You going down to the club?" Pearl asked as they walked down the hall.

"Yep. Daddy gets tired easier these days. He probably wants to come on home and go to bed." He gave Pearl a peck on the cheek. "He likes it when I can be around for Frankie's bedtime, though. Says it's important to tuck him in and kiss him goodnight."

"I think so, too."

See-Boy pulled on a jacket and opened the front door. "I'll try not to be too late."

Pearl rolled her eyes. "You're always late."

He winked at her as he pulled the door closed. "Business is good."

CHAPTER 33

Business *was* good at the club. The expanded size of the facility allowed for tables and chairs, and the space formerly taken up by the meat case had been converted into a bar. Alcohol selection remained the same—moonshine. But See-Boy heard talk of Prohibition ending. He wasn't sure how that might affect his business or if he could somehow transform the club into a legitimate enterprise.

He had time to decide, though. The wheels in Washington D.C. turned slow. In the meantime, he made good money and helped take people's minds off their troubles. Few folks these days, especially colored folks, could afford the price of a picture show or supper out. But most could squeeze enough for a taste or two of See-Boy's Sand Mountain Moonshine.

He could hear faint strands of music floating from the club as he entered the alley. Not very loud—didn't want anybody to complain—just enough to get the body swaying and toes tapping while folks sipped a refreshing beverage. A sliver of light bled from under the club's rear door, the only usable door at present. He pushed it open, immediately swallowed by the crowd. The clink of glasses and laughter sporadically interrupted the soft hum of conversation and music, and a gray cloud of cigarette and cigar smoke hung suspended a few feet above the tables.

Lawrence sat on a stool behind the bar pouring drinks as needed. All the tables and chairs occupied, a few folks leaned against the bar or wandered among tables chatting with seated patrons. See-Boy shook a few hands and patted a few backs, eventually making his way to the bar.

"Place is hopping tonight," he said to Lawrence.

"Saturday night." His father grinned and wiped his brow with a handkerchief. "Everybody wants to feel good."

"I reckon so." See-Boy moved around behind the bar. "You can go on home, Daddy. I'll take it from here."

"Thank you, son, I believe I'll do just that. These old bones can't perch on a stool near as long as they used to."

See-Boy massaged his father's shoulders. "Pearl's left you a slab of pecan pie sittin' out on the stove. Get you a piece and a glass of milk. I'll see you in the morning."

He watched as the older man sifted through the crowd, making good with the customers just like See-Boy had. A light-skinned colored man walked up and knocked his empty glass on the bar top. A regular, Calvin had been coming ever since See-Boy first opened in the maintenance shed years back.

"What'll it be?"

"Hmm, I believe I'll have a rye and ginger."

See-Boy poured the man a generous portion of moonshine.

"Tastes like moonshine," Calvin said after taking a sip.

"You just ain't got your mouth set right," See-Boy replied.

They both chuckled, and Calvin leaned back against the bar. "You know that phonograph thing you got is pretty good. I mean, ever'body likes a little music to drink by. I was thinking, though, what if you had a band come play? The phonograph is fine during the week. Most folks don't want to get too rowdy on weeknights, but on Friday and Saturday night? Some of us might just get up and dance."

"Band costs money," See-Boy said. "The phonograph is already bought and paid for."

"I know, I know. But think about it, son, folks be gettin' up and dancing, get all hot and sweaty. Get yourself one of those refrigerators, stock it with 'shine, they'll all be looking for a cool drink."

"So now I got to hire a band *and* buy a refrigerator?" See-Boy shook his head. "Even white folks can't afford to buy refrigerators no more. These are hard times."

"Well, you don't look like you're hurtin' too bad. It's just something to mull over while you're on your way to the bank." Calvin tossed a handful of coins on the bar, gave him a salute, and melted back into the crowd.

"Last thing I'd do," See-Boy said to no one in particular, "is put my money in a bank."

But it got him thinking. He'd like to have people dancing. And if what he'd heard was true, prohibition ending, it might keep his customers coming back anyway. Band might even have a singer. *That'd be nice. I might even croon a song or two on occasion.*

But then he got to looking around. With the whole place practically filled with tables and chairs, where would he put a band? Except … what used to be the meat cooler wasn't used at all now. Tearing down the interior walls to open it up hadn't produced enough space to make it worthwhile, but it might be just the right size for a band platform.

He served a few more customers, still thinking. He and Pearl had hung on to their old ice box even after they got the new Frigidaire. He could put it behind the bar and use it on weekend nights to chill the 'shine.

A man can't just stand still, See-Boy thought. *Got to keep moving or go stale.* He figured to bounce it off Pearl when he got home if she was still awake or, if she wasn't, first thing in the morning.

Pearl made scrambled eggs and skillet-fried toast, putting them on the table just as See-Boy finished dressing and came into the kitchen. After she poured up the coffee and seated herself, he told her about his conversation with Calvin the night before.

She listened closely, nodding every once in a while.

He loved that about her. When he talked to her, she made him feel like he was the only person in the world besides her.

When he finished, she said, "You're already making more from the club than you do working on the rental houses. Plus, this is really *yours*. You built it from scratch and expanded it to what you have now. I had a few doubts to begin with, but I've watched you build on an idea and make it work. Now you have another idea." She smiled and placed her hand over his. "Go make this one work, too."

See-Boy picked up her hand and kissed it. "That's why I love you, baby. You say all the right things."

She arched her eyebrows. "I mean everything I said. Don't you think otherwise, either."

"I can do most of the interior work myself. But I don't know any bands around here anywhere."

"Henry Schmidt is in a band," Pearl said. "I understand they are quite good."

"An all-white band, you mean."

"So what if it's white? In New York City, white people go to Harlem to see colored bands play. Look at Duke Ellington, for goodness sake. *Everybody* goes to hear him and his band. Seems to me colored folk could just as well enjoy hearing a white band."

"I think they mostly play high school dances," See-Boy said. "They might not want to play for a colored audience, especially in a speakeasy."

"See-Boy, you're the one keeps insisting it's a club, not a speakeasy. Anyway, I suspect Henry and his friends might like playing somewhere they could get a—what do you call it—a refreshing beverage, between sets."

"All right, then. I'll look into it. Maybe I can get a family discount."

Pearl grinned. "Now you're thinking like a businessman."

CHAPTER 34

Henry sat on his bed, eyes closed, hands moving imaginary drumsticks as he listened to a recording of Thelma Terry and Her Play Boys, featuring Gene Krupa as drummer. His absolute favorite drummer, Henry aspired to play just like Krupa one day.

A loud knock interrupted his reverie.

"Come in."

Fannie opened the door. "Telephone for you, Henry. It's See-Boy."

Henry frowned. He couldn't recollect See-Boy calling him before. He turned off the phonograph and hurried down the hall.

"Hello."

"Mr. Henry, I have a favor to ask," See-Boy said. "I wonder if you could meet me at my house around five o'clock this afternoon? I got something I'd like to show you."

"Well, sure, See-Boy. I guess I can do that. We're practicing at Jimmy's house early this afternoon, but I can be through by five."

"All right then. I'll see you here."

Henry hung up and wandered back to his bedroom. *What the heck does See-Boy have to show me?* He couldn't imagine. As a kid, he'd seen See-Boy all the time, working at their house and being buddies with Louise. Lawrence and See-Boy were the only men in his life he ever truly felt comfortable with, except for his grandfather, a vague memory in Henry's mind since he died so long ago.

He liked Murray all right but had never been around him much, him working away from home most of the time.

He went over to the phonograph and dropped the needle to restart Thelma Terry's "Mama's Gone, Good Bye." He loved the music, got lost in it usually, but throughout the rest of the day, his mind wondered what See-Boy had to show him.

He, Jimmy Farr, and the other band members practiced for a while, then Henry left and timed his arrival at See-Boy and Pearl's house at precisely five o'clock. He recognized the old obsession calling, wanting him to do everything a certain number of times, like stepping over a doorway threshold six times with one foot then six times with the other before going through. The therapy had helped, but they couldn't afford it these days. The music replaced much of that. When he played or practiced—sometimes just when listening—the music kept anything else from entering his mind.

He rapped on See-Boy's door five times, shoving the need to do so five more times deep down inside. Fortunately, the door opened almost immediately.

See-Boy extended his hand. "Mr. Henry, man, you are right on time. Come on in and say hello to Pearl, then we'll go for a little walk."

They stepped into the kitchen where Pearl shucked ears of corn in preparation for supper. Henry had always thought Pearl beautiful—caramel-colored skin, fine features, and lustrous black hair flowing to her shoulders.

"Hello, Henry," she said. "You've been so busy with your music I don't get to see you much when I'm helping Louise with the books." She winked at him, and Henry felt his cheeks redden. "I think you're going to like what See-Boy has to show you."

He mumbled a few words he knew sounded stupid, then See-Boy patted him on the back and ushered him out the front door. They walked two abreast down Bennett toward Dodds Avenue.

"You know I opened a club awhile back in your grandfather's old meat market? I needed more space than the maintenance shed offered. I want to show it to you, get your thoughts on something."

Henry couldn't imagine why See-Boy would be interested in his thoughts on anything, but he nodded and kept walking. Near the intersection, See-Boy turned right into the alley running behind the small strip of shops fronting Dodds.

When they approached the rear entry, See-Boy got out a ring of keys and opened the door. They stepped inside to the dark interior, then See-Boy flipped on lights, and Henry saw the packed room of tables, chairs, and a wooden bar.

"It looks a lot different."

See-Boy chuckled. "I did most of the work. Got a friend—guy who does cabinet work—to help me with the bar."

Henry ran his hand along the gleaming, smooth finish of the bar top. "Nice."

"Over here's what I want to show you." See-Boy moved to where the meat cooler used to be.

Henry took in the raised space about twelve by twelve with two small spotlights hung from the ceiling. When See-Boy flicked a nearby switch, the lights illuminated a gleaming hardwood floor.

"This is where the band will set up," See-Boy said. "They'll play Friday and Saturday nights from nine to midnight. That'll give my customers time to get in the mood and, hopefully, dance a little. What do you think of it?"

"It's very nice."

"Big enough, you think?"

"For a small band, sure, maybe not Duke Ellington, though."

"Well, I don't expect Duke Ellington would find this place big enough in general. What about your band? Do you think your band would like to play here?"

Henry felt light-headed for a moment. "You want *my* band?"

"Uh-huh, at least give it a go, then we'll see how it works out. I know you've been playing several high school dances. It's pay as you go. You won't get rich, but—if the crowd likes you—it's steady work. What do you think?"

"I think I'm in heaven," Henry said. "But your customers, they're … colored, aren't they? Wouldn't you want a colored band?"

See-Boy shrugged. "What I want is to make money. At this particular time, I don't know any colored bands, at least none I could afford. I do know you, so I'm giving you first chance." He flicked off the spots and walked back to the bar. "You think it'll be a problem for your buddies, playing in a colored club?"

"I don't know, See-Boy. I know it wouldn't be for me. Plus, we've hardly had a chance to play at all during the summer. I'll ask them and let you know, if that's okay."

"You do that. And let me know what you get for playing the school dances. I'll try to at least match it."

On the way home, Henry could hardly contain his excitement. If the band went for it, he could play steady. It would mean more money coming into the household. He'd finally be able to contribute. Louise would be so proud.

He telephoned Jimmy as soon as he walked in the door and told him the news. They decided to tell the others at tomorrow's practice session. That night, he lay awake in bed, thinking about the possibilities. He even forgot to flick the bedroom light switch fourteen times.

Watch out, Gene Krupa, Henry Schmidt is on the way up.

CHAPTER 35

L ouise and Pearl had just finished up the books for the end of the month when Fannie came in from the hallway. "I have wonderful news. The house in North Chattanooga sold."

"That *is* good news," Louise said. "How much did it sell for?"

"The asking price," Fannie said, hugging herself. "Seems one of the managers at Siskin Steel has transferred down here from up North somewhere. Home prices are higher there, and they felt lucky to get in here so cheaply."

Pearl placed a hand to her chest, batted her eyelashes, and said, "Why, ladies, I'm pleased to know a Yankee is finally good for *something*."

They all laughed.

Beneath Louise's laughter, a feeling of relief spread over her. Selling that house would provide ready cash, if and when they needed it. The further they got into the decade, the more worried she grew about their real estate holdings. With several renters far behind on payments, the reduction in cash flow had affected not only her and her family, but Lawrence and See-Boy's family, too.

With the pittance they'd received from the sale of her stock investments long gone, Murray's salary provided the only constant financial support they had at the moment. She needed a way to produce another income stream.

She broached the topic with Murray when he came home Friday evening. They sat in the parlor after supper, and Murray read the newspaper.

"It's quite a relief to have the money from Mother's house," she said. "But I worry we'll need it to supplement our regular income, then it'll be gone. Everyone says there's no telling how long these hard times will last."

"President Roosevelt says he can improve the economy." Murray showed her an article in the *Times*. "He has ideas that might work, I think."

"I know, but that may take years."

Murray retrieved a handkerchief from his pocket to polish his eyeglasses. "How many of your renters are behind?"

"Three right now, to one degree or another."

"Have you considered evicting them? Getting someone new in who can afford the rent?"

"Oh, Murray, I'd absolutely *hate* to do that. Many lost their jobs. They have families. What would they do? We can't just put them out on the street."

Murray put down the paper and took Louise by the hand. "I would hate to do it, too, but I know you. When it comes to protecting your family, you'll do whatever it takes." He locked his eyes on hers. "I'm the perfect example of that, aren't I?"

They never really talked about it, but they both knew she'd married Murray to save her family after they were forced out of their home. Both of them had compromised something to achieve their goals. For Louise, she'd kept her family intact. For Murray, well, he loved her but probably only tolerated the constant presence of her mother and Henry. She hoped he still felt good about that arrangement.

She leaned over and kissed him gently on the lips. "Given the chance, Murray, I wouldn't change a thing. I feel doubly blessed. I have Mother and Henry and Bobby, and I have you to thank for that."

She stood and smoothed the front of her dress. "Anyway, I thought you rather handsome, even if you were a bit too old for me." She darted toward the hallway as Murray leapt from his seat and swatted at her with the *Times*.

Despite her misgivings, Louise called See-Boy on Monday and asked that he drive her to see the past-due renters. The first house stood near the intersection of East Main and South Hawthorne Streets—a painted brick bungalow with a picket fence enclosing the small front yard. See-Boy waited in the truck while Louise went to the front door.

A middle-aged woman in a faded pink housecoat answered. "Can I help you?"

"I'm Louise Carlyon, Mrs. Frost. I'm the owner of Schmidt Enterprises, and I'm here because you're three months behind on your rent."

The woman pulled her housecoat tighter around her and looked behind her as if searching for someone else to deal with the problem. "I'm sorry," she finally said. "My husband has been out every day looking for work, but no one is hiring right now."

Louise nodded. "I understand. Times are certainly just awful right now, but I need you to understand we can't let this go on without your making the rent payments. My family has to pay utilities and buy groceries, too." As soon as she said it, a hammer of guilt drove a wedge into her heart. They weren't nearly as bad off as this woman and her husband.

"Hold on for just a moment, please," the woman said, turning away from the door. Then she stopped and said, "Won't you come in for just a moment? I'm sorry. It seems I've lost my manners."

Louise stepped inside the small living room. The furniture sparse and tattered, the room still appeared clean. On the mantle above the coal grate, a series of photographs showed the woman, and, Louise assumed, her husband. In a couple, he wore a uniform. Others depicted the couple in undoubtedly better times.

"Wait just a minute, please." The woman disappeared into the kitchen. When she returned a minute later, she clutched a few dollar bills and change in her hand. "Here, please take this. I know it's not nearly enough, but it's all we have right now."

Louise put out her hand, and the woman dropped four dollars and sixty-five cents into it.

"We were going to buy coal for the grate, but the fire is of no use if we can't stay in the house. Can you please give us just a bit longer? I've been taking in ironing, but most of the folks around here are about as bad off as we are."

Louise stared at the money, recalling when she, her mother, and Henry cobbled together change and wrinkled dollar bills to buy the cheapest cuts of meat they could find. *How could she put this family out on the street?*

"No, you keep this," she said, and fumbled in her purse to find a ten-dollar bill. "And take this, too, for coal or groceries. I'll give you another month to come up with the rent."

"Bless you." The woman smothered the money in her fist.

As she turned to leave, Louise said, "I hope your husband finds work."

"Yes, I hope so, too. Thank you, Mrs. Carlyon. Thank you for caring, and God bless you for your generosity."

When Louise climbed into the truck, See-Boy asked, "Did you get the rent money?"

"No, I didn't, and I gave the woman ten dollars."

See-Boy laughed. "I do believe Schmidt Enterprises has changed a lot under its latest management. I bet Mister Will would've looked under the sofa pillows to see could he get that rent payment."

"Probably so, but then Mister Will may well burn in the fires of Hell for all eternity."

See-Boy nodded. "You probably right."

The next two households were little different. Louise had hoped she'd find lackadaisical renters squandering their money on unnecessary luxuries. But all three families were simply victims of the increasingly poor economy, often standing in long lines for basic necessities and food. Murray said she would do whatever necessary to provide for her family. Maybe so, but whatever else she'd sacrificed, it had been hers to do so. These people's lives were not hers to risk.

CHAPTER 36

O n the way home, as Louise and See-Boy traveled down Dodds Avenue, Louise noticed a *For Sale* sign posted in the window of Chapman's Dry Cleaners and Laundry. "Pull over a minute, please."

See-Boy eased the truck to the curb, and Louise got out and walked across the street. When she entered the store, the acrid fumes of dry-cleaning fluid struck her, though the scent seemed less pervasive than she remembered. Mr. Chapman, looking much older and more haggard, stood behind the counter sorting clothes.

He smiled automatically at her entrance, then took a closer look and broke into a wide grin. "Why, Louise, I haven't seen you in a coon's age. How are you?"

She took his outstretched hand and closed both of hers around it. "Better than most, I think, Mr. Chapman. And you?"

"As well as can be expected, I suppose, considering the shape this world's in. Thank God, we're still the closest cleaning establishment to Missionary Ridge. The people living there still have enough money to have their clothes professionally cleaned."

"But the sign in your window. I thought perhaps business had fallen off."

Chapman let his gaze drift around the front of the store. "This is all I've ever done, Louise. It's been a good living, if not a great one, but I'm getting too old to put in the hours like I used to." He grinned at her again. "Plus, I can't seem to get the same high quality help I once had."

Louise returned the grin at his compliment. "If you don't mind telling me, how much are you asking for the business?"

"I don't mind at all." He took a pencil from behind his ear and flipped a cleaning receipt pad over to its blank side. He then jotted a number down. "This is the asking price I've advertised to potential buyers, what few I've had." He scratched his neck absently, looked up at the ceiling for a moment, then jotted another number on the pad and pushed it toward her. "And this is the one I'd give you."

Louise glanced at the two numbers. Both were more money than she had but the second figure a good deal less than the first. "I appreciate your offer. I wonder if I might be able to see your business ledgers for the past year."

"Certainly." He went into the rear of the store and returned a minute later carrying an accordion file full of business journals. "I'm sure you'll want to look these over carefully. You may take them with you if you like. I won't have to post anything until the end of the month."

"Thank you. I'll meet with my bookkeeper and take a look. I'll try to have them back to you in a week or so."

Chapman came around the counter and walked Louise to the door. "As I said, there's no hurry. And Louise … this has been my life for a great many years. If I must retire, I can't think of anyone more capable than you to carry it on."

"Thank you again." Louise offered her hand. "I'll be in touch."

Back in the truck, See-Boy asked what she had.

"It's Chapman's business records for the last year. I'm going to get Pearl to go over them with me. The business is up for sale."

"I thought you never liked breathing those fumes."

"These days, I guess we're all looking for ways to make money, no matter what we have to endure."

"Yes, ma'am," See-Boy said. "We are doing that."

Within two days, Louise and Pearl completed a thorough review of Chapman's files.

"It's marginally profitable," Pearl said, "and Mr. Chapman took a pretty decent salary from the gross income."

"Between you, See-Boy, and Lawrence, Schmidt Enterprises practically runs itself. I know how to run the dry cleaners, and you can help me with the bookkeeping. If I can scrape together enough to buy it, we'll have another source of income, and I can supplement your salary for the additional work."

"I appreciate that, Louise, but it wouldn't be that much more work. Besides, See-Boy's doing real well with the club."

Louise stretched and stood while Pearl gathered up her pads and placed the journals in Chapman's file. "Henry told me See-Boy asked about his band playing on the weekends there. I often think about how close our two families have been and how we continue to, in one way or another, depend on each other."

Pearl got up, too, and walked toward the front door. "Mama Jesse wouldn't have had it any other way, would she?"

"No." Louise sighed, feeling the acute sense of loneliness she always experienced whenever she thought of See-Boy's mother. "She wouldn't have allowed for anything else."

Louise, Fannie, and Murray sat around the kitchen table after supper while Louise explained her plan. "With the money we received from the sale of Mama Cornelius's house, we'd only need a few thousand more to purchase the dry cleaners. I can run it, and Henry and Bobby can help. We'd have enough coming in to support ourselves and make up for the losses in rental payments." She tapped a pencil on the notebook paper she'd used to figure income versus expenses. "The only problem is coming up with the extra cash."

"With the shape the country's in," Murray said, "I can think of only one way."

"What's that?" Louise asked.

"You won't like it, I'm afraid. I think you should put some of the rental houses on the market—those that aren't meeting the rent payments."

"But, Murray—"

Murray held up both hands. "I know, I know, but you simply can't be responsible for those people. They aren't your sheep for tending. I mean, what will you do when it comes time to pay the taxes on those houses? What if more of our renters fall on hard times? This way, you trade a loss of income for ready cash. The cash you'll need for the dry cleaners."

Fannie spoke for the first time. "Murray has a good point, Louise. And I don't want to seem callous, but if you sell, it will be someone else who decides what to do with the people behind on their rent—not you."

"That's a technicality, isn't it? I'm still the one abandoning them."

Fannie reached over and took Louise's hand. "Honey, you were the one who pulled Henry and me through the worst time in our life. You shouldered the load for all of us. You took care of us. But you can't take on the burden of our whole society. Sometimes, you just have to let people fend for themselves."

Louise put her face in her hands and rubbed her temples. "I need to think about it for a while, all right?"

"Of course," Murray said. He stood. "I'm going to get ready for bed."

"Me, too," Fannie said.

Louise remained at the table for a while, smoking and thinking about what might happen to those families she'd talked to. Later, after she slipped beneath the covers, she sought a seldom used counsel. She prayed.

CHAPTER 37

The fact he'd played several high school dances offered Henry little confidence as he and his fellow band members set up for their first time before an adult crowd—an adult crowd of colored folks at that. *Would they like the music? Would they feel as awkward as he felt right now?* His mind reeled with questions that would not, could not, be answered beforehand. He was in it. The whole band was in it. *They'd either live or die in less than an hour.*

Henry couldn't imagine how it might feel to play his music to an unresponsive audience. *What if they just sit there, unmoving, eyes showing impatience, and the only digits tapping are fingertips on table tops waiting for the torture to end?* A thin rivulet of sweat rolled down Henry's forehead and clung to the end of his nose. He jumped when he felt a large hand on his shoulder.

"Not long now, Henry." See-Boy stood by the small bandstand, a bar cloth in one hand, looking at the early arrivals populating the chairs. "Everybody's coming to see you all play. We put the word out so you'd have a full crowd tonight, probably standing room only." He laughed. "You boys do know a bunch of colored songs, right?"

Henry felt his world starting to go dark. See-Boy must have seen the terror on his face because he quickly added, "No, Henry, no. I'm just joshin' you. We all like the same music." He patted Henry on the back. "Look out there, Henry. Look at those people's faces. Do you see anything but a crowd of folks wanting to hear good music, maybe get up and dance a little? You and your band are going to make those folks happy. So, rest easy, Henry. You'll do just fine."

Henry swallowed, took a deep breath, and let his gaze travel over the crowd. They did seem happy and relaxed already, drinking and talking and moving around—shaking hands, slapping backs, and laughing out loud. The ones Henry actually made eye contact with smiled and nodded.

His heartrate slowed, his breathing returned to normal. *This is no different from what we've done dozens of times before, just an older crowd.* He looked at his fellow band members, wondered if they were apprehensive, too.

Glancing up, he noticed the clock mounted on the wall above the front door—the same clock that had been in the meat market years ago when his grandfather owned the place. It made him feel better to know that little part of his family had persisted over the span of time. He bet his grandfather would have been as proud of him as he had been of Louise.

Fifteen more minutes and they'd start playing.

It seemed much longer than that to Henry, and he felt grateful when Jimmy tapped the microphone and greeted the crowd.

"We're very pleased to be here tonight," their band leader said. "We want to start off with a little something from Duke Ellington called "Runnin' Wild." Hope you like it."

As soon as the band started playing, Henry forgot all about worrying. His mind went to a private place where nothing but the music existed. Beyond the bandstand lights, he saw men and women crowding the small dance floor. They looked happy and, like him, caught up as the music filled their bodies and minds and transformed them from ordinary folk into something really, really special.

They played two sets with a break in between. With no place to go during break, the band ended up mingling with customers. Henry smiled and tried to make small talk, but socializing wasn't one of his assets. He stayed close to the bar and See-Boy, happy to get back onstage for the final set.

Afterward, See-Boy paid them in cash and offered each a shot of moonshine. They all accepted, Henry sipping slowly for fear he might start coughing or tearing up. He managed to get it all down and actually felt pretty good as they prepared to leave.

"You did real good tonight, boys," See-Boy said. "I'll see you tomorrow, same time, same place."

Jimmy and the others were ecstatic. Henry shared their feeling of pure joy as they exited out the back. *And we've been asked back for tomorrow night.* Henry sighed with relief from that worry. How awkward, after their first night, if they weren't considered good enough to come back.

But they'd been good—maybe even great. He didn't really know, considering how the music consumed him. His mother and Louise would be happy and proud. It wasn't a lot of money, but unless something happened, it would be steady money, something the family needed.

He walked dark streets for the several blocks home, just able to make out the fronts of the houses, bathed in shadow, quiet as a cemetery. But the music still played in Henry's head, smooth and sweet as ever.

When he reached the house, he made out a soft glow from an interior light. He eased the front door open and slipped silently down the hall to the kitchen door.

Louise, Murray, and his mother all sat around the table playing cards, canasta, from the look of it—a game Murray played with his railroad friends in Cincinnati. Henry leaned against the doorframe, feeling a rare sense of confidence. "Kind of late to be up playing cards, isn't it?"

"We weren't sleepy," Louise said. "But since we are up, we might as well ask how everything went."

"Yes," Fannie added. "Did you have a good time?"

Henry knew that wasn't the question she wanted to ask. She really wanted to know: *Did the people like you? Did See-Boy like you? Are you being asked back?* He didn't blame her. He'd created a lot of worry, a lot of stress over the years. Now, he hoped to make up for that.

He pulled the money from his pocket and placed it on the table. "That's for tonight. And there'll be more tomorrow and in the weeks to come. I want to use it for whatever the family needs."

Louise smiled up at him—the kind of smile that said she was glad for his happiness. Even Murray, whose patience Henry knew he'd tried sometimes almost to the breaking point, looked pleased.

"Well done." Murray offered his hand to Henry.

They shook, then Henry bent down and kissed his mother on the cheek before turning to go. On his way out, he paused. "Yes, Mother, I did have a good time tonight."

Henry stopped at his bedroom door. The urge to step over the threshold or flip the light switch a certain number of times was there but not as strong. Crawling into bed, he thought he'd be too excited to sleep. He was wrong.

CHAPTER 38

L ouise wrestled with her options for almost a week. On Friday evening, after supper, she and Murray went for a walk. The days were getting longer, the promise of spring right around the corner, the breeze gentle as a caress. They held hands as they walked.

"I've given it a great deal of thought," Louise began. "And I've decided to sell two or three of the houses, at least the ones where the renters are so far behind on payments. It hurts me to do it, but I believe you're right. I can't carry everyone."

Murray squeezed her hand. "Good, I'm glad you've decided that way. If it makes you feel any better, at least you're being pro-active, doing something to help the family."

"Those people, the renters I spoke with, I can picture their faces. I've been where they are and know how they feel. I still find it hard to desert them."

"You're not deserting them," Murray said. "They were never in your care. You need to remember that." He stopped on the sidewalk, turned Louise to face him, and kissed her on the forehead. "But I do understand your feelings. You may be the most compassionate person I've ever known, and I love you for it."

They continued on, heading down Baily toward Bennett and the two houses where Louise had spent most of her youth. As they approached her grandparents' house, they saw the woman who rented it now sitting on the front porch. She waved, and they returned the gesture. Louise still couldn't recall her name.

Probably better that way, she thought.

After breakfast, Louise and Murray walked the same route they had the night before, this time continuing to Chapman's Dry Cleaners and Laundry. Mr. Chapman appeared from the back of the store when the bell over the door rang.

"Mrs. Carlyon," he beamed as he did every time they met. "It's good to see you again."

Louise introduced Murray, and the two men shook hands. She placed the file of business journals on the counter. "My bookkeeper and I have gone over all your numbers, and I have a proposition for you."

"That's good news. Tell me what you have in mind."

Louise pulled a check from her purse and smoothed it out on the counter. "My mother's house in North Chattanooga sold recently, and this check made out to you represents the proceeds from that sale. I know it's not the sale price you offered me, but I'd like you to keep it as a down payment on the laundry."

Chapman nodded and looked at Louise expectantly.

"I own several rental houses," she said. "I plan to put a few on the market, and when one or more sells, depending on what I can get for them, I'll have enough to pay you the remainder. I know times are hard, and I don't know how long it might take to sell, but that is our plan. I hope you'll consider it."

The store owner rubbed his chin and glanced at Murray, his eyes twinkling. "Sir, when I met your wife years ago, I knew I'd met someone special. I certainly hope you recognize that as well." He returned his gaze to Louise. "I will consider your offer on one condition. I would like you, or whoever you plan to use, to take over the operation as soon as possible, preferably within the next two weeks. Until you pay me the rest of the money, we'll split what profit there is after expenses."

Louise looked at Murray, who nodded. "Mr. Chapman, we have a deal."

On their way home, Louise told Murray there wouldn't be much profit to split, but, once the business became hers, the salary draw would be fairly significant.

"Of course, that will be split between Bobby, Henry, and me," she added.

"What about Fannie?" Murray grinned.

"I don't believe Mother is cut out for cleaning other people's clothes," Louise said, matching Murray's grin.

Louise placed an advertisement in the *Times'* classified section first thing Monday morning, offering three houses for sale. She also sat down with Bobby and Henry and worked out a schedule so at least one of them would be in the shop from seven in the morning until six in the evening. Louise would work half a day Monday through Friday, and Bobby and Henry would alternate mornings and afternoons. The two would work together on Saturday, and they'd close the store on Sundays.

Bobby still wanted to help See-Boy and Lawrence as needed during his off times, but, with luck, they'd have fewer houses to tend to before long. They agreed to start the following Monday.

The only hitch might be getting back and forth. None minded walking the several blocks from Chamberlain to Dodds Avenue on pleasant days, but opening the laundry by seven in the morning on rainy, cold days seemed much less appealing.

"Harry's away attending college," Bobby said. "His car's just sitting there. I bet he'd let me use it, or he might even sell it to me cheap."

Louise had seen little of Harry since the boys graduated from high school, but she remembered the car. "Does it still have the nicknames you gave yourselves painted on the side?"

"No, after we finished high school, we thought they seemed kind of silly."

"We won't have money to buy the car unless the houses sell, but see if Harry will let us use it until he comes home."

"Okay," Bobby said. "I'll call him this evening."

Louise sat back in her chair and studied Henry and her son. They seemed pleased by this turn of events. She especially hoped she was right about Henry. He'd been so happy playing in See-

Boy's club. Working at the laundry wouldn't interfere with that, and it would give Henry even more of a chance to feel good about himself. Maybe—hopefully—this would help him feel more at ease around people he didn't know well.

Now, if only the houses would sell.

CHAPTER 39

L ouise and her family crew started work on a crisp Monday
morning in early April. She and Bobby shared the shift,
and Mr. Chapman met them at the store to turn over the
keys and make sure Louise felt comfortable with all the equipment.

"I'll be around the house most of the time," Mr. Chapman
said. "Anything you need or have a question about, just give
me a ring."

"I hope you'll drop by on occasion to say hello, whether
we call or not." Louise gestured toward the name lettered in gold
paint on the front window. "You spent decades here, making your
business a success. I'd think your customers would love to see
you here once in a while. I know I'd like it."

Chapman nodded. "I'll try to do that. Probably, my wife
would enjoy it as well. She worries, now I'm retiring, I'll follow
her around the house from room to room like a dog." On his way
out, he stopped and pointed to the window. "I suppose once we've
finalized our deal, you'll want to have the name changed. Carlyon's
Dry Cleaners and Laundry has a good feel to it. Come to think of
it, you could leave the C and apostrophe, and just fill in the rest."

"Mr. Chapman," Louise said, "it's my belief you don't need
to change something that's been working so well over the years.
I hope you won't mind if we just leave the name as is. After all,
your customers have come to trust that name. In time, we hope
they'll feel the same about us, but for now let's not tamper with
success."

"Mrs. Carlyon, you are indeed a brilliant and engaging woman." He walked back to the counter and took Louise's hand in his. "You've made an old man feel rather good today. I know your customers will grow to appreciate you just as I have."

Her gaze followed him as Mr. Chapman strolled down the sidewalk. Like Murray, he'd been a godsend when she needed one. Maybe someone up there did watch out for her. Murray told her so on numerous occasions. More and more, she thought he might be right.

Bobby came out from the rear of the laundry. "It kind of stinks back there."

Louise raised her eyebrows. "You'd do well to get used to it. That's the smell of business, and business means money. At fourteen, I worked back there. It didn't kill me. It won't kill you either."

She took his hand and pulled him back to the rear of the shop. "Let me show you how all this works."

They'd been in back for a few minutes when the front door bell sounded.

"I'll get it," Bobby said.

Louise watched as he greeted his first customer, a good-looking young woman and apparently one of the house staff from a residence on Missionary Ridge. Mr. Chapman had been correct, she guessed, when he'd told her the folks up there had the money to keep his dry cleaners in the black.

Courteous and helpful, Bobby had a natural way with people, Louise thought. He'd be a valuable asset if he could stand the hard work and acrid fumes. He bagged the clothes and gave the young woman a receipt then stood watching as she disappeared down the sidewalk.

He handed the clothes bag to Louise. "Okay, so maybe the smell isn't all that bad after all."

Louise shrugged out of her coat and placed it on the hook just inside the front door. *Three days down, and my feet do hurt. Need to get them back in shape, I guess,* she thought as Fannie greeted her with a telephone number written on a piece of scrap paper.

"It's a realty firm. I've never heard of them, but they want you to call them back."

"Maybe they're interested in one of the houses. I hope so." It wasn't yet five, so she dialed the number and identified herself to the woman who answered.

"Oh yes, Mrs. Carlyon, thank you for returning my call. My name is Eleanor Brooks, and I'm with Houseman Realty. We've seen your advertisement in the *Times* and are interested in making you an offer."

Louise closed her eyes and silently thanked God or whomever or whatever had resulted in the call. "That's wonderful," she said. "Which house are you interested in?"

"Actually," Ms. Brooks said, "all of them."

Louise sat down. This was even better than she'd hoped. "Very well, then. Let me get a pencil and paper." She motioned to Fannie, who stood in the parlor doorway.

As Fannie brought her what she needed, Louise said, "Have you priced the houses separately or is your offer on all three?"

"All three," Ms. Brooks said. "Are you ready?"

"Yes, I'm ready."

Louise wrote the number down, frowning, as Ms. Brooks said, "Well, what do you think?"

"I think I'll need time to reflect on this. It's a good bit lower than what we're asking."

"You're right, Mrs. Carlyon. It's considerably less. You must realize, of course, how depressed our economy is right now. Houses are not moving quickly."

The North Chattanooga house had taken months to sell. Still, these three had been on the market less than a week. Should she hold out and hope for more or take this less-than-great deal?

"As I said, I'll need to think about this. Can I give you an answer next week? My husband works out of town and won't be in until Friday evening."

"I understand, and certainly you'll want to consult with your husband. I'll tell you what. I'm usually in the office on Saturday until around noon. Why don't you give me a call on Saturday morning?"

"Saturday morning? That's still not very much time."

"I'm sorry," Ms. Brooks said. "I know it's not much time, but we have other irons in the fire here. We'll need a decision by then."

Louise paused and took a breath. "I'll call Saturday morning."

After Louise hung up, Fannie asked, "How much are they offering?"

"They want all three, but it's only a little over half what we want."

"What are you going to do?"

Louise's mind raced. It seemed a shame to give up the houses for such a paltry sum. Who knew—the economy might strengthen and the renters find jobs and be a steady source of income again. On the other hand, they'd have a reliable source of income from the laundry once they'd finalized the purchase. And the offer from Houseman Realty would cover the rest of what they owed and leave a little left over.

Murray would be back tomorrow night. Until then, she'd just have to weigh it back and forth. She looked at her mother and shrugged.

"I really don't have any idea right now."

CHAPTER 40

On the third weekend, and fifth time Henry's band played See-Boy's club, the atmosphere was convivial, the band relaxed, and the patrons obviously pleased. The previous Saturday, one of See-Boy's customers bought a round of drinks for the band. Henry sipped the moonshine, but the music, not the spirits, had sent him where he wanted.

For the first time, Henry contributed to the family. At least that's how he felt about it. Louise and his mother never pushed him. He thought they probably feared he'd revert to his obsessive habits if he felt too much pressure. But he hadn't. Working at the cleaners and laundry wasn't too bad. The dry-cleaning fluid did smell pretty horrible, but he'd gotten used to it.

The best part of that job was getting to drive Louise to the shop. Bobby's friend had agreed to let them use his car. Either Henry or Bobby drove to work for the early half-day shift, then the other drove home at the end of the day. Louise had been nervous at first riding with either of them, but she'd finally managed to settle down.

"Hey, Henry," Jimmy said, "where's your head?"

Henry glanced up from where he sat behind the drum set. "What?"

"You look like you're dreaming, man, like you're somewhere else." Jimmy knelt and leaned in toward Henry. "Listen up. See-Boy told me there's a guy here tonight—somebody's cousin or uncle or something—who's in the music business in Nashville.

So do your best, okay? Who knows, he might like us, maybe get us other places to play."

"Sure, that'd be great," Henry said to be accommodating. He always *did* play his best. It's what he lived for, he thought it obvious, but maybe not everyone could tell. In truth, he wasn't sure he really wanted to play elsewhere. In just three weeks, he'd grown to feel really comfortable at See-Boy's, colored audience or not.

Still, if he wanted to be as famous as Gene Krupa, he guessed he'd need more exposure than playing in a speakeasy. He grabbed his sticks and listened as Jimmy counted off the beat with his right foot. Jelly Roll Morton's "Black Bottom Stomp" boomed from the bandstand, and the crowd piled onto the dance floor.

That same evening, Louise and Murray discussed the offer from Houseman Realty.

Murray paced in front of the parlor window, his arms crossed over his chest. "Those three houses are losing propositions right now. Chances are, the tenants won't find work anytime soon, which means they'll continue to be a loss for the foreseeable future. Even if you could evict them and find more reliable tenants, that would take time." He stopped pacing for a moment. "How long does it take to evict someone?"

She shook her head. "I don't know. It's never been necessary."

Murray sat beside Louise on the sofa. "And I'm sure it's nothing you'd want to do anyway. But the longer you keep those houses, the more income you're losing. If you take the offer, someone else will have that worry, and instead of losing rent payments, you'll have the capital you need for the laundry."

"I know," Louise said. "It's just hard to feel good about selling the houses at such a low price."

"Well, you sold your stocks for even less. Sometimes, you just have to make the best call you can and hope it all works out."

Louise leaned back against the sofa and cocked her head to one side. "When we got married, did you ever think we'd be talking about matters like these?"

Murray placed his hand on her knee. "Honestly, I had no idea." His face lit in a boyish smile that seemed to radiate warmth and love. "I suppose I could say I've never been surprised at anything you do, Louise. For most of every week, I sit around and play cards with a bunch of men who all do the same thing I do. Without you to come home to on Friday evenings, I'd probably lead a very uninteresting life."

"Thank God, you have a sense of humor."

"Yes," Murray said. "He has helped considerably on occasion."

Louise rang Houseman Realty Saturday morning and spoke to Ms. Brooks. "We are prepared to accept your offer for the three houses. How would you like to proceed with the legalities?"

"We'll have our attorney draw up the necessary documents and send them to your own for review. Once they're signed and notarized, we'll provide you a check for the agreed amount."

"Let me get back to you regarding our attorney," Louise said. "Our former attorney, Squire Adamson, died a few years ago. We've really had no need for legal services since then."

"Oh, yes, I remember hearing about that. What a shame for his family. Take the time you need. It will take a few days to prepare the documents. Just let us know who to send them to."

"I will," Louise said. "And thank you again." She hung up and turned to Murray, who watched her from the kitchen doorway. "She seems like a nice lady. I wonder if she'll feel guilty about forcing those families out of their homes."

"Better her than you," Murray said.

"We need to find another attorney," Louise said. "Someone who can review the closing documents on our behalf."

"Call Harrison Evers," Murray suggested. "He helped us find Squire Adamson. I'm sure he can recommend a good real estate attorney."

Louise thumbed through the lists of numbers she kept in the telephone stand. She found Evers' number but thought she'd wait and not try to reach him on the weekend. "I wonder where we'd be without all these different types of attorneys."

"A lot of people would probably say better off."

CHAPTER 41

President Franklin Roosevelt signed the Cullen-Harrison Act in late March, 1933. This forerunner of the full repeal of Prohibition allowed for the sale of low-alcohol-level beer and wine. See-boy took full advantage of the act, stocking and selling beer by the end of April.

Lots of folks said this "near beer" would never be popular, and he agreed. Nonetheless, he guessed his people might just enjoy a cold beer as a variant on the moonshine. He considered wine, too, but decided his customers weren't the wine-drinking type.

He'd already bought a commercial-size refrigeration unit, a large improvement over the leftover ice box he'd used in the beginning, and it would accommodate the new beverage just fine. If things kept going this way, the end of Prohibition seemed just around the corner. With luck, he hoped to be operating a legitimate, law-abiding business sometime during the coming year.

It might not be as interesting as running a speakeasy, wouldn't have that little thrill he often felt from operating outside the law, but it would sure make his daddy and Pearl feel better.

Sam, a regular at the club and good friend, drifted up to the bar and asked for a shot. See-Boy poured then used a clean cloth to polish the bar's surface. Still early Wednesday evening, the place wouldn't draw much of a crowd until later.

Sam tossed back the shot and wiped his lips on his sleeve. "My cousin, Odell, you remember him? Came in with me a few nights ago?"

"Uh-huh, had a green hat with a yellow feather in it."

"That's the one. He says he liked your band, thinks maybe they should make a recording."

"You don't say?"

"Yeah, says he got an eye for talent. Anyway, he's staying with my sister's people for a few days. He's coming back Friday, and if they're as good as they were when he first heard them, he's going to talk to the band leader, see if they want to go over to Nashville."

See-Boy leaned his elbows on the bar. "He works with white bands?"

Sam nodded. "According to him, he's got two other white groups, plus a stable of coloreds. His card says he's an agent. I guess that means if the bands make money he makes money."

"You think he's a straight shooter? I'd hate for them boys to get their hopes up then get disappointed. The drummer, Henry? He's kind of like family."

"Far as I know, Odell's all right."

See-Boy chuckled. "Wouldn't that be something to see? We'd be the place where they got discovered."

Sam nodded again. "It would indeed. Of course, you'd finally have to come up with a name for this place."

"Gonna have to anyway," See-Boy said. "Prohibition's ending soon. People be able to come in the front door for a change. Got to have a name by then."

As Henry and the others finished up their second set Friday night, a man wearing a chartreuse hat with a canary yellow feather protruding from the band ambled up to Jimmy and spoke to him. After a minute, Jimmy followed the man to one of the tables and sat down with him. That, in itself, wasn't unusual. The band had gotten to know a lot of the regulars and often joined them during breaks. But this fellow wasn't a regular. Henry remembered him from the previous weekend, the hat being hard to miss.

There wasn't time to find out what had been discussed before their third and last set of the night, but Henry couldn't help notice how the smile Jimmy wore coming back from the table never left his face. When they'd finished, Jimmy took the band out in the alley behind the club, his eyes blazing with excitement.

"The fellow I talked to is a music agent from Nashville. He likes us. I mean he *really* likes us. Wants us to go to Nashville and do a recording. He believes it will sell. We could be famous!"

Henry couldn't believe it. His heart raced, his mind immediately forming mental pictures of them playing before a huge crowd. The five of them wore white tuxedo jackets and red carnation boutonnieres, and already he could hear his drum solos on a phonograph recording.

Famous.

Jimmy would meet with the agent again tomorrow before they played their first set. They agreed to meet Sunday to discuss the details. Henry, still riding high, followed the others back inside for a celebratory drink.

At the bar, See-Boy poured a shot for each. "I heard the good news. I wish you all luck, and this drink's on the house." He then poured one for himself and held it up. "Here's to Farr and Away."

They all clinked glasses and downed the moonshine. It burned Henry's throat and made his eyes water, but it didn't matter. *Famous.* Like his idol, Gene Krupa. *Who knew? He might even meet the guy.*

By the time Henry got in bed, the first rush of excitement had ebbed. In its place, a new feeling slowly emerged—anxiety. Nashville was a big city, bigger than Chattanooga. Aside from the band members, he'd know no one. He'd be alone, away from his mother and Louise.

His heart pounded in his chest. Panic grabbed hold. What if he couldn't play? What if the need to count started again, to touch things, to step a certain way? What if it all came tumbling back down onto him?

Henry placed his hands over his ears and squeezed as hard as he could, but the feeling wouldn't go away. It grew. Jimmy and the others had never seen him this way. They *couldn't* see him like this. He turned his face into the sheets and felt something damp. Then he felt the tears on his face.

CHAPTER 42

Harrison Evers recommended Michael Peters, an attorney who specialized in real estate. Louise called and spoke with him, and he agreed to represent Schmidt Enterprises in dealing with Houseman Realty. Since he knew the attorney for Houseman, he would call and make arrangements to have the documents forwarded when ready.

Louise grabbed her purse and a light jacket for her walk to the laundry, having sent Bobby with the car to open up. The beautiful day, neither too warm nor too cool, made Louise glad to have the opportunity to be outside.

Before she left, she knocked on Henry's door. He'd seemed out of sorts the day before, quieter than usual.

"Henry?" She cracked the door and peeked inside. Henry sat on the side of the bed, staring at the floor. "Henry, are you feeling all right?"

He didn't look up. "I thought you'd be at work already."

"I had to speak with a couple of attorneys this morning regarding the houses I'm selling. I'm just getting ready to walk to the laundry. Are you okay? You didn't say much yesterday. Did something happen at See-Boy's club Saturday night?"

"No, nothing happened. I guess I just felt a little puny yesterday." He looked at her and smiled weakly.

"Do you feel better today? If you don't, I can stay and work your shift at the laundry."

"No, I'm better. I'll be there this afternoon." He stood and turned to the window before saying, "Have a nice walk."

Louise found Fannie in the kitchen drinking coffee at the table.

"I'm leaving for work," Louise said. "Did you think Henry seemed awfully quiet yesterday?"

Fannie looked up at Louise over the rim of her coffee cup. "Come to think of it, I suppose he did."

"He says he's all right."

"I'll check on him later," Fannie said.

Outside, Louise stopped for a moment by the house next door where a large old oak tree trailed tangles of purple wisteria vine from its limbs. Its fragrance filled her nose. She loved the spring when everything bloomed and painted the city in shades of green. It made her happy. And she *was* happy. But she couldn't quite get Henry off her mind.

Henry did his best to put on a good face for the rest of the day, having lunch with his mother before heading off to the laundry for his afternoon shift. He wanted to confide to Louise, the only person he felt comfortable talking to, but the afternoon brought a steady stream of customers. At six, they closed the door, and Henry and Louise climbed into Harry West's loaner car for the drive home.

"Would you mind if we talked for a minute before going home?" Henry asked.

"Mother's cooking tonight, so we don't have to be there right away. As a matter of fact, I've been thinking about you all day. I hope you'll tell me what's wrong."

"One of See-Boy's customers has a cousin visiting, a man who's a music agent from Nashville. He wants the band to go to Nashville and make a recording."

Louise reached over and squeezed Henry's arm. "Why, that's wonderful, Henry. That must be like a dream come true for a musician. I'm so happy for you."

Henry closed his eyes, leaned his head back, and let out a long breath. "I can't go, Louise. I've never been away from you and Momma. I'm scared. Scared of leaving Chattanooga, scared I'll panic, scared I'll mess up the recording. I'm scared of *everything*." He waited and watched as Louise stayed silent for a moment.

"But you love music and playing the drums," she finally said. "It's your chance to do what you've always wanted. It may only come this once. You'd be with your friends. You wouldn't be alone."

He shook his head. "It's not the same. I'm not comfortable with anyone but you and Momma—mostly you."

"But you've been doing so well. I'm sorry we had to drop the therapy sessions. I didn't want to, you know, they were just more than we could afford."

"I know," Henry said. "And I did do better, a lot better, until this came along." He clenched his fists around the steering wheel. "I'm twenty-seven years old, and I'm as frightened as a child."

Louise took his hand and pulled him to her, put her arm around his neck, and held his head against her chest, rubbing his back gently.

Henry breathed in Louise's smell, a mixture of soap, sweat, and dry-cleaning fumes. It felt so good. To be held like that. It made all the bad go away. *Like a child,* he thought. But it only lasted a moment. He couldn't take *her* to Nashville, although that's what he really wanted. With her there, everything else would be all right.

"I'll try to find a way to start the therapy sessions again. Would you like that?"

Henry nodded. It wasn't Nashville, but it was something.

After a few minutes, Henry sat up and tried hard to smile. "It'll be all right, Louise. Maybe I'll get another chance—after the therapy." He started the car and pulled onto Dodds Avenue. "Our band is pretty good, you know?"

"It must be," Louise said. "See-Boy knows how to back winners, I guess."

As they approached the house on Chamberlain, Henry said, "Let's not tell Momma what we talked about, okay?"

Louise hesitated for just a moment before answering. "Okay."

CHAPTER 43

The closing took place at the Houseman Realty attorney's office. John O'Brian's office, like many other attorneys', sat on a hill behind City Hall, its entrance on Cherry Street.

When Louise entered the reception area, a tall, slender, bespectacled man rose from one of the chairs and strode over to Louise.

"You must be Mrs. Carlyon," he said, offering her his hand. "I'm Michael Peters."

Louise noted his firm handshake. "How do you do, Squire Peters. It's always nice to put the face with the voice you've heard over the telephone."

"Please call me Michael. Squire sounds a little pompous, don't you think?"

"Perhaps," Louise said, smiling. "But I'm quite sure you've worked hard to earn the title."

The receptionist rose from her desk. "Squire Simmons will see you now." She opened the door to Simmons' office and gestured for them to enter.

O'Brian caught Louise's eye and mouthed the word *Squire* and winked. She bit her lip to keep from chuckling aloud.

Squire Simmons was everything Peters was not—short, portly, and almost completely bald. In contrast, a large, oak desk took up a third of the office while green velvet drapes graced the windows, and a thick oriental rug covered the floor. Bookshelves lined with legal tomes filled the wall space on either side of the room.

"Please come in, Mrs. Carlyon," he said and pointed to two guest chairs opposite the desk. "Hello, Michael, good to see you."

Surprised the realtor she'd spoken with wasn't there, Louise asked, "Will Ms. Brooks be joining us?"

"Unfortunately, no. She had other responsibilities, but everything requiring her approval and signature has already been taken care of."

Peters opened his briefcase and retrieved a sheaf of papers.

"I see you have the documents, Michael," Simmons said. "Shall we proceed?"

The three spent an hour going through the various papers and signing and initialing where needed. When they finished, Louise said, "There is a possibility I might want to sell another house soon. Do you think Houseman Realty might be interested?"

Simmons leaned back in his chair and rested his hands on his round belly. "I couldn't say for sure, of course, but I think possibly so. I can ask if you like."

"I'd appreciate that. Just let me know, and I can provide you with the particulars on what would be available."

They all shook hands again, and Squire Peters walked out with Louise. On the sidewalk, Louise thanked him again. "If I do decide to sell another house, I'll ask Squire Simmons to contact you."

"Please do, Mrs. Carlyon. I'll be happy to assist."

Louise caught the streetcar at Main and Cherry and settled herself into a window seat. She would have a little money left over after she paid Mr. Chapman, but, by itself, it wouldn't be enough to get Henry back into therapy for a reasonable length of time.

If she sold another house and dedicated the proceeds toward therapy, that should be enough to provide for at least another year. Maybe Henry wouldn't need it the whole time. She hoped that would be the case, but better to be prepared.

She wondered what Murray would think of her idea. He'd always let her handle Schmidt Enterprises however she felt best, but she also knew he wasn't particularly happy about the way she sometimes indulged Henry. Not that she thought of the therapy sessions as an indulgence. She believed they genuinely worked. Henry thought so, too, and she could tell the difference after he'd been in therapy for a while. Should she tell Murray the reason she hoped to sell another house? She'd agreed not to tell her mother about the band's recording offer and Henry's reluctance, but she didn't think it would be fair not to discuss it with Murray.

Louise told Murray the whole story after supper on Saturday. He listened quietly but didn't say much. He went back into the kitchen and brought both of them a glass of iced tea. Then he shook a Camel from his pack and lit it.

"Schmidt Enterprises is yours, Louise. You earned it. You deserved it. If you want to spend the proceeds on Henry's therapy, you should do it. He's had a hard time of it. You've told me a lot of what you went through with your father, and I suspect there's more you haven't shared. I suppose it's no wonder Henry's like he is. He's never been strong like you, and I doubt he ever will be."

He tapped an ash into the tray on the little table between their two chairs. "One thing arguing for your side is this: if you sell a house where the renters aren't behind on their payments, you don't have to worry about them being thrown out on the street."

"I hadn't thought of that," Louise said.

"On the other hand, you might be settling for a fixed amount of money against a long-term income stream. You might win in the short term but lose overall."

"I think I did know that," Louise said. "Houseman bought those other houses cheap. I probably can't expect to do much better on another one."

"But you really want to do this, don't you?"

Louise looked into Murray's eyes. "I told Henry from the time he was just a baby I'd always take care of him. I meant that, you know? Whatever else he is, he'll always be my baby brother."

Murray crushed out his cigarette and patted Louise's hand. "I know he is, Louise. Make the call."

After the band's final set, Henry pulled Jimmy outside in back and told him he couldn't go to Nashville. He didn't say the real reason. He just couldn't bring himself to confess something like that. Instead, he claimed he had to work, that he couldn't leave the laundry responsibilities to only Bobby and Louise.

"I'm really sorry," Henry said. "I just can't go."

Jimmy stood there, his arms crossed over his chest. "Yeah, Henry, we're *all* really sorry. Odell's still inside with his cousin Sam and See-Boy. I guess I'll have to go tell him we can't make the recording." He jerked open the door to the club and left Henry standing in the alley alone.

Once again, Henry felt tears sliding down his cheeks. *What was wrong with him? Why did God make him this way?* The other band members would hate him, resent him for causing them to miss what might be their one chance to be a success. He heard voices from inside the club nearing the door. He couldn't let anyone see him bawling like a baby. He moved quickly to one side and crouched behind a large trash can just as the door opened.

He recognized Jimmy's voice and peeked around the can to see the other voice belonged to Odell, the man in the green hat.

Odell put his hand on Jimmy's shoulder. "Don't worry, son. Nashville is overrun with session musicians. Drummers there are a dime a dozen, all waiting for a chance like this. You boys go ahead and plan your trip. I'll have a drummer lined up for you, and he'll be at least as good as yours, probably better."

"Thanks, Odell. I'll tell the others tomorrow. We'll make you proud. I guarantee it."

Odell laughed. "I know you will, son. I know you will."

Henry heard the door close and Jimmy's retreating steps going down the alley. *A dime a dozen,* Odell had said, and *probably better than yours.* The band members wouldn't hate him. They'd just forget him.

CHAPTER 44

After Murray left for the train terminal, Louise made calls to Squire Simmons and Michael Peters. She had gone through the list of her remaining rental houses and decided on a house on Thirteenth Street near Willow. The couple had only been renting the house for about six months. She knew their names but only from the rental agreement. Murray had been right. She wouldn't feel nearly as bad selling this house.

Squire Simmons agreed to present the offer and call her back when he had a response. Michael Peters assured her he would be glad to represent her interests once more. She needed only to call and let him know when she heard back from the realty firm.

Louise finished her morning coffee and left for work. Cool for June, she enjoyed the feel of a slight but insistent breeze on her cheeks as she walked. She thought about the turn of events that had brought about her current situation. Like many, she'd lost money in the stock market, but trading the non-productive rental houses for the dry cleaners and laundry had, so far, been a good move. She and her family were better off than so many.

If the house on Thirteenth sold, though, it would bring her remaining properties down to eight. See-Boy and his family had, for years, depended in part on the income they received for maintaining those houses. She wondered how much they depended on it still.

When she got to See-Boy and Pearl's house, she took a chance and knocked. Pearl opened the door almost immediately, smiling at her through the screen door.

"Good morning, Louise. What a nice surprise. Please come in."

Louise followed Pearl into the kitchen, declining her offer of coffee. "I won't be long, Pearl, I just wanted to talk to you about something."

They settled at the table and Louise told Pearl of her plans to sell another house. "I'm sorry to say I hadn't thought of it before now, but I've begun to worry about the loss of income you all might experience with fewer houses to maintain."

Pearl reached across the table and patted her hand. "Louise, honey, don't give it another thought. First of all, See-Boy's club is doing really well. In fact, he's spending much more time dealing with the club than he did when it first started. Daddy Lawrence can't do as much as he used to. Fewer houses would probably suit both of them. As for me, I'm doing the laundry books now, too, so we're all right."

Pearl poured herself another cup of coffee. "I hope I've set your mind to rest about this."

Louise nodded. "You have, Pearl. Thank you. And please give my best to See-Boy and Lawrence. I'm so glad the club is paying off." Speaking about the club brought Henry's problem to the forefront of her mind. *One more reason,* she thought, *to feel good about what I'm doing for Henry.*

Pearl walked Louise to the door and gave her a hug. "I'll have the totals from May for you by the end of the week. You can either stop by here or I'll come to you."

After waving goodbye, Louise continued to the laundry. *Now,* she thought, *all I have to do is make sure the house sells.*

Henry bagged a load of clothing, gave the customer a receipt, and took the bag to the rear of the laundry, where Louise prepared chemicals. Glad to be working, he appreciated anything to take his mind off all his troubles.

The band, except for him, would leave for Nashville on Tuesday, rehearse and record on Wednesday, and return on Thursday, back in time to play See-Boy's club Friday and Saturday. Jimmy had told him of their plans to use a session drummer, and he guessed he should be glad they could work around his absence.

But he wasn't. At least he'd play over the weekend as usual—and wouldn't have to explain to his mother why he wasn't at the club.

When he returned to the front, he saw Bobby and his friend, Harry, pull up at the curb. Harry had given the old Ford sedan to Bobby after his father provided him a used-but-newer vehicle from his car lot.

The guys climbed out, and Bobby held the door for a youngish-looking woman who crawled out from the rear seat. Plump, but not fat, Henry thought her pretty in a hard sort of way. Bobby slung his arm over her shoulder as they walked toward the laundry.

A little bell over the door announced their arrival, and Bobby said, "Henry, how's it going?"

"All right," Henry replied.

"Momma's in the back?"

Henry nodded as Bobby swung around the counter and disappeared to the rear of the store.

"Henry, this is Irene," Harry offered. "Irene, this is Henry, Bobby's uncle."

Irene thrust her hand out to Henry. "Pleased to meet you."

Her hand felt warm and slightly moist. Her blond hair fell in curls around her face, and she had an up-turned nose and green eyes that fixed on his. He realized he still held her hand and released it. "Glad to meet you, too."

She popped a piece of gum in her mouth.

"Irene is a new friend of ours," Harry said. She lives in a duplex close to the Cotton Patch Club. We're going to her place tonight to listen to records." He turned to Irene and pointed at Henry. "Henry's a drummer, plays with the Farr and Away Band."

"Are you really a musician?" Irene asked, a coy smile catching at the edges of her mouth.

Henry nodded. "Uh-huh."

She popped the gum again. "You can come, too, if you want."

Bobby appeared from the back then, and they piled into the car and left.

Henry rubbed his fingers together. He thought he could still feel a trace of moisture there from Irene's soft hand.

CHAPTER 45

Fannie barely waited for Louise to shed her purse before saying, "The attorney for the realty company called and said you should ring him at home. The number's by the phone."

Louise sat down at the telephone stand and removed her shoes. Then she dialed.

"Squire Simmons' residence," a woman's voice said.

"This is Louise Carlyon returning Squire Simmons' call."

A moment later, the attorney came on the line. "Mrs. Carlyon, I've heard from Ms. Brooks and indeed she is interested in the house. The house on Thirteenth is somewhat newer than the others she purchased, and that is reflected in the price she will pay."

Louise listened as Simmons quoted the offer—slightly more than the agreed prices for the others but less than she'd hoped. She had already committed to the idea of selling, though, and to securing more therapy for Henry.

"I'll accept the offer," she said.

"Excellent," the attorney said. "I'll draw up the papers and proceed. I assume you plan to use Squire Peters as your representative."

"Yes, I do."

"Excellent," he said again and rang off.

Well, Louise thought, *it's done.*

She went down the hall to Henry's room and knocked. When he didn't answer, she opened it to find the bedroom empty. Then she walked back to the kitchen and leaned against the doorjamb. "Where's Henry, Mother?"

"He called from the laundry after you'd gone and said he planned to go out with Bobby and Harry West."

"Is he really? That's a new one, his going out with them."

"I think it's good," Fannie said. "He needs to get out more and meet new people."

Louise couldn't help smiling. It really *was* nice of Bobby and Harry to include Henry in their plans. "Yes, I think so, too."

Henry rode in the back seat, with Bobby riding in front beside Harry, who drove. Henry felt out of place but nonetheless glad to be included—sort of excited, even.

"What kind of records does Irene have?" Henry asked.

"Jazz, I guess," Bobby said. "Maybe blues. I don't really know." He swung around to face Henry. "The truth is, we don't spend much time listening to her records." He smiled. "Irene's kind of easy … if you catch my meaning."

Henry wasn't sure he did, but he smiled back at Bobby and nodded like he understood. He'd heard the guys in the band talking—boasting, he thought—about being with women. It wasn't something he thought about much. Well, he *did* think about it but didn't figure it ever happening to him.

Harry turned onto Main Street, and, ahead on the right, Henry saw the sign for the Cotton Patch Club. He remembered Louise telling him his father used to hang out there before Prohibition caused its closure. In the club's parking lot, a couple of men in overalls packed a truck with painters' supplies. He could tell the building had a new coat of white paint. *See-Boy must be right,* he thought. Prohibition would end soon.

A few blocks later, Harry turned left off Main and eased to a stop in front of a beige stucco duplex. "This is it," Harry said opening his door.

Bobby slid out on the other side and pulled his seat forward so Henry could climb out. On the sidewalk, he clapped Henry on the back. "C'mon Henry, let the fun begin."

They were halfway up the walk when Irene, barefoot, opened the door. She wore a light blue off-the-shoulder blouse and matching shorts that stopped above her knee. "Hello, guys. Come on in."

Henry heard a record playing and knew the tune by Fats Waller's band. Small, the duplex was sparsely furnished but neat. A sofa, coffee table, and one upholstered chair sat in the front room. He saw beyond a bedroom, with a tiny kitchen area and bath squeezed into the middle space.

Irene grabbed Henry's arm, pulling him close. He felt the swell of her breasts and the back of his hand brushed her abdomen. Seldom touched by anyone, he almost jerked away but forced himself to relax. She pecked him on the cheek.

"Henry, I'm so glad you could come."

"Yes," Henry replied, very much aware of her body pressing against him. She smelled sweet, like cotton candy. "I'm glad, too."

He glanced at Bobby and Harry standing to one side, hands on hips, watching and smiling.

Irene finally let go of his arm. "Can I get us something to drink? All I have is near beer, but it's better than nothing, I guess."

"I have a better idea," Bobby said. "Harry and I know of a place where we can get real alcohol. We'll run out and get a bottle while you and Henry get acquainted."

"Okay," Irene said. She led Henry to the sofa and settled in beside him. "We'll do just that—get acquainted, won't we, Henry?"

Henry nodded. Things seemed to be happening so fast. He had no idea Bobby and Harry might leave him there alone. He didn't know what to do. Was he *supposed* to do something?

He heard the car start and pull away. Alone with Irene—this woman he didn't know, hadn't even met until that afternoon—his hands started to sweat.

Irene leaned over, and Henry felt her warm breath on his ear, her bosom pressing against his arm again.

"Why don't I get you and me a beer, Henry? It'll help us relax, okay?"

"Okay, sure," Henry said.

Irene went into the little kitchen area and came back with the beers. She handed one to Henry, said, "Cheers," and swallowed a mouthful of the liquid. She licked her lips and watched Henry take a drink. She set her beer on the coffee table, then took Henry's and did the same.

"I like the taste of beer," she said, then swung her right leg over and straddled Henry, kissing him on the lips. "I like the way it tastes on your lips, too."

Henry couldn't believe what was happening—until his body responded to Irene's weight on his lap. At first, he felt embarrassed. *What would she think?* Then the pressure began to build. She kissed him again, harder this time, and he felt himself kissing her back, moving his hands over her bare shoulders, not caring what she might think.

With her mouth still locked on his, Irene took one of his hands and guided it to her breast.

Something exploded inside Henry. He groaned as warmth flooded his loins and pulled away from Irene short of breath.

"Uh-oh," Irene said, first looking down at Henry's lap then sliding off him. "Let me get you a wash cloth or something."

Henry followed her gaze. His trousers were dark with stain. He stood. "I have to go. I need to leave right now."

Irene came out from the bathroom with a damp wash cloth. "We can fix that up. You don't need to go. Bobby and Harry aren't coming back for at least an hour. Next time, you'll do just fine."

He could feel the panic coming on. He had to go—right now. He snatched the cloth from Irene and stumbled to the front door, feeling the dampness of his trousers with each step. He swung the door open and stepped outside.

Irene followed him. "You really don't have to leave, Henry. It's all right. Either way, I'll still get my money."

Henry turned left at the sidewalk, not sure where he headed. It wasn't dark yet. What if he met somebody, and they saw what he'd done? He pulled his shirt out from the waistband of his trousers, but it wasn't long enough to cover the stain. What if his mother saw it when he got home? *What if Louise saw?*

He chose a roundabout way to cover the miles between Irene's duplex and the house on Chamberlain. He didn't want to come across Bobby and Harry. Didn't know what he'd say to them or how he'd be able to face Bobby at all. Why had they done this to him? He felt humiliated, just one more thing he couldn't do right.

CHAPTER 46

Henry lay awake in his bed when he heard the soft knock. He decided to ignore it. He'd made it home, crossing the street as needed to avoid coming face to face with anyone. By the time he arrived, the damp blotch had dried to a barely noticeable stain.

When the knock sounded again, he reluctantly answered, "Come in."

Bobby's figure appeared in the doorway, his silhouette framed by the meager hall light. "Hey, Henry, can we talk for a minute?"

Henry didn't really want to talk to Bobby but figured he might as well get it over with. "Yes."

Bobby stepped over to Henry's bed and stood beside it. "Irene told me what happened. I'm sorry you got so upset, man. It's not a big thing. Hell, almost everybody does it their first time. You should've stayed and tried again."

"I felt too embarrassed," Henry said, thinking now maybe he *should* have stayed. If he had, he might've done it right the next time. Then he wouldn't be hiding under his bedcovers.

"Okay if I sit down?" Bobby asked.

Henry shifted to make room. "Harry and I are sorry you ended up feeling bad. We thought being with a woman would be good for you."

"It might have been, but I can't do anything right. Whatever it is, I'll mess it up."

"That's not true, Henry. You're a really good guy. You do just great at the laundry. And you're a musician, man. That's talent, something to be proud of."

Not if you can't bring yourself to even leave your home for a couple of days to cut a record.

"I'd like to make it up to you," Bobby said. "How about we go back and see Irene again, just you and me? Harry doesn't even have to know. I'll sit outside on the porch or in the front room while you and Irene go in the bedroom. What do you say?"

Henry remembered the feeling of Irene kissing him. And he had wanted to touch her breast—and more. But he couldn't live with *that* happening again. "I don't know. What if..."

Bobby chuckled. "Believe me, Henry, sooner or later you'll get it right. And so what? It still feels good, doesn't it? There are lots worse things."

"Is Irene a prostitute? She said she'd still get paid."

"Irene worked at Miller Brothers selling dresses, but she got laid off when the economy went sour. She's just like the rest of us, trying to make ends meet doing whatever she can."

Henry lay there trying to make up his mind.

"She told me she liked you. It upset her you left. Thought maybe she'd done something wrong. She asked me to ask you to come back and see her."

"Did she really?"

"Yes, she really did."

"Well, I suppose it wouldn't hurt to try again. When do you think we could go back?"

Bobby got up off the bed. "Tomorrow after work, if that sounds okay."

Henry smiled. "I think that sounds good."

Bobby walked over to the door. "Leave your trousers on the bed in the morning. I'll make sure they're cleaned and pressed."

"Thanks, Bobby."

After the door closed, Henry lay awake staring at the ceiling. He still felt embarrassed, but, according to Bobby, this sort of thing happened all the time. Next time he'd get it right—or maybe the time after that.

L ouise walked the few blocks from Chamberlain to McCallie Avenue to catch the streetcar downtown. With Christmas approaching, she wanted to find Murray something special. Bobby and Henry had both agreed to work the morning shift at the laundry, giving her the time to shop.

She debated between a nice leather wallet and a belt, both of which she'd seen advertised in the *Times*. As the streetcar neared the intersection of Highland Park Avenue, she noticed a *For Sale* sign in the window of Lackey's Grocery. She'd worked there for a while years before and enjoyed the job. Then her stepmother died, and with her arrested for the murder, Old Man Lackey had worried it would affect business and fired her.

She wondered if the store had gone out of business, or if perhaps Lackey passed away. He'd been overweight and florid-faced when she knew him, probably had high blood pressure, so it wouldn't surprise her. She got a pencil from her purse and jotted down the number on the sign. It couldn't hurt to inquire. The fragrance of fresh fruit and other produce sure beat dry-cleaning fumes.

L ouise made her purchase at Loveman's Department Store— a nice pair of gloves, the rich leather so supple it felt like velvet. Riding the streetcar home, on a whim, she got off at the corner of Highland Park Avenue and walked down to the empty grocery store. The ice cream parlor, attached to the grocery and also owned by Old Man Lackey, appeared to be open. She went inside.

"Hey there," a female voice said. "Please come in."

Louise looked around but saw no one, then, as she stepped further inside, a plump dark-haired woman rose from where she'd been doing something below the level of the counter.

"Sorry," the woman said. "I just—" Her eyes grew wide and her mouth hung open. "Louise! My God, I thought I'd never see you again."

Louise grinned. Juanita, who'd run the ice cream parlor for Old Man Lackey, had, for a time, been Louise's closest friend and confidante. "Hello to you, too!"

Juanita rushed around the counter and smothered Louise in a hug.

"I saw the sign in the window and thought I'd take a look at the grocery. You'll have to tell me what's going on."

Juanita pulled out one of the wrought-iron chairs, its metal tubing entwined to form a heart shape of the backrest. "Sit down, honey, and I'll make us both a milkshake and tell you all about it."

Henry followed Irene from her bedroom into the front room and stood waiting as she opened the door and invited Bobby back inside. She wore a flimsy nightgown, barely held together by a narrow fabric belt of the same material. He could see the imprint of her nipples through the gown, nipples that had grazed his chest just minutes earlier.

Bobby looked from Irene to Henry. "Well, how'd it go?"

Irene glided back over and put her arm around Henry's waist. "What do you think, Henry? Did it go all right?"

Henry nodded, feeling color rise in his cheeks. "It went just great … I think."

"Uh-huh," Irene said. "I think Henry and I are going to become good friends."

CHAPTER 47

L ouise sat in the parlor wrapping Murray's present. The coal grate cast a warm orange glow throughout the room, and the flames made shadows dance on the walls. The summer of 1933 had gone by quickly, and fall had followed suit. Sometimes, she marveled at how life slipped by almost without her knowing.

She'd sold the house on Thirteenth as planned. Once again, the closing had been conducted in Squire Simmons' office with only Louise and the two attorneys attending. She wanted to thank Ms. Brooks, but according to Simmons, she was a very busy lady. Louise imagined her as one of those people who really did think time equaled money and niceties an unproductive nuisance.

At any rate, the sale provided funds to begin Henry's therapy again—a wise investment since, for the first time, he seemed truly content, even confident. She didn't know who came up with his form of therapy but certainly felt grateful.

Fannie came in and stood over Louise, who sat on the floor with her scissors, wrapping paper, and ribbon. "Can I bring you anything?"

"I don't think so. I'm just enjoying the fire while I wrap presents." She tied a strip of blue ribbon, made a bow, then ran the blade of the scissors down over the loose ends so they would curl.

"What have you gotten Murray for Christmas?"

"Fur-lined leather gloves. He doesn't need them much around here, but it gets so cold in Cincinnati."

"That fire does feel nice. I think I'll join you." Fannie pulled a wooden rocker from the corner and placed it near the grate. "Have you heard any more from your lawyer or Old Man Lackey's estate?"

"Nothing new, I'm afraid. After the old man died, his nieces and nephews got into a squabble about what to do with the grocery. Part of them wanted to reopen the store and others wanted to sell the ice cream parlor and the grocery."

"Looking for a nice piece of cash, I expect. Get something for nothing without having to work for it."

Louise's thoughts flashed back to her father's funeral and what Kaye had told her about Sylvia and Edith. "There's a lot of that going around, I guess. Anyway, Squire Peters says this kind of conflict could drag on for months."

"I admire your ambition, running the laundry and wanting to take on the grocery store, too. It takes gumption, especially with the poor economy these days."

Louise got up from the floor and placed Murray's giftwrapped package under the tree the two of them had picked out last Saturday and decorated Sunday. To her, it transformed the room into something from the past, like the trees she remembered from her childhood, when her grandparents were alive and the space under the tree packed with gifts for her and Henry.

"You know I like to stay busy, Mother. Bobby and Henry can practically run the laundry by themselves now, and I always loved working at that grocery store." She turned and looked at Fannie. "Do you know what Juanita told me? She said the store never did as well as when I worked there."

"I'm not at all surprised. You're not only smart and ambitious, you're good with people—colored, white, whatever—you make your customers feel good about themselves."

Her mother rarely handed out compliments, Louise knew. "Thank you, Mother."

Fannie nodded. "I just hope you don't get in over your head."

That's more like it, Louise thought. "I suppose we'll just have to wait and see, won't we?"

Henry retrieved a bundle of clothing and made change for the customer. "Thank you for your business," he said as the man turned for the door. He still preferred working in back, but he'd gotten better at customer service.

The therapy helped him understand what seemed obvious when he thought back on it. From toddler to preadolescent, he'd lived with the notion that not only did his father despise him but wanted to kill him. *Who wouldn't be messed up by that?*

He loved his mother and his grandparents, but he'd only ever truly trusted Louise. His attachment to her was both beneficial—she calmed him—and restrictive, in that he felt he couldn't survive without her. His therapist termed it paradoxical. He'd looked the word up in the dictionary but still wasn't sure he understood it fully. Even so, his visits made him feel better.

Better, but not as good as visits to Irene's. He went as often as he could afford, once a week. He'd felt bad about spending his money on Irene when Louise spent her money on his therapy, so he and Irene worked out a bartering system. She gave him a discount as a frequent visitor, and Henry laundered and dry cleaned her clothes for free.

He'd asked her to come down to See-Boy's club and listen to the band, but she'd told him she didn't think she'd be comfortable there. Instead, they listened to records at her place. She had some pretty good ones, and other times Henry brought his own.

He never thought of her as a prostitute. Like Bobby said, she was just trying to keep her life together any way she could.

Just like him.

What else did he have to spend money on, anyway?

He'd heard the band's recording on the radio a week ago. Although he felt he'd have done better on the drums, it sounded really good. Jimmy talked about the agent, Odell something or other, setting the band up to go on the road. It would either happen or not, Henry figured. If therapy helped enough to join them—and they wanted him back—that would be great. If not, though, he still had his job, and he had Irene.

He wondered if he should get her a Christmas present. They weren't like girlfriend and boyfriend. He knew that. But, for the first time beyond Louise, he felt close to a woman, business arrangement or not. He could ask Bobby, but his answer would likely be no. He certainly couldn't ask Louise. He thought it funny that, over the past few months, his sister had remarked more than once how he seemed so much better. She chalked it up to the therapy. And the therapy had helped—his therapist's version and Irene's own unique brand as well.

A record, that's what I'll get her for Christmas! That wouldn't be awkward. They both loved music.

As he returned to the rear of the laundry, he whistled—something he'd done very little of during his twenty-seven years. It felt good, really good.

See-Boy took a final look at the estimate and signed off. *Not a bad price,* he thought. But then, most folks just wanted a job, any job. A depressed economy dictated depressed wages—good for him, in that his renovations would be very affordable, and the men doing the work would get a couple weeks' work and a few extra dollars.

He handed the estimate back to James Woodall, the contractor. "When can you get started?"

"We can start tomorrow, if you like."

See-Boy nodded. "The sooner the better, as far as I'm concerned. I'd like to have everything done by Christmas Eve, so we can have a nice, big party here."

"We'll have it done," Woodall said and left See-Boy sitting at a table.

See-Boy stood and walked to the bar, feeling pretty good. With the repeal of Prohibition ratified by Utah earlier in December—the last state needed to affect the change—his business became legitimate. But See-boy had seen it coming months before, and had already made plans for the club's renovations.

The bar would be moved to allow easier entry and exit through the front door, the door that hadn't been used since the building had been a meat market. He'd add a back bar as well, to show-case the now-legal liquor. New lighting, parquet tiles for the dance floor, and an upgraded restroom rounded out most other improvements.

His planned changes to the front of the club excited him the most—a new door flanked by twin gas lighting fixtures with a green canvas canopy above. The front windows, painted over during Prohibition to hide the interior, would be scraped clean and the club's name hand-lettered on each one. He'd spent a lot of time tossing around ideas but finally came to the conclusion the name would honor his first moonshine bar in the maintenance shed: The Hanger.

He'd booked the Farr and Away band for the big party on Christmas Eve to celebrate the club's grand opening, though See-Boy wasn't sure how long they'd be around after that. Odell had a plan to take them on the road for a while. He might have to see if he could find another group, a colored group this time maybe, and possibly even one with a singer. That would be nice.

Anyway he looked at it, 1934 promised to be a good year.

PART THREE

A PRELUDE TO WAR

CHAPTER 48

Louise sat in the reception room at Squire Peters' office thumbing absently through a copy of *Life*. Eleanor Roosevelt graced the cover of the May 29, 1939, issue, and an accompanying article told of the visit to Hyde Park by King George and Queen Elizabeth. Though not much interested in English Royalty, Louise did admire the First Lady.

Normally, she didn't have to wait for her attorney, but this morning he'd been called to court at the last minute. His receptionist and secretary, Flo, apologized and made her a cup of coffee. She put *Life* aside and picked up a copy of *Time*, scanning a few articles related to the economy. It had been up and down over the past few years, and, while times were still hard for many Americans, the despair gradually lifted.

Louise hoped for a continued recovery but remained wary. She'd read in the newspaper about the chancellor of Germany threatening that country's Jewish population. She couldn't imagine President Roosevelt doing something like that. Germany was a world away, of course, but she couldn't help remembering the past war in Europe and Murray's prolonged absence when he went overseas. *The war to end all wars.* For Bobby's sake, for everyone's sake, really, she prayed that was true.

Squire Peters swept in and closed the door behind him, his face bright as he greeted Louise. "Hello, Mrs. Carlyon. I'm sorry to keep you waiting."

"It wasn't a bother," Louise said. "Flo gave me coffee, and I caught up on world events."

He gestured toward his office. "Please, let's go inside."

They settled in, Peters behind his desk and Louise in one of the client chairs opposite.

"Well, Louise, this is your big day. It's been a long time coming, hasn't it?"

Louise nodded and smiled. "Indeed it has, Michael. Thank you for helping me along the way."

Peters slid a document across the desk: an executed, notarized deed for the grocery store. Louise picked it up and took a few minutes to read the paper thoroughly.

It *had* been a long time coming to fruition. Old Man Lackey's relatives had squabbled months away over whether to sell or keep the grocery in the family. None, though, had either the business sense or inclination to work the hours required to make the store an ongoing profitable venture.

Squire Peters had approached the estate with Louise's offer to manage the store fulltime and pay one fifth of the final asking price on an annual basis. During that five-year period, the grocery continued to carry the Lackey name.

As Squire Peters said after the family agreed on the proposal, "Everyone got part of what they wanted, but no one got it all."

And now, Louise had made the last annual payment, the store finally hers in full. Over the last five years, she had sold off five more rental houses to help make the annual payment. Three renters had been behind on their rent, but Louise hadn't felt the same sense of guilt she'd experienced years before. She supposed she'd grown used to the idea everyone had to fend for themselves.

"So, Louise, are you planning to change the name of the store now that you're the owner?"

"There's no reason not to, so yes, I'm having a sign painted now—Carlyon's Grocery. It has a nice ring to it, don't you think?"

Peters leaned back in his chair and rested his hands on his lap. "I certainly do. It'll go nicely with the laundry and dry cleaners."

Mr. Chapman, the laundry's former owner had passed away two years ago, and Louise had finally changed the name to her own. Chapman's had a large customer base when she bought the shop, and she thought at the time keeping the name would help retain it. Over the years, though, she, Bobby, and Henry had earned their own brand of loyalty.

"What are you thinking about doing with the last three houses?" Peters asked.

"I guess I should go ahead and sell them, too. Between the grocery and the laundry, I don't have much time to think about those houses. With only three left, there's very little maintenance needed, and my crew has other interests now, too. They probably think it more of a bother than a source of income."

"I've always heard that the role of landlord is not an easy one—some renter always wanting this or that done at precisely the most inconvenient time."

"It really wasn't like that. I practically grew up with the colored family that handles the repairs and maintenance." Louise smiled, thinking back on those times. "The mother worked for my grandmother as a cook and maid. The father worked in my grandfather's meat market. And their son—only a few years older than me—helped with the rental houses. Anyway, whenever I've needed a repair, I had only to call and they took care of it."

"It must be nice to have people like that you can rely on."

"They're like family," Louise said.

"Well, back to the business at hand. All the houses you've sold so far have been to Houseman Realty. Shall I contact Squire Simmons, or would you care to think about it further before you decide?"

"I'll get you the information on the last three houses. Once you have it, you can make the contact."

"Very well." Peters rose and walked Louise to the door. "Do you ever think it a little odd Houseman is always ready to buy when you're ready to sell?"

"I've thought about that," Louise said. "I could probably have gotten more had I waited and seen what other offers came in. But the money was put to good use, and right there when I needed it."

"True enough. And certainly they're a legitimate realty firm. I suppose it's just the lawyer in me trying to find an angle."

Louise grinned. "I've heard about you attorneys—a suspicious lot, aren't you?"

Peters grinned and opened the door. "It's what we get paid for."

CHAPTER 49

Henry stepped back a few feet to admire his work. He had hand painted the small sign reading *Schmidt's Radio Repair* and affixed it over the door of the maintenance shed in Louise's back yard. *Not bad,* he thought, *not bad at all.*

After Jimmy and the band went on the road with Odell, Henry had been lost. He still had his drums, but they weren't doing him any good without a band. He still worked at the laundry, but that job gave him no real pleasure. He'd been looking for something to occupy his time when, one night in between songs, the announcer advertised a manual on radio repair: *"Make hundreds of dollars working from your own home."*

It sounded good. With hundreds of dollars he could do a lot. The manual arrived a few weeks later in the mail, and, after studying it, he'd bought the necessary equipment and a supply of tubes and wires, then advertised his services in the newspaper.

The shed, little-used these days, still housed a lawn mower and gardening tools, but plenty of space remained since Bobby's airplane went away.

Henry turned the counter See Boy built for Louise as a potting area into a work counter for his new venture, adding a chair and an oscillating fan, which provided a breeze in the summer. He'd replace the fan with a small electric heater during colder months. Now, he just had to wait for the broken radios to pile in.

He closed the shed door and went back into the house.

Fannie, reading the paper at the table, looked up when Henry entered. "Your ad's in today's classifieds." She handed the section to him. "It's down near the bottom on the right."

Henry ran his finger down the page until he found it. He read it over and smiled. "I should probably start getting calls or people coming by soon."

"I hope so, dear," Fannie said.

Henry made himself a ham and tomato sandwich, then sat at the table with half an ear listening for the telephone to ring. It would be silly, he knew, to expect too much, but he couldn't help hoping his new business would pay off soon.

He would work the afternoon shift at the laundry, and then had plans to visit Irene after work. Of course, he might miss a few calls, but his mother had told him she would take messages if anyone called or get the necessary information if someone came by and dropped off a radio.

Business affairs settled for the time being, his thoughts shifted to Irene. During all the time they'd been "seeing" each other, Henry had never quite known the true nature of their relationship. She saw other guys, he knew but tried not to think about. And true, he paid her for making love to him, but it never felt like just that. They listened to records or the radio. Sometimes, he brought sandwiches and they'd eat and drink a beer together. Maybe he should ask her out sometime, a movie or supper, or both. The more he thought about it, the more he wondered why he hadn't already done so.

Finished eating, he rinsed the plate and placed it by the sink. In the hallway, he stuck his head into the parlor. "I'm going to the laundry, Momma, and then out with friends after work." It had become his customary excuse for evenings spent with Irene. His mother and Louise both seemed pleased he interacted with friends.

"All right. I'll see you later this evening."

Just then the telephone rang, and Henry snatched it up—then paused, momentarily unsure how to answer. Should he simply say hello, or—

"Schmidt's Radio Repair," he blurted out, then, as he listened, he felt his mouth stretch into a smile. "Yes, ma'am, it's on Chamberlain just a couple doors down from Fairleigh Street. I won't be in this afternoon, but you can leave it with my mother, and I'll start on it first thing in the morning. Yes, ma'am, and thank you for choosing Schmidt's Radio Repair."

He hung up and peeked into the parlor. "It's starting," he said, still wearing a wide smile.

Fannie lowered her newspaper. "Good for you, Henry."

Bounding up the steps to Irene's small front porch, Henry could hardly wait to tell her the good news. When Irene opened the door, she wore white shorts and a blouse dotted with tiny nautical flags.

"I have good news." Henry took her hand and led her to the sofa.

"My goodness," Irene said. "Tell me about it."

"I've opened my own radio repair shop. My office and work room are in a separate building from the house. I have all the tools and equipment I need." Henry paused to take a breath, thinking, *What if she wants to come over and see it? I'm probably making it sound a lot fancier than it is. Maybe I can put a coat of paint on the inside.* "I have a technical manual for reference. I even have a soldering iron."

Irene pecked him on the cheek. "Well, it certainly sounds wonderful, but I have no idea what a soldering iron is."

"It welds wires together. And you know what? I got my first repair call today."

"Oh, Henry. I'm very happy for you. With your shift at the laundry and starting a new business, it sounds like you're going to be very busy."

"I'll be busy, but don't worry, not too busy to see you."

Irene unbuttoned the top of her blouse to reveal a lacy white bra underneath. "I have good news, too, Henry, but let's wait until after we make love to talk about it, okay?"

"Sure," Henry said, starting on his buttons.

Half an hour later, Irene brought Henry a beer and set it down on the bedside table. She sat beside him and rubbed his chest with her hand.

Her hand felt cold from the beer, but Henry didn't mind.

"My good news," she said, "is that I got my old job back today. Ladies Dresses at Miller's called me this morning and said they'd like me to come back. I start on Monday morning. Isn't that just something?"

Henry got a funny feeling in the back of his brain. He took a sip of beer, then asked, "What about you and me? We'll still be able to … spend time together, won't we?"

Irene leaned over and kissed Henry's forehead. "I won't need to do this kind of thing anymore, Henry. Aren't you glad for me?"

Henry swallowed hard, felt his Adam's apple working up and down. "Sure I am, but I thought we had something special between us. I wanted to ask you to supper and a movie or something."

"Oh dear, I think that might be sort of awkward. That would be dating. That's a different thing. I hope you're not disappointed. You're a really sweet man. We had something sweet, too, in its own way." She laughed. "You might say I'll be working on my feet again instead of my back."

Henry tried to smile. But suddenly, radio repair didn't seem so exciting.

CHAPTER 50

Louise second-guessed her decision to part with the last three rental houses. Not because she had any real reason to keep them, but always before she'd informed See-boy in advance to make sure the loss of income wouldn't hurt his finances. He'd assured her every time they'd be fine, and that he spent so much time with the club he wouldn't miss either the work or the money.

Of course, she hadn't sent the information to Michael Peters yet, so there'd been no contact with Houseman or their attorney. She decided to call and find out when would be a good time to let See-Boy know of her plans.

Pearl answered, and they traded helloes before Louise asked about coming over.

"How about Monday evening?" Pearl said. "See-Boy doesn't open The Hanger on Sunday and Monday nights, so we'll all be here. In fact, why don't you come for supper? I'll make something good."

"I'd love to. I haven't seen Lawrence in months. Or Frankie, either. I'll bet he's grown like a weed."

"Uh-huh, just turned sixteen and won't listen to a word his daddy says. Thinks he knows it all already. But I guess maybe it's like that with all sixteen-year-olds."

Louise remembered Bobby at that age. He'd been confident, too, until he got Squire Adamson's daughter in trouble. "Yes, I think you're right about that. Hopefully, it's just a phase they pass through."

"Lord, I hope so," Pearl said. "We'll see you Monday after work."

Pearl, as good as her word, baked a roast with peeled potatoes and carrots, and made a batch of black-skillet cornbread. Louise had forgotten how much she enjoyed being with See-Boy and his family and told them so.

"We had some happy times," Lawrence said. "A few bad times, too, but we got through all of 'em, didn't we?"

"Yes, we did," Louise said. Lawrence's hair had turned almost all gray now, and his eyes had lost a little of the sparkle they'd once had. Louise thought the latter derived more from Jesse's passing than age.

She waited until after Pearl served each of them peach cobbler to bring up the sale of the last houses. "I just wanted to be sure you all wouldn't be affected negatively by it." She studied See-Boy's face. "You've done so well with your club. I know you love having your own business, but I'd still feel better about getting out of the landlord business if I can do it with your blessing."

See-Boy wiped his lips with a napkin and placed it back in his lap. "Miss Louise, I don't think you would ever do anything to affect us in a bad way. Fact is, it's like we're all almost joined at the hip. You got Pearl doing your books for the laundry and the grocery now. And I had Henry playing for me at the club until Odell took the band on the road. We're like family, always have been, and I suspect always will be. So, yes, you go ahead and sell those houses and concentrate on your other businesses." He gave her a wide grin and reached out and clasped hands with Pearl and Lawrence. "We will be just fine."

Frankie looked up from his pie. "What about me, Daddy? I planned to work with Granddaddy, helping him keep those houses in shape."

"Wouldn't be enough work with those last three houses to keep you and your granddaddy busy. Besides which, you're gonna finish school like I wish I'd done." He narrowed one eye. "If you need something to keep you busy this summer, we'll find it."

"Uh-oh," Frankie said, spooning up another bite of cobbler. "Looks like I better keep my mouth shut."

After they'd finished dessert, See-Boy and Lawrence walked Louise to the door and hugged her goodbye. Lawrence lingered for a moment after See-Boy went back inside.

"I just want you to know how proud of you I am. Jesse and me, we thought of you and loved you just like if you'd been our own daughter. All my family, blood kin and otherwise, have done real well for themselves."

"I have to say the same, Lawrence." Louise hugged him once more. "Are you sure you're okay with my selling the houses? What are you going to do now?"

"I'm gettin' on up in age, you know. I imagine I'd of had a hard time climbing ladders and going under houses and such— even with Frankie helping me. So it's fine. Tell you the truth, the only thing I'll miss is talking to folks. Most of your renters, back when you had a bunch, talked to me just like they would a white person. We got to know each other pretty good."

Lawrence turned his face up to the dark sky, and Louise saw the moon reflected by the tears forming in his eyes. "It's good to have people to talk to."

As she walked home, Lawrence's words kept repeating in her ears. *How he must miss Jesse,* she thought, trying to imagine her life without Murray. The more she thought about it, the more determined she became to do something about it.

CHAPTER 51

"Go ahead and send the information on the last three houses to Squire Simmons," Louise told Peters. "I've decided for certain to get out of the landlord business. It's only one more thing to concern myself with, and I need to focus on the laundry and the grocery store."

"All right, Louise, I'll send the information today. With any luck, we'll hear back later this week."

That done, Louise told Fannie goodbye and walked over to McCallie Avenue, where she caught the streetcar to the grocery. Still too early to open, she entered the ice cream parlor through a shared storage and ice cream processing center in the rear.

Juanita stood behind the counter stacking plates and glasses and arranging various condiments for the grill. "Good morning, Louise, can I fix you something?"

"No thanks, but I'd like to run something by you."

Juanita pulled a hairnet from the pocket of her dress and stuffed her black curly hair underneath, her round face already showing a fine patina of perspiration. "I'm all ears."

The two women talked for several minutes, Louise mostly while Juanita nodded every so often in agreement. Louise left to open the grocery as Lackey's nephew—who managed the ice cream parlor since his uncle passed away—entered the building.

Just before noon, Juanita slipped into the grocery through the shared rear entrance. She pulled a pack of Old Golds and matches from her apron and lit up, blowing a plume of smoke toward the ceiling. "He says okay as long as you're paying for it."

"Mighty generous of him," Louise said.

Juanita took another drag on her cigarette. "As you know, he don't much care for the coloreds. That's probably why they were willing to part with the grocery store. Me, I'll just be glad to have help cleaning up—white or colored, it don't matter to me."

"I appreciate your talking to him about it," Louise said.

"Hey, us girls have to stick together."

The next Sunday, Louise called See-Boy's house and invited herself to Monday night supper again. "But this time, I'll bring the food," she told Pearl. "And let me tell you in advance what I have in mind, okay?"

She spent Sunday afternoon preparing a chicken casserole. On Monday, she brought bread rolls and vine-ripened tomatoes home from the grocery and loaded everything up in Bobby's car. Bobby helped her unload, said his helloes to See-Boy's family, and took off.

"You know you didn't need to do this," Pearl said. "You're always welcome here."

"I know that, but I wanted to return the favor."

Pearl helped set the table and lay out the food. "Well, just so you know, I made dessert anyway—pecan pie this time."

"My mouth is already watering," Louise replied.

After they finished stuffing themselves with casserole and pecan pie, Louise said, "I've been thinking that I could use some help down at the grocery. I've got this meat case where I keep a lot of sausage, baloney, olive loaf, and such as that. I've also got this electric meat slicer which I'm about half afraid to use. I mean, one slip and I could slice off the end of my finger."

She turned to look at Lawrence. "So, I thought maybe you could work part time at the store and help me with all that. It's not much like what you did at Granddaddy's market, but I think you'd be good at it. And it would really help me out."

Lawrence looked around the table, first at See-Boy, then at Pearl. "Well ... I guess I might could come in from time to time and help you out. After all, Miss Louise, you helped us out when we needed it."

See-Boy and Pearl tried to hide their smiles. See-Boy stroked his chin. "That would be good of you, Daddy. And it'd give you the chance to get out of the house, too, stay out of Pearl's way, you know?"

"All right then," Lawrence said. "I guess I could do that if you need me to. Meat slicers are powerful sharp. You don't want somebody fooling with those unless they know what they're doing."

"Thank you, Lawrence. I'm very relieved." Louise glanced at See-Boy, purposefully not looking at Frankie, who poked at a piece of pecan pie crust with his fork. "We're also looking for someone to come in and help out during the summer and on weekends after school begins. It would be stocking canned and other shelf goods, filling the drink box, keeping the floors clean, that sort of thing. It'll mostly be for the grocery, but the ice cream parlor could use a little help, too."

She cocked her head to one side. "See-Boy, can you think of anyone who might be interested?"

"I'd be interested," Frankie said, leaning forward in his seat. "Can I do it, Daddy?"

"I guess it'll be up to Miss Louise who she wants to hire," See-Boy said, suppressing a grin.

"You know—" Louise turned her gaze on Frankie "—that just might work out well. You and Lawrence could ride together to the store."

See-Boy cleared his throat. "Speaking of, Miss Louise, now that we'll not be looking after the houses anymore, I guess you're gonna want that truck back."

"Why don't you keep it?" Louise said. "We've got the car Bobby's friend let us have. It does just fine getting us around."

"I can pay you whatever you think it's worth."

Louise shook her head. "Having Lawrence and Frankie help me at the store is worth much more than that truck."

"All right, then," See-Boy said.

"When would you like us to start?" Lawrence asked.

"Can you start as early as tomorrow? I've got deliveries from Libby's and Ray Moss Farms coming in, and we'll need to price a lot of canned goods."

Lawrence looked over at Frankie, who nodded vigorously. "I guess we'll see you in the morning then."

CHAPTER 52

Henry perched on a four-legged stool next to the counter in his newly created repair shop. Since opening two weeks ago, he'd fixed two radios and had four currently waiting to be repaired. Not exactly overwhelming, but that and working at the laundry kept him busy. A good thing because staying busy meant he didn't constantly think about Irene.

He finished soldering a wire, wisps of smoke filling his nostrils with a metallic-but-pleasing odor. He let it cool a moment then plugged the cord into a receptacle and turned the little Philco table-top radio on. Static at first, but then he rotated the tuner and the stations began coming in one after another. *All right*, he thought, *another satisfied customer.*

He reached for the plug but stopped when the radio announcer mentioned Farr and Away would be playing in the Read House ballroom over the coming weekend.

Henry's shoulders sagged as "Handful of Keys" by Fats Waller filled the room. He'd performed it many times when still part of the band. *But look at me now.* Jimmy and the boys preparing to play at the Read House while he breathed dry-cleaning fumes and solder smoke all day. On top of that, he'd lost the woman he thought he loved. He couldn't do *anything* right. *A coward and an emotional cripple. My life is shit.*

He switched off the radio and laid his head on the countertop.

See-Boy leaned forward, elbows on the bar, and glanced casually over the Wednesday night crowd at The Hanger. *Not bad at all for middle of the week.* He served as bartender most of the time, although one of his waitresses could pour drinks if he needed. He liked being behind the bar. It gave him a nice vantage point to gauge how the people—he'd come to think of them as *his* people—felt. And usually, they seemed to be feeling just fine.

Dorothea, his only weeknight waitress, came up with a drink order. See-Boy fixed the two rum and Coca-Colas and one rye and ginger, marveling at his good fortune.

Who'd have imagined, back when he first invited the neighbors over for a sip of moonshine in his shed, he'd be the owner of a nightclub? His daddy had doubts about the venture, Pearl, too, but they'd mostly been afraid he'd be arrested and thrown in jail. That thought had crossed his mind once in a while as well, but never enough to stop.

Even Louise—he thought of her as just Louise but couldn't shake the habit of calling her *Miss* Louise when he talked to her, though she'd been married for years—had worried. He appreciated what she'd done for Daddy and Frankie, giving them something to feel good about and put a little jingle in their pockets, too. He hoped her life was as content as his.

The telephone behind the bar rang and See-Boy heard Abernathy's voice when he picked up. The young man led the band See-Boy had engaged to play since Farr and Away left and got semi-famous—in the South, anyway.

"See-Boy, I got bad news, man. Darrell's gone. His momma got bad sick so he caught a Greyhound to Opelika. Don't know when he might be back, or even *if* he's coming back. I can't find a replacement before Friday. You know anybody? We can't play without a drummer."

See-Boy paused, knowing who to at least ask. "Let me think on it, Abernathy. I'll call you back."

"Please see can you find somebody quick. We'd all appreciate it, man."

Hmmm, See-Boy thought. *Wonder how that might work.* He gave it the night to consider then called Henry the following morning.

"It's See-Boy for you," Fannie said handing the phone to Henry.

"You still got your drums?" See-Boy asked.

"Sure I do. I just don't have any reason to play them."

"You just might, if you want. I got a band whose drummer just took off for Opelika. You have any problem playing drums in a colored band?"

Henry's heart fluttered like a caged bird trying to escape. "No, no I don't—none at all."

"All right then, come on down to the club after work today, and I'll have Abernathy—he's the band leader—and the others here to meet you. I suspect they'll be surprised to find out you're white, but they'll get over it when they hear you play. I imagine you and them will want to practice a little before tomorrow night. Sound good?"

Henry's eyes closed tightly and his knees felt wobbly. "It sounds great, See-boy. Thank you."

"You'll be helping me out. I appreciate it. See you later today."

Henry hung up and sat at the telephone stand with his face buried in his hands. He'd been feeling so low, needing something, anything to come his way. He looked up to see his mother watching from the parlor doorway.

"Henry, are you all right?"

He stood and grabbed her around the waist, twirling her like a dance partner. "Momma, I'm about as right as rain."

CHAPTER 53

L ouise met Peters in front of Simmons' office at eight-thirty, giving her time to sign papers and open the grocery by ten. Traffic edged along the street, automobile horns blaring periodically. Exhaust fumes hung low over the already rush-hour-clogged downtown streets.

Peters grinned at Louise as they approached the office. "I suppose we'll have to stop seeing each other now you're divesting yourself of rental property."

Louise laughed. "It's been my experience you never know when you might need a good attorney." She paused as he opened the door for her. "But seriously, it has been a pleasure knowing you. I appreciate all your help."

Peters nodded. "Call me anytime. I won't charge you for telephone advice."

Simmons welcomed Louise and Peters into his office and slid a sheaf of papers across his desk. "Look these over, Michael." He handed Louise a fountain pen. "Hopefully, we'll have you out of here in plenty of time to get to your store."

"I'd hoped to finally meet Ms. Brooks, but it appears we aren't fated to do that. Please pass along my thanks for her readiness to take these houses off my hands."

Peters looked up from the papers. "At about half their worth, I might add. I'd think Ms. Brooks—any realtor, really—would be extremely happy with the selling price."

Simmons chuckled. "Surely, counselor, you're not maligning my client."

Peters shook his head. "Not at all; I'm merely pointing out the obvious."

"Well, in the end," Louise said, "I guess we both got what we wanted. That's not a bad way for everything to turn out."

Peters passed part of the stack of papers to Louise. "You can begin signing now."

Henry unloaded his drums from the car and arranged them on the small performance stage before the band members arrived. See-Boy had assured him again it wouldn't matter him being white.

"Music is music," See-Boy had said. "We got white bands and colored bands both playing the same kind of music, the same tunes. Why not mix?"

The band members came into the bar carrying their instruments but stopped short just inside the door when they spotted Henry sitting behind his drum set. One of them looked over at See-Boy, who stood behind the bar washing glasses.

"See-Boy?"

"Uh-huh, He's white. When you called, Abernathy, you told me you had to have a drummer so you could play like always. Now you got one. And he's a good one, too." See-Boy came out from behind the bar and stood halfway between Henry and the band. "You heard of the Farr and Away band, haven't you? Uh-huh, yes, I see heads nodding. Henry here played drums for them for years before they went on the road. He couldn't go because of family obligations, lucky for you. He's here now, and he's what you need."

See-Boy turned to Henry. "Play somethin' for them, Henry."

Henry coughed a little, his throat parched, and he felt sweat trickling down his ribcage, but he picked up his sticks and did part of a drum solo from Benny Goodman's "Sing, Sing, Sing."

When he finished, the echo of the drums still hanging in the air, the one called Abernathy spoke first. "Well, shit, I reckon we got ourselves a new drummer."

Stepping to the band stand, they introduced themselves and unpacked their instruments. The five-piece band consisted of a trumpet, trombone, saxophone, and bass player, and now Henry as the drummer. Abernathy—last name Jones—had pulled the group together and named it, simply enough, Abernathy Jones' Jazz Band.

After shaking hands with the band members, Henry glanced toward the bar where See-Boy now spoke to an attractive colored woman. He hadn't seen her enter but thought she must have been behind the others when they came in. She wore peach-colored pants ending mid-calf and a startlingly white high-collared blouse tied into a knot just above her waist.

She laughed at something See-Boy said and looked over at Henry. See-Boy patted the woman's shoulder, then she walked over and held her hand out to Henry.

"Hello, Henry, I'm Lawanda. I sing with the band."

Henry took her hand. "Henry Schmidt. It's nice to meet you."

"Farr and Away didn't use a singer, did they?"

"No," Henry said, "we only did instrumentals. I guess a lot of jazz bands are like that."

Lawanda picked up one of Henry's drum sticks and tapped it lightly on his cymbal. "You're going to have a lot to get used to, aren't you?"

Henry watched as she turned and began talking with Abernathy. *She's right,* he thought, *there's a heck of a lot to get used to.* But he thought he'd enjoy it just the same.

"So, how does it feel," Fannie asked, "not having the rental houses any longer?" She and Louise sat alone in the kitchen eating leftover stew. Henry had gone to See-Boy's club after work, and Bobby was out with Harry.

"A little strange, I guess, but it's not like I sold them all at once. I've had time to get used to the idea."

"No more Schmidt Enterprises," Fannie said. "The only good thing to ever come from your father, and he inherited that."

Louise took a sip of iced tea and dabbed at her lips with a napkin. "Mother, I believe you're forgetting about Henry and me."

Fannie reached over and patting Louise's hand. "Honey, I prefer to think of those two events as immaculate conceptions."

CHAPTER 54

Bobby opened the rear door of the laundry, then walked to the front and propped that door open. With September cooler, the cross breeze helped to rid the place of the strong chemical odors.

He grabbed a copy of the *Times* from the metal rack located just outside the laundry. He never paid for them, just put them back when he'd finished. He figured *no harm, no foul.*

He spread the paper on the counter and read the first headline. Germany had invaded Poland a few days earlier. Almost immediately, Britain and France declared war on Germany. The big news today focused on the United States' declaration of neutrality.

Bobby couldn't help but be a little disappointed. He knew from his father about the hardships suffered by the soldiers during World War One, and he wouldn't wish that kind of pain on anyone, but *damn*. He'd always wanted to fly an airplane.

He remembered the one See-Boy put together for him. A pedal-driven plane—quite a treasure at the time, though it didn't leave the ground. He'd later built wooden models and hung them from the ceiling in his room. And the balsa wood gliders—now those were really fun. He could make them do different tricks just by position-ing the wings forward or back. He'd used cellophane tape to affix kitchen matches to the underside of the glider. That way, when it finally landed and skidded to a stop on the concrete, the matches ignited and the plane burst into flame.

Then he got to be too old for that kid stuff. And he ended up working at the dry cleaners and laundry. Of course, he was thankful.

Lots of people didn't have jobs or much of anything still. But working in a laundry … not exactly what he pictured himself doing at twenty-six.

Eventually, he refolded the newspaper and stuck it back in the rack. He'd just returned to the counter when a sleek black '39 Ford Convertible eased up in front and Harry climbed out. After college, Harry started working at his father's Ford dealership. Seems he had a new car every year, sometimes sooner.

"How's it hanging, man?" Harry said.

Bobby grinned. "To the left, just like always."

They shook, then Harry hiked one hip on the counter. "I got us two saucy chicks lined up for the lake on Labor Day. You probably remember them from high school: Ruth Lewis and Annie Killough. They graduated the year after us. Ruth—she's mine—works at a bookstore downtown. Annie works for the telephone company."

"So I don't get a say in whose chick is whose?"

"What do you want, buddy? I got us the dates. Frankly, I can't wait to see Ruth in a bathing suit. She's stacked like one of those Hollywood starlets."

"I remember Annie, I think. Auburn hair and freckles, maybe not so stacked but okay. We might've had geometry together."

"Yeah," Harry said, hopping off the counter. "They're best friends, so wherever one goes, so goes the other."

"Okay, what does that mean?"

Harry smiled his best car salesman's smile. "I think that means we'll be working in tandem."

Bobby watched as Harry slipped behind the steering wheel and maneuvered the shiny Ford back into traffic. Impressive car, for sure. And he could think of less pleasing ways to spend the holiday. He hadn't seen Annie Killough in years and wondered what she looked like now.

Then he pondered the idea of joining Britain's Royal Air Force and becoming a fighter pilot. *Could you do that?* Not that the answer mattered. He had no way to get to London. And, obviously, America wasn't going anywhere.

Being the only white man in a colored band wasn't so bad. The band sounded great, maybe even better than Jimmy's, and most of the crowd at The Hanger remembered Henry from before. And Lawanda sure had a voice, clear and strong and melding with the music perfectly. She set toes tapping belting out "Carolina Shout" and then turned around and broke hearts caressing that microphone and crooning, "Everybody Loves My Baby."

Abernathy told Henry she'd been working in a restaurant off Baily when he heard her singing to herself while she waited tables.

"We was pretty lucky to get her before somebody else heard her and snatched her up," he told Henry. Then he looked off in the distance. "I suspect somebody will hear her and sweep her off one day before too long. A voice like that is hard not to notice."

He smiled and shook his index finger at Henry. "You pretty good, too. Could be that same somebody might hear you and take you both off somewhere. Then where would we be?"

"I don't think you have to worry about me going anywhere," Henry said. "I'm kind of a homebody these days."

Abernathy winked at him and picked up his trumpet for the next set.

The first song, a slow, torchy number, had Henry using a lot of broom on the drums to capture the mood. He'd done it in practice the night before and remembered how Lawanda moved her body in time with the *swish, swish, swish* of the brooms. It was definitely worth a great deal of practice just to watch her move.

CHAPTER 55

Bobby rode with Annie in the cramped backseat of the convertible, the wind whipping their hair around their heads. Harry's date, Ruth, turned in her seat and shouted to Annie to be heard over the wind. "Don't you just love this car?"

"Yes," Annie said, "but I wish I'd thought to bring a scarf like you did."

"Well," Ruth said, "if it makes you feel any better…" She pulled her scarf loose and held it up over the windshield where it rippled in the rush of air like a pennant at the baseball stadium. Then she let it go and the cloth disappeared behind them.

Bobby and Annie both turned in their seats to see the scarf tumbling down the road, only to be whisked back into the air by the car behind them. "Why'd you do that?" Bobby asked.

"Who cares?" Ruth replied. "It's only a scarf." She turned back around and shifted closer to Harry.

He took one hand off the steering wheel and slipped it around her shoulder.

Bobby put his arm around Annie's shoulder, too. She looked at him and smiled, snuggling under his arm. Bobby had been curious how Annie would look almost ten years out of high school, and he'd been impressed. She still had auburn hair and freckles, but she'd lost the gawky teenage look, filling out nicely. Not "stacked" like her friend Ruth, but with curves in all the right places.

He had to admit he looked forward to seeing Annie in her bathing suit—Ruth, too, for that matter, even though Harry had already called dibs. *No harm in looking.*

They pulled off the main highway and found a tree-covered gravel road where they could access the lake and spread out a couple of blankets. The girls brought a picnic lunch of fried chicken, fruit, and soft drinks. Harry and Bobby had a cooler of Rolling Rock beer iced down in the trunk. The Labor Day weather provided the perfect temperature for getting in the water but not hot enough to get sweaty just sitting around. Of course, both Bobby and Harry had more in mind than just sitting around.

They reached their destination in less than five minutes and piled out of the car. Ruth and Annie spread out the blankets and brought out the picnic basket while Bobby carried the cooler over, settling it between the two blankets, and pulled an opener from his pants pocket.

"Who's up for a cold one?"

"Definitely me," Harry said.

Annie and Ruth glanced at each other. "I'll have one, too," Ruth said.

"Me, too, I guess. No use being the odd one out."

"That's the spirit," Bobby said, digging down into the ice and bringing out four cold, green bottles. He opened each and handed the bottles around.

Harry lifted his bottle. "Here's to Labor Day and us."

They clinked and drank the toast. When they'd finished the beer, Bobby and Harry went on the other side of the car to change into their bathing suits.

"You're next, girls," Harry said.

Ruth and Annie began undoing the buttons on their blouses. Ruth grinned. "We wore our suits under our clothes."

Bobby and Harry watched as the girls finished removing their shorts and tops. Ruth stood tall, arched her back, and put one hand on her nicely developed hip. "What do you think, Harry?"

Harry cocked his head. "I think you'll do just fine, Miss Lewis."

More discreet, maybe a little shy, Annie simply dropped her outer wear on one of the blankets, let her arms fall by her sides, and smiled sweetly.

Bobby took it all in and returned her smile. He didn't say anything, but he thought *all right, all right, all right.*

Henry sat beside Lawanda on the edge of the bandstand during break. Abernathy and the others had gone out to the alley to cool off, they said, and have a smoke. It stayed rather warm inside, what with the crowd and the overall closeness of the club, but Henry suspected the band had something other than ordinary cigarettes to smoke.

Lawanda's skin glowed with a fine film of perspiration. Her hair, straightened, fell to her shoulders with a row of bangs cut over her forehead. Tonight, she held her hair up with her hands to let the air dry her neck.

She turned to Henry. "How do you like playing with the band?"

"I like it a lot. I thought I might go crazy when Jimmy and the guys left to go on tour." He turned to find her dark eyes staring into his own. "Music, playing the drums, is about the only thing in my life that makes me feel worthwhile."

"Why do you say that?"

He shrugged. "I don't know. I've just never been very good at anything except playing the drums."

"You are good at that," Lawanda said, grinning. "But you have a job, too, don't you?"

"I work at the laundry and dry cleaners my sister owns, but it's nothing special. Plus I repair radios. I have my own shop in back of my sister's house."

"Now see," Lawanda said, "you have a lot going for you. Lots of people out of work, you got three different jobs."

"One of which, working here, I really like," Henry said. *And I worry about how long this will last,* he thought. *What if you all go on the road? What if, like Abernathy thinks, an agent hears you sing and takes you away? What then?*

Someone got up and put a coin in the Wurlitzer juke box. See-Boy had just purchased the big box a few months back, and it held a limited number of tunes. The song began, a slow number, "Quiet City" by Aaron Copland. A few couples got up and moved onto the dance floor.

He reached over and touched Lawanda's arm. "Would you like to dance with me?" His heart pounded inside his chest.

Lawanda took his hand and gave it a squeeze. "I would like to, Henry, but … I don't think that's a good idea right now."

Henry nodded. "It's okay. I just thought maybe…" He let the sentence trail off and got up from the bandstand. "I think I'll go to the restroom before we get started again." *What is wrong with me? Why can't I do anything right?* He pushed open the restroom door and leaned with his forehead against the wall, eyes clinched tightly shut.

CHAPTER 56

L ouise rang up the grocery items, made change from the cash register drawer, and handed that with the receipt to the customer. As she bagged the groceries, she repeated her mantra: "Thanks for coming in. Please come back and see us again."

Her customer, a middle-aged colored lady named Sally, laughed as she gathered up her grocery sack. "Now, Miss Louise, you know I come in here regular two or three times a week. Where else you think I'm going to get my groceries?"

"I know you do, Sally. I've said it so long, I just can't help myself."

They both laughed then. Sally opened the screen door with her hip and backed out. "See you soon, Miss Louise—you, too, Lawrence."

Lawrence waved to her from behind the meat case. "Bye, Sally."

After Sally had departed up the street, Louise left the register and walked back to Lawrence. She slid open the meat case window and breathed in the cool air. "Lord, I wish it would rain or something. This is one of the hottest Augusts I've ever seen."

Lawrence pulled a handkerchief from his pocket and wiped his forehead. "I know what you mean. Could just about fry an egg on the sidewalk."

Louise picked up a section of the *Chattanooga Times* and fanned herself with it, glancing idly at one of the headlines in the world news section. More and more articles appeared each day concerning the war, and the radio coverage seemed nonstop, too. The Germans had taken Holland, Belgium, and Paris during the first six months of 1940. Now, they engaged in a battle for air superiority over Britain. *What a horrible mess.* Louise felt for all the people going through it. Thank God, the United States had stayed out of it.

Even so, Congress currently debated legislation requiring men between the ages of twenty-one and thirty-five to register for the draft. It gave her cold chills to think of Bobby or Henry drafted.

Then she spied another article...

Just then, the small bell over the front door rang, and Lawrence said, "Good morning, Clarice."

"Morning, Lawrence, morning Louise."

Louise said hello, put the newspaper aside for later, and went to tend to her customer.

The afternoon had been busy, and Louise didn't get a chance to look at the article until she arrived home that evening. She turned on a lamp in the parlor and began to read. At first, she didn't believe her eyes, but the more she read, the more deflated she felt.

Houseman Realty had announced the location of two new "strip" shopping areas in the Ridgedale and Highland Park communities. The article, accompanied by artist renderings of what the developments would look like when completed, highlighted a design based on similar developments at various places in California and in large cities like Dallas and Baltimore. The locations would include grocery stores as "anchor" tenants, along with pharmacies, cloth shops, barber shops, dry cleaners, and the like. The concept, according to real estate agent Eleanor Brooks, would provide a central spot where customers could find many of their household and personal needs. She went on to say the available lease space at both sites was already over eighty percent under contract.

Several houses Louise had sold to the realty firm had been clustered geographically in groups of three or more, and had fronted well-traveled streets. *But they'd been zoned for residential housing only.* She didn't understand.

Fannie came into the parlor and sat down across from Louise. "What's the matter with you? You look ill."

Louise handed her the newspaper and pointed to the article. "Read this."

Fannie did, eyes narrowing as she read. "Well, I'll be damned. Looks like you should've hung on to those houses after all."

"How could I have seen this coming?" Louise said. "They were zoned residential."

Fannie rested the paper on her lap. "Not anymore, apparently." Then she showed Louise another, smaller article on the same page. "Take a look at this." The title read: *Not Everyone Happy with New Strip Centers.*

A man named John Acres told the *Times* reporter he and his family had been forced out of their home to make space for the proposed shopping center. Louise recognized the name from her bookkeeping journals. Another man reported much the same happening to him and his family. Louise remembered talking to his wife when she first thought of selling houses.

They never even fixed nothing that went wrong with the house. The roof leaked so much I had to use buckets to catch the rain. Used to be we'd ask about something and it'd be taken care of, but not with the new owners.

"I talked to this man's wife right before I sold the house they lived in. They were behind on the rent, so I ended up making that family somebody else's problem. It seems pretty callous now."

"As I recall," Fannie said, "you were feeling awful guilty for making a business decision instead of carrying along a bunch of people who couldn't pay the rent. That wasn't being callous; that was self-preservation."

"You're right, I know, but I can't help feeling bad—about the people forced out, about settling for less than the houses' worth. I feel like I did something stupid, like I should have seen or known about something else going on. But I didn't."

Fannie got up and walked to Louise then bent down and hugged her. "You've never been stupid. If you've got anything wrong with you, it's that you feel too much. And I don't know *what* side of the family you got that from."

"Nevertheless," Louise said, "I'm going to call Eleanor Brooks and talk to her. Maybe it's just plain luck things happened like they did for her, but I can't get past feeling like I've been taken somehow."

"Trust no living body and walk carefully by the dead," Fannie said. "That's always been my mantra."

Between customers calling for their laundry and dry cleaning, Bobby laid the *Times* out flat on the counter. Things had really heated up in Europe. The German air attacks had shifted from airfields and factories to Britain's major cities. According to the newspaper sources, Germany had plenty of pilots but not enough planes. Britain's situation was reversed—plenty of airplanes and not enough pilots.

Something burned fierce and bright inside Bobby's soul. *If only I had a way to get there,* he thought. *I'd blow those Krauts out of the sky.*

CHAPTER 57

L ouise made the call to Houseman Realty the following morning, identifying herself when Eleanor Brooks answered. "I wanted to talk to you about the new commercial developments I saw in yesterday's newspaper."

"Oh really," Ms. Brooks said. "What about them?"

"All those houses, the ones I sold to you, where the new developments are taking place, they were zoned for residential only."

"Surely you realize zoning designations can be changed as the need arises."

"I know it can happen," Louise said, "but I'd like to know when it *did* happen."

"It's all public record, Mrs. Carlyon. Just check with the city clerk's office."

Louise pressed the phone to her ear with one hand and rubbed her temple with the other. "Why were you always so eager to take these houses off my hands?"

"What makes you think we were eager? We certainly didn't pay top dollar for them. Perhaps you were the eager one."

"But why *mine?* I'm sure you don't purchase every house for sale in Chattanooga. What made mine special?"

The woman on the other end paused briefly. "This is rather difficult to explain over the phone. If you really want to know, I suggest you come by our office so we can discuss this in person."

"I'll do that," Louise said. "But I work from ten to six every day except Sunday."

"It's not a problem. We can meet with you before or after work. Unlike many people, real estate agents even work on Sundays."

The band practiced every Sunday afternoon at The Hanger. They could have practiced any morning before the bar opened, but none of the members liked getting up any earlier than they had to. Henry still opened the laundry three times a week, alternating with Bobby the other three days.

Henry thought of it as a mixed blessing, really. He saw Lawanda three days in a row, but then he had to wait four whole days before seeing her again. It had become a necessity, like needing to flip the light switch a certain number of times or step over the threshold a certain way. He hadn't succumbed to those compulsions in a while, but this one felt overwhelming.

Around Lawanda—like now—he could hardly restrain himself from touching her caramel-colored skin. Smooth and faintly glowing, she seemed bathed in liquid sunshine.

"Okay," Abernathy said, breaking into Henry's thoughts. "Let's do 'Mood Indigo' one more time, then we'll take a break."

A few minutes later, when the others drifted outside to smoke or to another part of the room, Henry walked over to Lawanda, who stood by the club's big front window using a piece of sheet music as a fan. "Can I get you a Coca-Cola?"

She turned from the window and smiled. "Yes, Henry, I'd like that. Thank you."

Henry went behind the bar where See-Boy kept colas and other mixers, and got two bottles dripping with ice. He opened them, went back to the window, and handed one to Lawanda.

She took a swallow. "God, that's good. My throat gets parched from singing, you know?"

I love the way your throat looks, parched or not, Henry thought. "I could listen to you sing forever."

"What a lovely thing to say."

Henry paused, feeling his heartrate speed up. "Do you like me, Lawanda?"

"Of course I like you. Why do you have to ask?"

"Then why wouldn't you dance with me when I asked you?"

Lawanda took a deep breath and set the bottle on top of the bar. "You do know you're white, right? And I'm colored. People don't like for us to mix. You know that."

"But I've been around colored people all my life. See-Boy's mother and father were like family to us, still are. As a child, I saw Lawrence more than my own father."

Lawanda touched Henry's arm. "That's different. They worked for your family. That's not like you and me dancing together in a public place."

Her touch made Henry's arm tingle. He wanted so much to feel the softness of her skin. "But these people like me. I've played for most of them dozens of times. They wouldn't mind."

"Most probably wouldn't," Lawanda said, "but a few might. And those kinds of feelings run hot sometimes."

"I really like you, Lawanda. I'd like to get to know you better."

"And I like you, too," Lawanda said, her smile beaming. "We can always talk. We'll get to know each other. Just give it a little time, okay?"

Abernathy called out from the bandstand, "Let's get back to it, guys."

Lawanda winked at Henry and walked across the room. As he watched, Henry had a small epiphany. He'd thought he loved Irene. Thought he couldn't go on without her. But he wanted Lawanda more. He wanted her so bad he ached.

Harry and Bobby talked about the prospects of the coming "conscription" on their way to pick up Ruth and Annie. Everyone they knew seemed convinced it would pass Congress and be signed into law almost immediately.

"I don't know why they're doing it when we're at peace," Harry said. "We've already declared ourselves neutral in the European conflict."

"Better safe than sorry," Bobby said. "What if the krauts bomb us like they're doing to Britain?"

Harry laughed. "They'd have to cross the Atlantic first. That's a hell of a long way."

"I read where the Germans have pilots to spare," Bobby said, "but not enough planes, and Britain's air force has more planes than pilots."

"I know, I know. You want to go to Britain and fly for them, right?"

"Is that so bad? And think how I'd look in an air force uniform. I'll bet the women would be impressed."

Harry slowed to make the turn onto Ruth's street. "What would Annie say about that?"

Bobby shrugged. "Hopefully, she'd be impressed, too."

Harry pulled the convertible to the curb in front of Ruth's house. She and Annie waved and started down the steps while Harry and Bobby got out.

"I see your point about the uniform," Harry said, adding, "I've always heard that women love men in uniform."

"Maybe you and I will get drafted together," Bobby said as Annie rushed into his arms.

CHAPTER 58

L ouise arrived at the Houseman Realty office shortly after six on Thursday. She'd thought briefly of making the appointment for Sunday afternoon but hated to miss any time with Murray.

Houseman's location, across McCallie Avenue near Erlanger Hospital, warranted her taking a taxicab, considering the streetcar would have taken far too long. Even so, she'd left Lawrence to close up the grocery.

Fittingly, the office occupied an old house—probably built about the same time as her house on Chamberlain—converted for business use. White azaleas graced both sides of the walkway and steps leading to the porch. A sign in the front yard identified the office and proclaimed that the firm dealt in both residential and commercial realty.

Louise approached the front door, where she found a small placard that advised: *Please Come In.* She entered a good-sized foyer that served as a reception area. A young girl with dark, shoulder-length hair sat at a secretarial desk, tapping away on a Royal typewriter.

"Hello. How may I help you?"

"I'm here to see Ms. Brooks. I have an appointment. Louise Carlyon."

"Oh, yes, Mrs. Carlyon." She gestured to a door on the left. "Go right in. You're expected."

Louise walked to the door, open a few inches, knocked lightly, and heard, "Come in."

The woman who sat behind a large mahogany desk stood, and Louise paused for half a second as the realization set in. She'd last seen "Ms. Brooks" at her father's funeral nearly twenty years before: her stepsister, Edith.

"Louise," the woman said.

"Hello, Edith." Louise stepped closer and narrowed her eyes. "You identified yourself as Eleanor. In fact, you were quoted in the paper as Eleanor."

Edith smiled—a lazy confident smile. "Eleanor is my middle name. Brooks is my married name." She waved at a chair. "Have a seat if you like."

"I think I'll stand."

"Whatever you wish."

"Why did you try to hide your identity from me?"

Edith chuckled. "I didn't hide anything. I just didn't make it a point to tell you. There's nothing wrong with that."

Louise looked down at Edith. "Why were you so anxious to buy my houses?"

"Really, Louise, this is becoming monotonous. I'd say you were anxious to sell."

Louise walked over to a grouping of photographs and plaques adorning one wall. One showed Edith shaking hands with a man she recognized as the mayor of Chattanooga. Another had Edith and a tall man with rimless glasses standing in front of the Chattanooga Chamber of Commerce.

"It seems you've done well for yourself." Louise turned back to her stepsister. "How did you come up with the name Houseman Realty? Is that something else you made up to throw me off?"

"Oh, Louise, don't you remember? Or, I suppose it's possible you didn't know. Houseman was my mother's maiden name. We named the business to honor her."

"We? Are you partners with someone?"

As if on cue, the office door opened and Louise's oldest stepsister entered the room. "Hello, Louise."

Louise let out a breath. "I should have known it would be you."

Sylvia swept past Louise and perched one hip on the desk, a smarmy grin playing at the edges of her mouth. "Edith tells me you're upset about something. Please, tell us all about it."

"Why the big charade? Why did you go to all this trouble to fool me? Surely, you're not still harboring a grudge about my father's transferring his business interests to me." Then she remembered what Fannie said about the two girls learning at the knee of their mother. "No, now that I think about it, that's exactly what this is all about."

Sylvia exchanged a glance with Edith. "When we saw your first ad in the *Times*, we knew we had to do something. Those houses would have been ours, or at least partially ours, if your grandmother's Negro maid hadn't poisoned our mother. So we said 'let's see how cheaply we can buy those houses.' As it turned out, we bought them for less than half their worth."

Louise felt the heat rise in her body, color flooding her neck and cheeks.

Sylvia continued. "I didn't imagine it would be so easy, but you never even waited for other offers. That's really kind of funny. I never knew you to be lazy."

"I invested the money from that sale in purchasing a business. And my brother needed counseling," Louise said, immediately sorry her anger got the best of her. "That's why I sold the houses."

"Yes, I remember Mother talking about your brother, Henry, isn't it? He's mentally ill, isn't he? How's the counseling working?"

Louise stepped toward Sylvia, stopping two feet away. She hadn't necessarily meant the move as a threat, but maybe her face gave her away. Sylvia eased off the desk corner and went behind it to stand by her sister. Louise spoke slowly and distinctly. "Henry is not mentally ill. He simply had emotional problems stemming, I'm sure, from the way our father treated him."

"All right then," Sylvia said. "I'm sure you're right. At any rate, we bought those houses and all the rest over the years. All at bargain prices, too. Now that the economy's gotten better, new businesses are starting up. As it happened, the city planning commission granted a request to rezone several properties for a commercial developer interested in constructing strip shopping centers. He approached us about purchasing the land the houses were on."

Edith spoke then, for the first time since her sister had entered. "We tripled our original investment."

"How nice for you," Louise snapped. "I suppose you didn't hesitate to toss out the people living there."

"They didn't own the houses," Sylvia said. "They were just renters. I'm sure they found somewhere else to live. So, Louise, even though you got your father to sign over everything he had to you, we not only got it all back, in the end we made a killing off it."

"You know," Louise said, "I thought something was odd about this whole thing, about never meeting the mysteriously busy Eleanor Brooks, about Houseman always being ready to purchase my houses. I admit it never occurred to me you two were behind it." She shook her head. "How you must have hated me, to harbor this quest for revenge over all these years."

Louise smiled for the first time since she'd entered the office and recognized Edith. "But hate burns hot in your minds. I can't help thinking you'll end up poisoned by it, sort of like your mother. The only difference—hate takes longer to kill you."

She walked over and stood with one hand on the doorknob. "By the way, Edith, now that I think about it, I'm not at all surprised I didn't recognize your voice when we spoke on the phone." She pointed at Sylvia. "She always did the talking for you—the thinking, too." As Louise opened the door, she added, "I hope you both enjoy seeing your mother again. My father will probably be there as well. You know where I mean, right? You can be just one big happy family again."

As she passed through the reception area, the secretary said, "Goodnight, Mrs. Carlyon, I hope you have a pleasant evening."

"Oddly enough, I think I will." Louise closed the outer door behind her and only then remembered she had come by taxi. *Oh well,* she thought, *I'm not going back inside there to make a call. The walk will do me good.*

CHAPTER 59

L ouise awakened still tired Friday morning, having spent a good portion of the night going over all she'd learned. She made coffee, then scrambled eggs and toast and sat at the kitchen table reading the paper while she ate. The more she thought about her stepsisters' actions, the more she became convinced their success came from more than luck and timing.

Coming home last night, she'd also had the niggling feeling she'd missed something, a little detail she should have thought of before she left the realty office. This morning she remembered. She didn't know if Sylvia was married, or, if so, her married name. She'd need that to go snooping around.

Fannie came in and poured herself coffee then sat with Louise. "Are you still thinking about Sylvia and Edith?"

"Just about all night." Louise had vented to her mother just after arriving home. "I keep thinking they *must* have done something illegal, or at least shady."

Fannie lit a Lucky Strike. "What are you going to do about it?"

"I'm not sure, but I think I'll do a little poking around and see what I can find."

"Let me know if I can help," Fannie said. "I'd hate to see those two get away with something."

Bobby and Henry shuffled down the hall and into the kitchen, both yawning. "What's for breakfast?" Bobby asked.

Fannie got up and started for the refrigerator. "Revenge, I hope."

Bobby and Henry exchanged glances. "Huh?" Bobby said.

"Nothing," Fannie said as she pulled out a carton of eggs and turned the oven on for toast.

Louise checked her watch, drained the last of her coffee, and went out into the hall to the telephone stand. She found the number she wanted in the stand's drawer. A few seconds later, the secretary's perky voice answered. "Good morning, Houseman Realty. How can I help you?"

"This is Louise Carlyon. I came in last evening and met with Ms. Brooks and her sister, Sylvia."

"Oh yes, Mrs. Carlyon, I remember."

"Well, silly me, I wanted to send a thank you note for all their help, but I've forgotten Sylvia's last name. Can you help with that?"

"Of course I can. Sylvia's my mom. Our last name is Parkinson. You know, like Parkinson Construction Company? You've probably heard of it. It's one of the biggest commercial development firms in the county. That's my dad, Ray Parkinson."

Surprised, both at the information she'd just happened upon and that such a friendly, helpful girl came from her stepsister's body, Louise pondered the implications "Thank you so much. You're very kind."

"You're very welcome." The girl rang off.

Parkinson Construction Company, Louise thought. *How very interesting.* She went back into the kitchen where Fannie spooned scrambled eggs onto Henry's and Bobby's plates. "I've got to get ready, Mother. Maybe there is something you can do for me while I'm at work."

"Anything that'll help," Fannie said. "Just let me know before you leave."

Murray arrived home before Louise Friday night. She took several minutes filling him in on what she'd found out from her meeting and subsequent call to Houseman Realty. They decided to wait until after supper to discuss it further. Bobby would be out with Annie Killough, his most recent girlfriend, and Henry playing at See-Boy's club.

Retiring to the parlor later, Fannie settled into the chair across from Louise and Murray on the couch. "I went down to the city planning commission and got a copy of their zoning ordinance and minutes from the last few meetings." She handed Louise a sheaf of papers. "Look at the beginning where it lists which members were in attendance and which absent."

Louise quickly scanned the first sheet then eyed her mother. "Arlen Brooks is chairman of the planning commission. That has to be Edith's husband."

"Uh-huh, "Fannie said. "As if that weren't enough, they've got a color photograph of him hanging on the wall. Not a handsome man, I can tell you, but I suspect he's about the best she could hope for."

"An interesting combination," Murray said, "the head of a construction company and the head of the planning commission each married to one of the sisters." He picked up one of the meeting minutes and ran his forefinger down the page. "Let's find when the zoning change requests were made and by whom."

Fannie and Louise each took minutes and scanned them. After a few moments, Murray said, "Okay, here's one of them. It's the Willow Street development, affecting five houses, three of them you sold to Houseman." He squinted and held the sheet up to the light. The requesting party was Parkinson Construction Company, representing a chain grocery store out of Nashville."

"When did they make the request?" Louise asked.

"In July, on the seventh. You closed on those last three houses in June, if I recall correctly. So right after that."

"Here's another," Fannie said. "The three houses bordering Main and Cowart Streets are among others where they requested to rezone as commercial." She looked up and smiled. "Parkinson Construction made the request on behalf of Western Auto, Incorporated, in August."

"All right," Louise said. "We know Parkinson and Brooks have to be working together to push through the zoning changes. But does that prove anything?"

"Collusion, maybe," Murray offered. "Or perhaps something illegal if money changed hands, but how could we know if it did? I think they call that influence peddling."

"I could call Michael Peters," Louise said. "See if he has any thoughts on the whole thing."

"You might as well," Murray said. "He should at least know if there's anything illegal about it."

Louise shuffled the pages of minutes, putting them back in chronological order. "I wouldn't be surprised if the two sisters hooked up with those husbands to do what they did. How much anger and resentment could they have felt over all these years?"

"I'll be darned if I know," Murray said.

Fannie's eyes flashed. "I'll be *damned*."

Louise glanced at Murray who, having grown up the son of a minister, didn't particularly care for cursing.

His mouth twitched, the slightest hint of a smile playing at the corners of his mouth. "Probably," he said.

CHAPTER 60

Between sets again, the two leaned against the bar—Henry drinking a beer, Lawanda an Orange Crush, juke box playing in the background.

"Have you ever wanted something so much," Henry asked, "you felt you'd be completely lost without it?"

Lawanda took a moment then said, "To sing, I guess. If I couldn't sing anymore, I'm not sure I'd have a purpose in life. Waiting tables was never my plan."

"That's exactly how I feel about you."

"Oh, Henry, we're too different. It's taboo. No one would accept a white man and a colored woman together."

"I don't care about color," Henry said. "I only care about you."

"Other people care. Almost everyone else cares." Lawanda turned and set her Orange Crush on top of the bar. "We've had this conversation."

"I'm going to keep on trying until you at least dance with me." He held his hand out to her. "Please, just one dance?" A new record started: "I'll Never Smile Again"—Frank Sinatra and the Tommy Dorsey orchestra. Henry beckoned with his fingers. "Please, Lawanda."

She let her chin slump toward her chest for a moment, took a deep breath, then slowly took Henry's hand.

A few couples danced, but most sat at their tables, refreshing their drinks or mopping sweat from their foreheads with handkerchiefs or napkins. Henry threaded his way through the couples already on the dance floor, Lawanda trailing behind him. In the center, he turned and pulled her to him.

The feel of her in his arms was so powerful he thought he might burst. He'd danced with a few women in his life, like when he and Jimmy Farr had played the high school proms and spring dances, and a couple of times with Irene to songs on her record player. But it never felt like this.

Every inch of her body nestled against every inch of his. Whichever way he turned, he felt her, like a second skin. Her hair smelled of apples. Her perfume, mingled with the moist heat of her body, acted like an elixir, and Henry shut his eyes to let his other senses take over.

When the song ended, he didn't want to let her go. She pulled away, and it felt like his own flesh being peeled from his body. He opened his eyes to find them alone on the dance floor. Lawanda moved toward the bar immediately.

He stood there by himself a moment before following. He'd hoped the dance would finally quench his thirst for her, but he'd been wrong. It only made his obsession worse.

See-Boy watched as Henry led Lawanda onto the dance floor, having overheard much of the conversation preceding Henry's move. He'd known Lawanda a while, Henry all the man's life. Lawanda, while friendly with the customers, had sung with the band for several years but maintained a professional distance and never flirted.

On the other hand, See-Boy had seen firsthand the abuses Henry suffered from his father and knew the profound effect it had on his emotional state. As a boy, he'd been compulsive and delicate, occasionally reclusive, as if he lived in his head a lot of the time.

From the overheard conversation, See-Boy figured out Henry's obsession with Lawanda, and it worried him. This could be troublesome for one if not both of them.

Thinking back, See-Boy recalled that, about every time the band took a break, while the others cooled off out back, Henry always made it a point to be close to Lawanda. He'd seen the way he looked at her, adoration in his eyes. But until now, there'd been nothing as obvious as the two dancing.

Probably, the folks in the bar might think it surprising, but they'd grown used to Henry as the white drummer and known him from the other band. This, however, pushed the boundaries too far.

See-Boy's gaze swept the room. Good, law-abiding folks mostly—maybe a drink too many every now and then, a little rowdiness on occasion; he'd even walked a few home, but he'd never had to break up a fight or throw anybody out. He surely hoped his luck would hold.

As usual, Henry left the bar last, the others carrying their horns home with them. Only he and Cecil, the bassist, left their equipment in the club, in a small storage room off the dance floor. Cecil finished first, slapping hands with Henry, who still moved his drums.

"Need any help?" Cecil asked.

"Thanks anyway, but I've got it." Henry put the last drum in place and leaned the cymbal stand against the wall. Walking across the bar, he waved to See-Boy—who offered 'goodnights' to a few closing-time stragglers—and headed out the front. He turned left outside and had nearly passed the alley entrance when someone grabbed his collar and jerked him into the darkness.

"What's going—"

A hard punch to his stomach left him bent forward at the waist and sucking air. A pair of hands wrenched his shoulders backward and someone punched him hard in the face. He felt blood run into his mouth.

"Please, please stop," he gasped. "I don't have any money."

One of the men shoved him up against the brick wall and held him there with a powerful forearm. "We know you're friends with See-Boy, but you need to learn not to mess with our women, you hear me? You stay away from Lawanda or you'll hear from us again. And next time, it'll hurt a lot worse."

Henry felt the pressure on his chest lessen, then the men disappeared into the alley's shadows. He slid down the wall, feeling the cool, rough grain of the brick through his shirt. He touched his nose, his hand coming away bloody. His stomach ached, but he didn't think anything felt broken.

After a few minutes, he stood slowly. He heard the last of the crowd leaving the bar and stepped further back into the alley. He didn't want to be seen this way. Once all became quiet, he moved onto the sidewalk, producing a handkerchief and wiping most of the blood from his face.

He was always last to arrive home Fridays and Saturdays because of the club staying open late, so he didn't worry about running into anyone. Tomorrow morning would be another story, though. He'd have to think of a way to explain the damage without telling the whole truth.

He felt the lingering pain as he undressed and slipped under the covers, but then he remembered how it felt dancing with Lawanda. *It was worth getting punched,* he thought. *Damn right it was.*

CHAPTER 61

enry walked into the kitchen to find his mother cooking eggs and grits. He had the early shift at the laundry, so as yet, no one else had made it to the kitchen.

"Good morning, Momma."

Fannie glanced up from the pot she stirred. "Good lord, Henry. What happened to your face?"

He'd checked it out in the bathroom mirror before coming out and thought his swollen nose barely noticeable, but the dark circles under both eyes were hard to miss.

"Putting away my drums last night, I accidently bumped Cecil's bass. The darn thing slid and hit me right on the nose."

She left the stove and came over to examine the damage close up. "Well, at least your nose doesn't seem broken. You're going to look like a badger for a few days, though."

"It doesn't hurt much," he said. *But my stomach does. Good thing she can't see the bruise there.* He ate a hurried breakfast and left. It would be easier if his mother related the story to the others. That way, he wouldn't have to lie as much.

See-Boy finished breakfast and asked Pearl for another cup of coffee. As she poured, he told her about Henry and Lawanda dancing together the previous evening. "It might be nothing, but if you'd seen the way he looks at her, watching her all the time practically. It might not sit well with some folks."

Pearl sat down beside See-Boy and blew on her coffee. "There are those who would say it's not really your business."

"I can't help it. I've looked out for that family since I turned twelve. It's hard not to worry when I sense trouble coming."

"Will you tell Louise about it?"

"I'm not sure what I'd say. And I'm not sure what she could do, either. Henry and Lawanda are both adults."

Pearl took a sip of her coffee. "Maybe the best approach is to keep a close eye on things for the time being. Keep an ear open, too. Listen for any grumbling."

See-Boy nodded. "You're probably right. For the moment anyway, I don't know what else to do."

When Henry arrived at The Hanger, he kept his head down while setting up, knowing all the while nothing would shield his black eyes from anyone who cared to look.

Abernathy noticed first. "What the hell happened to your face?" Then the others crowded around to take a look.

Best to get it over with as soon as possible, he thought, relaying the same story he'd invented for his mother. They seemed to buy it—all but Lawanda. She stared, her head cocked to one side as if measuring him. She didn't say anything, though, just kept looking at him like she knew something the others didn't—which, in this case, happened to be true.

See-Boy wandered over and took a minute to examine him. "What happened?"

"I bumped into Cecil's bass. It fell and hit me on the nose."

"Huh," See-Boy grunted and walked away.

Before the band started, Lawanda cornered Henry away from the others. "What really happened to you, Henry? And don't lie to me. I mean it. I need to know."

"Two guys dragged me into the alley last night as I left the club. They punched me a couple of times and told me to stay away from you."

"Did you recognize them? Were they from the club?"

"Too dark to tell."

Lawanda reached out to touch Henry's face, then drew her hand back and glanced around at the quickly filling tables. "I've

been afraid this would happen. We shouldn't have danced together. That's what caused this."

"I'd do it again," Henry said. "I'd do it every night if it meant
I could keep on dancing with you. When I held you last night, I
felt like I might explode. It means that much to me."

Lawanda stared at him, searching for something in his eyes,
his battered face. Then she nodded and walked away.

Henry scanned the crowd, wondering if his attackers were
out there. Most likely, he should be afraid. He'd spent most of his
life being afraid of one thing or another. But right then, he wasn't.

See-Boy kept his eyes on Lawanda and Henry before and during
the first set. He saw nothing worrisome. Still, when the set
ended, he caught Lawanda's eye and signaled for her to come
to the bar. He hoped Henry wouldn't follow.

When Lawanda walked up, See-Boy asked, "You want something to drink?"

"Just a Coca-Cola right now."

He dug a cold bottle from the cooler, popped the cap, and
handed it to her with a napkin. "Henry tell you what happened
to his face?"

"Uh-huh, Cecil's bass fell and hit him when he was putting
his drums away."

"I saw Henry leave last night. He waved on his way out, and
he didn't appear to be holding his nose or have a handkerchief
to it at the time." He leaned an elbow on the bar. "You'd think
I would have noticed if he'd been hurt."

Lawanda shifted and looked back at Henry still sitting on
the bandstand. "Maybe it didn't start bleeding until later."

"Maybe, but usually nose bleeds start right away."

"I guess so," Lawanda said.

"I watched you two dancing last night during the break. I'm
not sure that's a wise thing. You know how people are, sometimes
emotions run high. I don't mean to tell you what to do, but I'd
appreciate it if you wouldn't. I think a lot of you, Lawanda, and
I've known Henry all his life. I don't want anything bad to happen
to either of you."

"You don't need to worry. We won't dance together anymore. I'll make sure of it."

See-Boy reached over and patted her hand. "That's my girl."

Henry thought Lawanda avoided contact with him all night. He'd hoped, when she saw his face, she'd understand how serious he was about her. He watched as Lawanda and See-Boy chatted at the bar, See-Boy patting her hand. Though he'd grown up with See-Boy, respected him as much as anybody, except for Louise, he couldn't help feeling jealous of even that small gesture of affection.

Lawanda returned to the bandstand, reached into her purse, then scribbled something on a piece of notepaper. She folded the paper and slipped it to him as the band members picked up their instruments.

He took it and read it hurriedly. It said: *Come to my house after practice tomorrow if you want to.* The address scrawled below was only a few blocks from the club. Henry felt a surge of pure joy wash over him.

CHAPTER 62

L ouise, Fannie, and Murray sat finishing breakfast, sipping coffee, and reading different sections of the newspaper. Bobby and Henry slept in, often their habit Sundays. Henry played late, and Bobby had been out with Annie. Fortunately, Annie's parents had imposed a midnight curfew. At first, it had struck Louise as odd, Annie being an adult and holding down a job as a long distance operator, but she guessed as long as the young woman lived with her parents, they could make the rules. The deadline seemed plenty late.

Murray folded his section and handed it to Louise. "Have you seen this yet?"

She glanced at the column headings. "Not yet."

He pointed to a headline above the fold. "Read this."

Louise took the paper. When she finished, she looked at Murray. "Does this mean what I think it does?"

"I'm afraid so."

Fannie took a sip of coffee then placed her cup back into its saucer. "What are you talking about?"

"Congress passed the Selective Service and Training Act," Louise said. "I read they were debating it, but I didn't think it would pass so quickly." She read from the column, "All men, ages twenty-one to thirty-five, are required to register with specially appointed local draft boards beginning in October. Selections will be based on a national lottery."

"We're not at war," Fannie said. "Why would they do that?"

"To be ready, I suppose," Murray said, "just in case anything changes."

A shiver traveled up Louise's spine. "God forbid that happens."

Murray nodded. "I wish we could be more certain it won't."

"I'd hate to think of Bobby being drafted and having to go to war," Louise said.

"Henry, too," Fannie said. "What's the maximum age again?"

"Thirty-five," Murray said.

Fannie blew out a breath. "Henry turns thirty-four next month. I'm not sure he'd cope with being drafted."

Murray rose, rinsed his cup, and left the kitchen. Louise knew, though he wouldn't say anything, he had little patience with Henry's quirks. Her mother was right, though. Louise doubted her brother could survive being ripped away from his home, let alone fight in a war.

Henry hardly looked at Lawanda during the band's practice session for fear his excitement would be obvious to everyone. She had ignored him as well. He reached into his shirt pocket and caressed the note. No, he wasn't dreaming. The note was real.

He waited until the others left before heading out. The address Lawanda gave him was about midway between the club and his house. As he walked, he wished he had brought along something—flowers, perfume, candy—to give her. But, it being Sunday, nothing close would be open. *Next time, though, if there's a next time.*

He reached the address, a small one-story house with dark green shingles and white trim. Boxwood hedges separated the structure from the houses on either side. On the way from the club, he'd seen several people sitting on their porches enjoying the still-warm September weather. Closer to Lawanda's house, the whites grew progressively fewer, and, for the last block or so, only colored people appeared about.

He wondered what the neighbors would think, a white man visiting Lawanda's house. Then he put that thought aside and stepped to the front door.

Lawanda answered right away. She'd changed her clothes from the practice session and wore a pale blue blouse with matching pants cinched tightly at her waist. On her feet, she wore open-toed flats.

"Come in, Henry."

He followed her to the living room, furnished with a green and yellow flowered sofa, low-backed upholstered chair, and walnut occasional table. A radio sat on the table, Peggy Lee singing, "Why Don't You Do Right?" softly from the speaker.

"This is nice," Henry said, looking around.

Lawanda smiled. "What, the room or being here?"

Henry looked her in the eyes. "Both, I guess, but being here for sure."

"Let's sit," Lawanda said, leading Henry to the sofa and getting straight to the point. "You know we can't dance together at the club anymore, right?" She lightly touched the purple-ochre smudges under his eyes. "We can't let this kind of thing happen again."

"I don't care what happens to me as long as I can be with you."

"What do you mean when you say 'be with me'?"

Henry reached out and let his fingers rest on Lawanda's arm. "It means whatever you will let it mean. I think about you all the time. I want to be in your presence all the time. But when I'm with you, it's like torture knowing I can't touch you, embrace you, feel your body next to mine. I ache inside."

He held her gaze. His fingers, resting on her forearm, tingled at the smooth softness of her skin. "I'll take whatever you can give. If that turns out to be nothing more than watching you perform, I'll die a little inside every time we play, but it will be the sweetest damn death I could hope for."

"Oh, Henry..." Lawanda left her thought either unfinished or unspoken. Then she said, "There's no way our being together, whatever way, can turn out well. There's no future for us. Don't you understand that?"

Henry shook his head. "I understand what you're saying, but—"

She put her forefinger to his lips. "There's only today. I can't promise you next month, next week, or even tomorrow—only today. Can you live with that?"

Henry nodded—her eyes pools of dark water calling him to submerse himself in their depths. "I can live with that."

She rose from the sofa, took Henry by the hand, and led him to the bedroom.

Harry stopped on their way to the lake to gas up the Ford. Bobby followed the women inside the service station while the attendant pumped gasoline. Looking for peanut butter crackers, he spotted the newspaper rack next to the cash register. The headline made him do a double take. He slid a coin into the slot, dragged out the *Times*, and scanned the article.

He stood by the rack, still reading when the women returned from the restroom.

"What is it?" Annie asked.

Bobby grinned. "Congress passed a draft act. Who knows, I might get to be a pilot after all."

CHAPTER 63

L ouise called Michael Peters first thing Monday morning and told him what they had uncovered regarding the link between her stepsisters, their husbands, and the rezoning of the previously residentially zoned housing clusters.

"We don't know that they've done anything illegal," Louise said. "It just seems a little too much to write off as coincidence."

"Let me do a bit of checking," Peters said. "I doubt it's anything illegal, but I'll see what I can find out. I'll call you at the grocery later this afternoon."

Louise hung up and finished getting ready for work. She kissed Murray goodbye and promised to call him that evening with whatever she found out.

Busy as usual after being closed on Sunday, Louise rang up sales and bagged groceries nearly nonstop, all the while thinking about her stepsisters. *Am I working myself up over nothing? The whole matter is so convoluted.* She wasn't even sure what she wanted Peters' checking to reveal, if anything.

True to his word, Peters called her at three. "I've verified the facts as you told them," he said. "Further—and I should have remembered this when we talked this morning—Ray Parkinson is this year's chairman of the Chattanooga Chamber of Commerce."

Peters paused to let that sink in then continued. "The Chamber is the private sector body charged with attracting commercial and industrial development for the city. So, Parkinson is well within his rights seeking out investment in the community, including the grocery store chain out of Nashville and Western Auto. Firms like those pay taxes, provide local jobs, and help attract other investments."

"You're telling me everything they've done is not only legal but good for the city."

"Essentially yes. In cases like this, the participants have occasionally been accused of, and sometimes convicted of, influence peddling or payoffs. But it's difficult to prove. And, in most of those instances, the participants are not as closely related as your stepsisters' husbands. Why risk doing anything illegal when they both profit—through their wives' business—doing the very things they're charged with doing?"

Louise felt deflated yet relieved. She'd seen enough of the insides of courtrooms to last a lifetime. She'd have let it go immediately if not for her wounded pride.

"I guess I've been outplayed. I'm holding a pair of deuces and they've got a full house."

"I didn't realize you played poker," Peters said.

"Just Mother and I sometimes, and Lawrence and I at the store when things aren't busy. This time I overplayed my hand."

"I'm sorry, Louise."

"Don't be. I'm not sure how I wanted it to turn out, anyway. I think we'll chalk this one up as a learning lesson."

"And what have you learned?"

"Something I should have learned a long time ago. It's one of my mothers' favorite sayings. Trust no living body and walk carefully by the dead."

Peters laughed. "Louise, you continue to be one of my favorite clients. I hope we'll do more business together. Next time, hopefully, it will be profitable."

She hung up the telephone and sat for a moment staring at nothing. Then the bell on the door rang, signaling a customer, and Louise fixed a smile on her face. "How can I help you this afternoon?"

Henry spent most of Monday afternoon alone in his repair shop, thinking about his evening with Lawanda. They'd made love in Lawanda's bed, lighted candles atop a dresser, chest of drawers, and a night stand. It struck him that the candles were already lit when she led him to her bed.

Did she know in advance she would sleep with him? Maybe she kept candles burning all the time when home, but that seemed unlikely. He wondered, but it didn't bother him either way.

The experience—watching her undress, the smoothness of her skin as the candles flickered, casting both light and shadow on her curves and hollows, the exquisiteness of feeling her body pressed to his. He couldn't stop seeing her face in his mind or hearing her soft cries in his ears.

Though everything he'd hoped for, he couldn't help feeling bad when it was over and she gently told him to go. Irene and he had listened to records, danced in the living room, and shared beers. It seemed to him, at the time, they were friends as well as lovers. In the end, he'd found out differently, of course. But he wanted that same sense of familiarity with Lawanda.

That's so like me, he thought. He'd told her he would accept whatever she was willing to give. Now, though, he wanted more. He would do the best he could to contain himself. Try not to go too far and ruin what he had. *But do I really have anything?*

Lawanda promised him yesterday, nothing more. He might not see her beautiful body again or feel its warmth and smoothness or taste the sweetness of her mouth. He knew down deep he would never be able to accept that. *He could try, though, couldn't he?* Most things were easier said than done; other things were near impossible.

His mother broke in on his thoughts, calling from the back porch steps. "Henry, the telephone is for you. Someone has a radio that needs repair."

Henry left the shed and climbed the steps to the porch. He remembered when his new venture as a radio repairman had meant so much to him. Things were different now. He knew how much love could hurt—and how things like radios, tubes, and soldering irons meant little in comparison.

CHAPTER 64

B obby and Harry, among the first eligible to register with the recently appointed local draft board, stood in line at the downtown office talking and joking with other young men about the prospects of being shipped off to parts unknown. Several bragged how they would show the Krauts or the Japs a thing or two. Others managed only a grim smile.

Bobby himself felt conflicted. From newspaper and radio reports, he knew the likelihood of the United States joining with the Allied forces. Many supposedly in the know leaned toward the idea that it was only a matter of time.

Unlike some of the registrants, Bobby didn't fear going to war. Perhaps he should, but he still saw the whole experience as nothing more than a grand adventure. His father had gone overseas and fought in World War One and come back unscathed. Bobby had prompted his dad to tell him stories about that war, but the few he told were more about the soldiers than the battles.

His only reservation had to do with Annie. They'd been dating for more than two months, and he felt more than he'd felt with any of the girls he'd dated previously. He'd never been in love before, even with Helen, but he thought now he just might be.

Nevertheless, his dream of flying counterbalanced his desire to be with Annie. *I want both,* he thought, *but lots of people want lots of things.* If he had to make a choice right now, for the first time in his life, he wasn't sure what it would be.

B y mid-November, the draft fully underway across the country, each eligible man had been assigned a number. Those numbers went into a large bowl in the oval office, and, as individual numbers were drawn, President Franklin D. Roosevelt read them aloud over the radio. Young men everywhere reported for examinations and paperwork prior to being inducted in one of the branches of service.

Like many mothers, fathers, and grandparents throughout the nation, Louise and Fannie listened to the draft lottery broadcasts, sitting on the parlor sofa, shoulders hunched, hands clasped together in their laps, heads down. The tension Louise felt as she waited compared only to when she'd been on trial, accused of murdering Will's second wife.

Henry registered not long after Bobby. Though he'd said nothing, Louise could see the angst and fear on his face. Neither he nor Bobby chose to listen. Louise understood that. For Henry, she imagined it would be like having his neck in a guillotine, waiting for the blade to fall. And as for her son, he seemed oblivious to the potential for tragedy Louise feared so much. She thought it better that way. Worrying about what might happen to Henry was enough. With Bobby, she might be devastated, but her son would go along, apparently unconcerned with fate.

The numbers drawn and radio turned off, Louise sighed. "One more night we can rest and not worry until the next drawing."

Fannie lit a Lucky Strike and dropped her match into an ashtray. "It's a hell of a way to live, not knowing when or if it's going to be one of our men. What happened to the Germans, anyway? Your Grandmother and Grandfather Schmidt had German heritage and they were two of the finest people I've ever known."

Louise shook out a cigarette for herself. "I guess Hitler happened—this time anyway. Last time, it was the Kaiser. It seems we're bound and determined to be in a war with someone every few years."

Fannie got up from the sofa. "I'm going to bed. I don't know how Bobby and Henry can sleep not knowing. I couldn't."

"I don't know, either, Mother. I suppose it's a good thing. They've got us to worry for them, so they don't have to."

Louise lit her cigarette and watched her mother disappear down the hallway. A few minutes later, she crushed out the cigarette and got up to get ready for bed. She paused on her way down the hall at Bobby's door. A slant of light from the hall angled across the bed and up the opposite wall. She could just make out his shape under the sheets. He snored softly.

How nice it must be to sleep with the confidence of youth.

She stopped at Henry's door, too, but it was closed and she heard nothing. Just as well. She'd rather think of him sleeping peacefully than find out otherwise.

Henry lay awake in the dark. He heard his mother then Louise as they prepared for bed. No one had knocked on his door after the lottery broadcast, so he must be safe for now.

He wondered if others felt as he did—like a beast lurked in the shadows ready to lunge at any time and clamp its jaws around his neck. The image lingered, ever-present in his mind, except when he played his drums or made love to Lawanda.

Though she'd promised him only that day the first time they made love, he'd visited her every Sunday afternoon since. He didn't know how to form the nature of their relationship in his mind. He couldn't take her willingness to be with him for granted, and he couldn't bear the thought of it ending.

He lived one day at a time, two dire specters hovering over his head, either of which could blow his world apart. He envied Bobby, who seemed to take everything in stride.

Henry remembered when, years ago, all he'd needed to feel loved and safe was for Louise to slip an arm over his shoulder or give him a smile and a wink. Before his life became so complicated. He turned onto his side, pulled his knees up as close to his chest as they would go, and waited for sleep to crowd everything else from his mind.

CHAPTER 65

By December, the German blitzkrieg hammered away at Britain's cities, and Hitler finalized his plans for the invasion of Russia. Tensions ran high between the United States and Japan, whose leaders continued to take advantage of the war in Europe to advance their own ambitions in the Far East.

Despite pressures on the global scale, Louise managed to find relief from worrying by preparing for Christmas at the Carlyon house, the laundry, and the grocery.

The laundry proved easiest to decorate—only the door and two big plate glass windows on either side of the entrance. She and Bobby had done the work early on Sunday. She draped garland from the top corners of each window and hung a wreath with a big red bow on the door. Bobby used white washable paint to simulate frost—though he called it snow—collecting on the bottoms of the windows and creeping up the sides.

Bobby wielded the paint brush to the lower portions of one of the windows. "What am I going to get Annie for Christmas, Momma?"

"I don't know," Louise said. "What does she like?"

He grinned, his dimples reminding her of why he'd always had a handful of young women vying for his attention. Aside from the time he'd gotten into a fix with Helen Adamson, Annie had lasted the longest of any.

"You mean besides me?"

"Yes, dear, I mean besides you."

"That's just it. She likes everything: clothes, jewelry, perfume, *everything*."

"Does she read?" Louise asked.

He shrugged. "You mean, like books and such?"

"Yes, like that."

"I don't know. She doesn't talk about it if she does."

One of Louise's few regrets where Bobby was concerned. Somehow, he'd missed those genes from her and Murray, both avid readers.

"A nice book is always good, but if you don't know what she's interested in, you'd probably do better with something else."

Bobby got up from the floor and stretched his back for a moment. "I don't know anything about women's clothes, jewelry, or perfume. I'm back to where I started."

Louise adjusted the bow on the wreath, making both the ends the same length. She finished and gave her son a smile. "Well, candy is always nice."

Since the grocery had more windows along the front and vegetable bins backed up to those windows, decorating required moving the bins and repositioning them afterward.

She and Frankie tackled that job on Friday, after he arrived from school. Louise loved seeing the light in Lawrence's eyes when he watched his grandson working. *He's certainly bright and a hard worker,* she noted.

Like his father and grandfather, Frankie called her Miss Louise. She guessed no matter what her status or what others called her, she would always be a 'Miss' to the three of them.

She still had Thanksgiving specials painted on the windows, so Frankie moved the bins and washed off the old paint to prepare for the new. He would turn eighteen before long, and despite trying to keep her focus elsewhere, her thoughts returned to the draft.

"Are you worried about being drafted after your birthday next month, Frankie?"

"No, ma'am. I'll have to register, but from what I hear, they're not drafting colored men."

Louise thought of asking how he felt about that but decided against it. In her mind, being drafted wasn't nearly as troubling as the reasons might be why colored men got passed over.

"Anyway," Frankie added, "I guess it's good I don't have to worry about fighting in a war way out there across the ocean."

Louise nodded, thinking, in many ways, he'd probably have enough to fight here at home.

They both looked up when the bell rang. The man who drove the Coca-Cola truck came in carrying a full-color, life-size cardboard Santa Claus whose dark eyes sparkled and rosy lips grinned in satisfaction as he lifted the familiar, frosty bottle. Since she'd purchased the grocery, this had always been her favorite holiday promotion piece.

Frankie looked up from his work and put his hands on his hips. "Look there, Miss Louise. Now the Christmas season can begin."

The December moon, round and bright and golden, floated like a Florida orange against the black backdrop of sky. Parked in the old Ford on a bluff overlooking the Tennessee River, Bobby and Annie watched as the lights from North Chattanooga stretched long and ghostlike on the black surface of the water. The paddle wheeler Delta Queen sounded its steam whistle. To their immediate left, the Hunter Museum of Art marked the highest point downtown and shielded the couple from passersby on the street.

Bobby leaned with his back against the driver's side door. Annie nestled under his right arm, her head resting on his chest. Earlier in the evening, they'd seen Spencer Tracy in *Northwest Passage* at the Tivoli Theater. The bluff provided their favorite place to park afterward.

They'd dated steadily for more than three months but hadn't yet made love. If it had been anyone else, Bobby would have moved on long before now. He could tell she wanted to as much as he did, yet she always seemed able to stop before they went too far.

"I've been thinking about what I'm getting you for Christmas," Bobby said. Actually, he'd been thinking of almost nothing else for days.

Annie twisted to look up at him. "Have you decided?"

"Not so far. Uh … do you read books? My mother and father both love to read, but I'm not much for it. Momma thought you might enjoy a good book."

Annie used her forefinger to trace a line from his chin to the hollow at the base of his throat. "I might like a book. I do read novels, but not as much as I go to the movies. I like records, too."

Bobby's heart thudded. Annie must have felt it, too, because she leaned up and asked, "Are you all right?"

"Records would be good, but I've been thinking about a ring."

She tilted her head to one side, her eyes bright with the orange glow of the moon reflected in them. "What sort of ring are you thinking of?"

"An engagement ring," he said, watching as Annie's lips parted in surprise. "But if there's another kind you'd rather have…"

Annie leaned forward and took his face in her hands. "Are you crazy? Of course I wouldn't rather have another kind." She kissed him hard on the mouth.

"I love you so much," he said when she broke the kiss. Or maybe she said it first. Her warm body pressed against him. She felt as smooth and soft as a pillow.

Wow, Bobby thought. *Momma and Daddy are going to be surprised.*

CHAPTER 66

Bobby and Annie agreed to wait until his mother's forty-second birthday celebration to announce their engagement. Though the seventh of January actually fell on Wednesday, they held the party that Friday so Murray could be there. Fannie made a chuck roast with sweet potatoes and turnip greens and had baked a chocolate cake for dessert. Mouth-watering scents wafted through the warm kitchen.

Bobby, happy and nervous at once, watched as his mother blew out the candles on the cake. After they'd finished dessert, the whole family moved to the parlor.

"So soon after Christmas," Louise said, taking in the pile of gifts. "I really didn't need anything else." But she opened all the presents with delight and gushed over them as only dedicated wives and mothers do. When she finished, she thanked everyone.

Then she looked at Annie, who had given her a pair of coral-colored cameo earrings. "Annie, sweetheart, I'm so glad you're here with us, and thank you again for your precious gift. The earrings are lovely."

Bobby reached over and took Annie's hand. "Mother, Daddy—" He let his eyes sweep over Henry and Fannie as well. "All of you, we have something to tell you. Annie and I are engaged. We plan to marry in June."

His father's mouth dropped open as his eyebrows went up. He turned to his wife. "Did you hear that, Louise? Bobby and Annie are getting married."

Louise grinned as she rose from the sofa and took both Annie's hands in her own. "Well, of course I heard it, Murray." She pulled Annie up and hugged her tightly. "I'm so happy for you both."

Murray got into the hugs next, embracing first Annie then Bobby. Fannie and Henry followed suit.

"Have you told your parents yet?" Louise asked.

"Not yet. We wanted to let you know first, but if you'll excuse us, that's where we're going next."

"Well, I hope they'll be as happy as we are."

Bobby took his mother's hand. "I hope you don't mind we chose your birthday party to make our announcement."

"I can't think of a better time," Louise said. "It's the best birthday gift I've ever had."

Henry couldn't shake feeling envious. *Why is it always someone else? When will it be my turn?* Sometimes, he wondered exactly what his family felt for him. He considered himself a failure in almost every way. When had he ever done anything to bring his family the kind of joy he'd witnessed tonight?

His radio repair venture had turned into a joke, barely making enough money to buy the soft drinks and cheese crackers he drank and ate while in the shed. He'd also begun slipping magazines and paperback books into the shop to read while he pretended to work.

The money he made playing in the band wasn't much either, and his pay from the laundry came straight out of Louise's pocket.

But money wasn't really the problem. He always wanted what he couldn't have. It had been Irene first, and now Lawanda. What would his family say if they knew he'd been sleeping with a colored woman? Could he bring her home for supper like Bobby did Annie? He knew the answer.

The worst part, though, was the knowledge that, even if he could, Lawanda wouldn't come.

Saturday afternoon, Fannie caught the streetcar as far as Bennett then walked the rest of the way to See-Boy's club. She knew from what Henry had told her, See-Boy spent most of his time there, if not working the crowd then working in a small office he'd remodeled shortly after the place went legitimate.

She stopped in front and tried the door. Finding it open, she stepped in and let her eyes adjust to the dimly lit interior. At first, she saw no one, then, from a doorway across the room, she caught a glimpse of See-Boy looking out at her.

"Good lord, Miss Fannie, I haven't seen you in I don't know how long. Come in, come in." He traveled the room's distance and offered his hand. "Can I get you something to drink? Is everything all right at home?"

"It's good to see you, too, See-Boy. I'll pass on the drink. It's a bit early yet." She smiled to let him know she was kidding. "But I will take a seat at the bar if you have a few minutes."

"Sure I do." He led her to one of the stools. "How can I help you?"

"I'm worried about Henry. A few months ago, he came home with two black eyes. He told me he'd done it putting away his drums. At the time, I had no reason not to believe him. But since, he's been moodier than usual. I know his band practices Sunday afternoons, but lately he's gone much longer than usual those days."

See-Boy nodded but waited for her to continue.

"I'm pretty sure he was seeing a woman for a while, but I think that's over now. He never mentioned it to me, but I'm not dumb. I can put things together. And now … I suspect the same thing is happening again. Not there's anything wrong with his seeing someone, of course."

She took a cigarette from her purse.

See-Boy struck a match and lit it for her.

She looked him in the eyes. "I hoped you might know something one way or the other."

He took a cloth from his back pocket and wiped down the bar top, avoiding her gaze. "I can't say as I do, Miss Fannie. There's been no trouble here. Whatever else might be going on, I wouldn't know about."

Fannie watched him a long moment. She wasn't sure she believed him, but if he lied to her, it wouldn't be for lying's sake. He'd have a reason. She knew him well enough to be certain of that. She took a last drag on the Lucky Strike and put it out in the ashtray.

"All right, then. But, See-Boy, if you do see or hear anything, please let me know. I know you like Henry, and you've been good to him. I just don't want anything bad to happen to my boy."

"Oh, yes, ma'am," See-Boy said. "You can count on me for that."

See-Boy walked Fannie to the door and closed it behind her. On the sidewalk, Fannie took a deep breath and let it out. See-Boy knew something. But he wasn't telling. She hoped his protective nature extended to Henry as well as Louise.

CHAPTER 67

As the band finished its practice session, See-Boy waited in his office, working on orders for the coming week and paying first-of-the-month bills. He enjoyed hearing the band, even though he usually heard the same numbers several times over. Sometimes, they took a new tune and practiced it over and over until they got it just right. All good musicians, he appreciated their efforts.

He came out as Henry put away the last of his drums. "About ready to head for home, are you, Henry?"

"Pretty soon, I guess. It's nice outside for mid-January, though. I might walk for a while first."

See-Boy leaned forward with his elbows on the bar. "Yep, it's always good to take advantage of being outside when you can. Well, you have a good week and tell your momma and Louise I said hello."

"I'll do it," Henry said as he walked out the door. "You have a good week, too."

Pulling on his brown leather jacket and matching felt fedora, See-Boy waited until Henry had walked a half-block ahead before starting his truck and easing along behind him. If Henry was indeed just taking a walk to enjoy the weather, he seemed to do so with purpose. See-Boy watched the neighborhoods change gradually, the houses becoming smaller, older automobiles or no autos at all.

When Henry stopped at one house in the colored section and went up to the porch, See-Boy edged next to the curb a few houses up—the vantage point allowed him to watch without being observed.

About an hour later, the front door opened, and Henry came out onto the porch, Lawanda hovering in the doorway briefly as she pulled the door closed. See-Boy nodded to himself and chewed on his lower lip. He hadn't seen it coming, but it didn't surprise him either. Lawanda had kept her word—no more dancing together at the club—but this promised a lot more trouble.

He debated what to do. He'd like to talk with Pearl, see what she thought, but the memory of their similar conversation lingered. Maybe Lawanda's doings weren't his business, but Henry's were a different story.

After a while, he pulled the truck up in front of her house, made his way up the walk, and rang the bell. Lawanda's smile turned to surprise when she opened the door.

"See-Boy," she said, putting her hand to her throat, "what are you doing here?"

"I'd like to talk to you. Can I come in?"

She stepped back, allowing him entry. Barefoot, she wore a burgundy robe. "I'm just getting ready to take a bath, but it can wait." She gestured to the sofa. "Would you like to sit down?"

See-Boy sat on the sofa as Lawanda eased into the chair.

"I followed Henry to your house this afternoon."

"Oh, yes," Lawanda said, "he stopped by to pick up some sheet music. We're doing a new song, and then we started talking and…"

"Doesn't he come by every Sunday afternoon?" See-Boy asked.

Lawanda looked down at the floor. "How did you know?"

"I didn't, really, until today. But his mother came to see me. She suspected he's seeing someone. After what happened before— when you two danced together—I figured it must be you. He tries not to show it, but he still looks at you like you're the only person in his world."

She folded her hands in her lap. "He told me he didn't care what happened to him as long as he could dance with me. I was afraid for him. This seemed … better, I guess. At least we're not out in the open."

See-Boy leaned forward, resting elbows on thighs. "Do you love Henry?"

Lawanda looked at the floor again. After a moment, she shook her head. "No, I'm not in love with him. I like him. I like going to bed with him. He's so considerate and gentle. He makes me feel like a queen."

"I'm pretty sure he loves you," See-Boy said. "But you need to understand this arrangement can't end well. If people, *some* people ever found out, Henry could get hurt. He might not escape with black eyes next time."

She sighed. "I don't want him to be hurt. That's why I did what I did. But I think, if I stopped seeing him this way, he'd be hurt from that, too."

See-Boy nodded. "I understand, but at least he'd be alive. You're a lovely woman, Lawanda, and a wonderful singer. I have a friend in the music business, an agent, comes by the club when he's in town. Suppose I give him a call and see if he'd be interested in taking you on as a client, maybe get you an audition in Memphis or Nashville?"

"With the band, you mean?"

"Not with the band, just you. They're good musicians, but they're happy enough playing weekends at The Hanger. You could be somebody, maybe even famous. You're that good."

"You're willing to do all this for Henry, to protect him?"

"Not just Henry," See-Boy said. "I'd be doing it for you, too. I meant what I said. You're that good."

Lawanda looked around the sparsely furnished living room. "Would I have to move?"

"Let's not get ahead of ourselves. I'll make the call. We'll see what happens." He reached over and took Lawanda's hand. "But if you're as good as I think, you might want to. The music scene is bigger and better in Nashville and Memphis—lots more opportunity there. If you get a contract or go on the road, and if you end up moving, I'll help you with that, help you get set up somewhere new."

"In the meantime," Lawanda asked, "what do I tell Henry?"

"I can't stop you from seeing him. If and when something happens with your career, then you can tell him whatever the truth turns out to be. Henry would never stand in your way of becoming successful. He wouldn't like it, of course, but he probably loves you enough to let you go."

"I never promised him anything, except for the time we find ourselves together."

"That's good." See-Boy got up and walked to the door. "I'll call after I talk to my friend. And Lawanda, I'd just as soon Henry never find out about this conversation."

Back in his truck, See-Boy wondered if he'd done the right thing. He hoped Odell would be as successful with Lawanda as he'd been with Jimmy Farr's band.

Might cost him a bit of money to set Lawanda up somewhere else, but what the hell, he had a bunch of it these days.

CHAPTER 68

A soft pink dawn spread color across the trees and rooftops as Henry stood looking out the kitchen window. The beautiful June day—Bobby and Annie's wedding day— only reminded him he'd probably never be a groom.

The house had buzzed with activity for the last week. Louise, Henry's mother, and Bobby—along with Annie's mother and sisters—had been on the phone or in various stores and shops, arranging for food and flowers, wedding photos, and clothes.

Henry watched impassively as the others scurried hither and yon, always smiling, hugging, and pecking each other on the cheeks. He stayed on the sidelines, the loner, the wallflower, the man who wasn't there.

He heard a noise and turned from the window.

"Good morning, Henry," his mother said.

"Good morning, Mother." He turned back to the window. "It's a beautiful morning. Bobby and Annie will be pleased."

Fannie placed her hand on his shoulder. "Would you like coffee and breakfast? Better eat something soon. The day is just going to get busier as it goes along."

"Not right now. I woke up early, had a hard time sleeping. I think I'll lie down for a little while."

"All right then," Fannie said. "I'm going over to the church later to help with the flowers. I'll check on you before I go."

Henry went into his room, sitting on the edge of his unmade bed. Though hungry, the thought of bacon and eggs somehow made him nauseous—just another way he felt hollowed out inside.

Lawanda had left town in late February, bound for Nashville. Odell only had to hear her once and placed her with a Nashville-based band getting ready to play fairly large venues. He'd heard a rumor from one of his band members she and the new group might cut a record soon.

Henry hadn't seen it coming. Even though he'd promised to honor her caution about not planning on the future, it nonetheless devastated him when she left. One Sunday, they were together, and the next Friday a *For Sale* sign stood next to her porch steps.

He'd asked See-Boy about it, but See-Boy told him that's just the way it was with musicians—always on the move, looking for the next big step up. In a way, Henry felt the same about himself: there one minute, gone the next.

Henry played with the band twice more but couldn't continue without Lawanda, so he'd piled his drums into Bobby's car and settled them back in the shed next to his radio repair equipment. He didn't even set them up.

He got up from the bed and opened his closet, looking at the suit of clothes he'd wear for the wedding that afternoon at Saint Andrew's Methodist Church. Fannie had purchased the suit at Miller Brothers' Department Store. A nice suit—rich brown fabric with faint cream-colored pinstripes. He wished he could find pleasure in wearing it. He wished, too, he could feel at least a spark of happiness for Bobby and Annie. He loved Bobby and had grown to like Annie very much. When they were together, she always tried to include him.

To accommodate the newlyweds' brief honeymoon in Gatlinburg, Tennessee, Henry would work full days at the laundry. *Good,* he figured, *anything to keep busy, to keep my mind off my troubles.*

Louise enjoyed meeting Annie's family: Ned and Grace, her parents, Margie and Jenny, her sisters, and brother, Edward. Her father worked for the Standard Oil Company, Margie, the eldest daughter, at Fowler Brothers' Furniture Store, and Jenny worked alongside Annie at Southern Bell Telephone. Edward, Annie's oldest sibling, had worked for years as a mechanic at Newton Chevrolet.

They welcomed Bobby into their midst like one of their own, as had Louise with Annie. She remembered Bobby's birth and the complications. If it hadn't been for Jesse, See-Boy's mother, he'd probably have died that night. At the time, she'd been so frightened she wouldn't consider having another child. But since, she sometimes wondered if that had been the right decision. Having Annie in the family would give her another chance—the daughter she secretly wanted.

Now, as she sat with Murray, Fannie, and Henry on the groom's side of the aisle waiting for the service to begin, she felt she might overflow with happiness. No crying on this side of the aisle, but she might have seen Grace, across the way, dabbing at her eyes with a handkerchief once or twice.

Light filtering in through the stained-glass windows filled the sanctuary with a honeyed glow and lit up the beautiful flowers. Behind the chancel, a huge pipe organ rose almost to the ceiling. Louise wondered wistfully if Murray missed church. He hadn't spoken of it. She supposed he might not want to give up any of the limited time he had at home with her and Bobby. Or maybe he had enough growing up as a minister's son.

The organist began, and, shortly afterward, Bobby came in through a side door followed by Harry, his best man. If Bobby felt nervous, he didn't show it.

Once they found their place, "The Wedding March" began. Annie's two sisters and her best friend, Ruth, preceded her down the aisle. Annie followed, escorted by her father. The bride looked as beautiful as her surroundings, radiant as an angel. They all stood as Annie passed, her eyes locked onto Bobby.

Louise squeezed Murray's hand. "Isn't she beautiful?"

Murray glanced at her. "They both are."

Louise turned briefly and scanned the rows of pews. In the rear of the sanctuary, she saw Lawrence, See-Boy, Frankie, and Pearl. See-Boy winked and flashed a brilliant smile. She wondered if there could possibly be a better day than this one.

But always, somewhere in the back of her mind, she worried about the war in Europe and the ever-present specter of the draft. She'd been so busy for the past several weeks preparing for the wedding, it had almost slipped her mind—almost. She wondered if Annie's family worried about Edward, also draft-eligible.

As the ceremony reached its end and Bobby and Annie shared their first kiss as husband and wife, Louise managed to put her worries aside. Too much joy spilled from the church to let anything else intrude.

The happy couple left amid showers of rice. This time, instead of "Ace" West and "The Flash" Carlyon, the Ford's sides sported white shoe polish slogans proclaiming *Just Married* and *Hot Springs Express.*

Louise felt her eyes moisten as the car disappeared around a corner. She brushed it away. Still much to do. The newlyweds would take up residence in the Carlyon household for the foreseeable future, and she and Annie would redecorate Bobby's room into something that reflected more of a woman's touch.

Murray hugged her to him and let her head rest against his chest. "Happy?"

"Very," she replied.

CHAPTER 69

T he envelope addressed to *W. Henry Schmidt, III* with a return label reading *Selective Service and Training Board, Chattanooga, Tennessee Branch* arrived Tuesday.

Fannie stood on the front porch staring at it a full minute before she opened the screen door and went inside. She dropped the rest of the mail on the stand in the hall and took Henry's letter to the kitchen. Pouring herself the last of the coffee, she lit a Lucky Strike and continued staring at the envelope.

The coffee and her cigarette long gone, she finally retrieved a kitchen knife and slit the top, then unfolded the white paper and began to read.

Henry had to report to the local draft board in one week: *October 14, 1941.* The date glared at her as her hands started to shake. He would receive a physical examination and be tested for suitability of service. If found suitable, he would be inducted into the United States Army and sent to Camp Campbell, near Clarkesville, Tennessee, for training.

One week, Fannie thought, *dear God, what will we do?*

She thought of calling Louise at the grocery, but Louise could do nothing while at work, and why ruin her day before necessary? On the other hand, she would be the only one in the house when Henry came home from the laundry around one. She wouldn't tell him—not before she'd talked to Louise—which meant she'd be alone with the knowledge until after the grocery closed. She hoped she'd be able to keep her fears at bay until then.

L ouise arrived at the house at six-thirty. Annie, who'd walked in not long before, sat alone in the parlor with her shoes and nylons off, rubbing her feet. Louise couldn't understand why Annie wanted to wear heels to sit before a switchboard and place telephone calls for eight hours, but she guessed that's what young women did these days.

Bobby wouldn't be home for another hour or so, and, from the aromas drifting from the kitchen, she guessed Fannie already busy with supper. Louise dropped her purse on the telephone stand, said hello to Annie, and walked into the kitchen.

"What's for supper?"

Fannie stopped basting a chicken, stuck her head into the hallway and looked both ways, then whispered to Louise, "Henry got his draft notice today. He doesn't know it yet, but he has to report in a week. One week, Louise. What are we going to do?"

Louise hung her head, closed her eyes, and sighed deeply. She could still sense Fannie's presence, hovering beside her, waiting for an answer. "I don't know, Mother. Give me time to think."

She retraced her steps to the parlor, picked up her purse, and went into her bedroom. Dark earlier now, the tawny light of early evening crept through the window and across her bed. She hung her purse on one of the bedposts and sat on the side. Then she lay down with her clothes still on and draped one arm over her eyes.

She wished she could have answered her mother's question, but, in truth, what could she do? She only knew what being drafted might well do to her brother. Louise lay there in the growing dusk until she heard Bobby come in. Then she got up and changed for supper. Even if she had a solution, nothing could be done tonight. So she might as well act as if nothing was wrong. She just hoped she could eat.

When they'd finished supper, Bobby and Annie helped with the dishes while Louise got the letter from her mother and returned to her bedroom, reading it over twice. Surely the same wording went to hundreds or thousands of young men all across the country.

With everything going on to prepare for the wedding, she and her mother had stopped following the draft lottery with such tenacity as before. She wondered when Henry's number had been drawn. She wasn't sure how long it took for notifications to go out. Maybe it was best this way. Otherwise, the anxiety would be spread over a much longer period.

She looked at the sheet of paper once more, which listed the names of the draft board members along the side. She didn't know any, of course, hadn't even heard their names before. One, though, had the initials *Esq.* following his name—an attorney. She wondered if Michael Peters knew the man. It was a desperate hope, but at the moment, it was all she had.

The following morning, before she left for work, Louise made two calls. Lying awake half the night, she thought of Henry's on-again-off-again therapy. It had continued sporadically since his teenage years—the longest stretch without during the nineteen thirties—until just over a year ago.

With the first call, she reestablished Henry's bi-monthly therapy sessions, beginning the following day. The second she made to Michael Peters, who took her call immediately.

"It's not anything having to do with the law," she told him. "It's something personal."

"Louise, do you know how boring it can be to have a real estate-oriented practice—nothing all day long but title searches and endless paperwork? I make my living that way, but when you call me, as seldom as that is, I've come to expect something to break the monotony. So, tell me, how can I help you this morning?"

Louise told Peters as much as she could about her brother's emotional problems, beginning with his childhood, up through the present, including his previous and newly reinitiated therapy. She told him of the draft board letter and her conviction he wouldn't be able to function in the armed forces. Finally, she asked if he knew the attorney on the local draft board.

"As a matter of fact, I do," Peters responded. "I know most of the members of Chattanooga's Bar Association. However, I don't think I know him well enough to influence his or the board's decision regarding a potential inductee."

"If I were able to get a letter from Henry's therapist detailing his mental and emotional problems, would you be willing to pass it along to your acquaintance on the board?"

Silence for a moment, then Peters said, "Yes, I would, as one attorney to the next. I see no harm in providing information he might wish to consider before casting his vote on the suitability of the prospective inductee. I can and will do that."

"Thank you, Michael. You'll never know how much this means to me."

"As I've said before, Louise, it's always interesting and always a pleasure to hear from you."

CHAPTER 70

After supper, Louise and her mother spoke with Henry once Bobby and Annie had retired to their room. The three sat at the kitchen table, where it seemed most family business happened. Louise held the envelope upright between her hands, its edge resting on the table top, return address facing her.

Henry's eyes had not left the rectangle since he sat down. "It's my draft notice, isn't it?"

"It is," Louise said, "but don't panic yet. I have a couple of things in mind."

Henry's head fell forward, his chin reaching almost to his chest.

Louise could only imagine the eruptions of fear, anxiety, dread, and, indeed, panic coursing through his body. "It's not an automatic induction. You have to be mentally and emotionally able to serve as well as physically able. You've been in therapy off and on since you were a boy. I've spoken to Doctor Ingram and you're re-enrolled as of tomorrow afternoon. I'm going with you. Lawrence is covering for me at the store. I hope to obtain a letter from Doctor Ingram saying that, in his opinion, you are not suitable for military duty."

As Louise took a breath, Fannie added, "She's contacted Squire Peters, who has an acquaintance on the draft board. He's going to forward the therapist's letter to him."

Henry's eyes searched both their faces. "When do I have to go?"

"A week from yesterday," Louise said. "There'll be plenty of time to do what we can before you report."

The following Wednesday, Henry and Louise took the streetcar downtown to the draft board offices. Several young men stood or sat around the spacious lobby area, waiting to be called for their physical exams and other paperwork. The air inside thick with cigarette smoke, the faces of the men showed a mélange of emotions: fear, excitement, disbelief—all the things he'd felt since receiving the notice.

"Do you want me to stay?" Louise asked.

Henry looked around once more. No women. A few men glanced in their direction. *Yes, please, stay with me.* "No, you can go back to the store. I'll be all right."

"Lawrence is filling in again. I'll be at that diner across the street. When you come out, we'll have a cup of coffee and maybe a piece of apple pie with vanilla ice cream." She exited through the door and left him alone.

Henry removed his coat, but the only coatrack he saw looked overburdened. His knees wobbly, he found a place to sit, folded his coat onto his lap, and removed his hat, placing it on top of the coat.

The man sitting to his left offered Henry a cigarette. "Chesterfield? Looks like you could use one."

Henry didn't smoke, but he took one anyway, and the man lit it for him. "Thanks for the smoke," Henry said. The hand holding the cigarette trembled. It made the smoke from the glowing tip waft upward in little curls like finger waves in a woman's hair.

"I'm hoping to get the Army Air Corps," the man said. "You know they'll assign you to whatever branch they think you'll fit best, right? What do you want?"

Henry shook his head. "I don't know."

"It's pretty exciting, huh?"

Henry just nodded and tried to hold his hand steady.

He waited two hours before a man came to the office door and called his name. His heart thumped like a poorly loaded washer and his knees felt so weak he wasn't sure he could stand. The room had cleared considerably, so at least no one noticed as he walked unsteadily to the door leading to an interior office.

When he entered, he saw five men sitting behind a long, narrow table filled with stacks of papers, pads, and files.

"Name, please," said the man in the middle.

Henry stammered out, "William Henry Schmidt, III." He spoke so low he could hardly hear himself.

"You're thirty-four years old. Is that correct?"

"Yes, sir, it is."

"Too bad for you, you almost missed the cut."

Henry closed his eyes. *This is really happening. I'm being drafted.* Because his eyes were tightly shut, he missed it when one of the men—dressed in dark slacks, a white shirt, and burgundy suspenders—retrieved a letter from the file in front of him and passed it to the man next to him.

"Mister Schmidt," the man said.

Henry opened his eyes.

"I have a letter from Doctor Lester Ingram, a psychologist who says you've been in therapy for a mental and emotional disorder for a good portion of your life and that you are currently receiving therapy. Is that correct?"

"Yes, sir, that is correct."

Another man asked, "Do you have a job?"

"Yes, sir, I work for my sister at Carlyon Dry Cleaners and Laundry."

The man with the burgundy suspenders took the sheet of paper and passed it along to the other men. When they'd all had a chance to see it, the man in the middle spoke. "Mr. Schmidt, do you wish to be excused from military service?"

Henry let out his breath. "Yes, sir, I do."

The five men spoke to each other in hushed tones for a minute, then the man who seemed in charge said, "Very well. You will be classified as 4-F, Mr. Schmidt, and excused from service at this time. You may go."

Henry made eye contact with the men. Their faces showed nothing—not that it mattered to Henry—except for the man in suspenders, who smiled faintly in Henry's direction.

"Thank you very much." Henry vacated the office as fast as he possibly could. Ten minutes later, he sat across from Louise in the diner. She ate apple pie with a scoop of vanilla ice cream on top. He sat with his head down staring at a cup of rapidly cooling coffee.

"Are you sure you don't want pie?" Louise asked. All the previous signs of tension had disappeared from her face.

He wished he could feel the same way, but he knew the men at the draft board pitied him. That knowledge proved almost as hard to bear as being afraid to fight and die. With Louise's help, he'd gotten what he wanted. But he'd lost his dignity in that room, along with whatever shred of respect he'd previously possessed.

Henry gave his sister a tired smile. "I'm sorry, Louise. I guess I just don't feel much like celebrating."

See-Boy spent the better part of an hour walking around inside the vacant building, making notes and drawings on a clipboard. He'd be able to use a few pieces of the old equipment, but his thoughts on remodeling and decorating extended well beyond previous projects. The place had been in disuse for several years, a victim of Prohibition that never got back on its feet.

But it would return to life in fine fashion now, when he got through with it. He stood at one of the windows and looked out. It even had a parking lot, something of a problem at The Hanger, which had only street parking.

The old sign on the pole out front would have to go, of course. The Cotton Patch had been one of Will Schmidt's hangouts. See-Boy felt a bit of justice when he signed the papers buying the old bar. Too bad the old man had passed. He would have liked seeing Will's face when he learned his watering hole had been purchased by a colored man. And not just any colored man but the one who'd once dragged Will out of his own house and into his yard while the man screamed, "Let go of me, nigger!"

He turned around and leaned against the wall, surveying the interior. The bandstand would be bigger, and the dance floor twice the size of that in the converted meat market. He also toyed with the idea of having a short order kitchen installed. That way, he could get the lunch trade, too.

He hoped to have the place ready before Christmas or at least by New Year's Eve. *Two, two and a half months should do the trick.* He hummed a little tune as he continued planning. Life looked pretty good.

The atmosphere during supper stayed light and happy. Louise felt such relief that Henry wouldn't be drafted, and Fannie appeared ebullient. They'd decided not to mention the draft board proceedings to Bobby and Annie. They weren't aware of the draft notice, and Louise felt the less said about Henry's status, the better.

Bobby and Annie seemed particularly upbeat themselves. Louise noted the sly grins and sideways looks pass between them. After the meal, as Fannie and Henry cleared and washed dishes, Annie grasped Louise's hand, touched a finger to her lips, and whispered, "Come with us."

In their bedroom, Annie led Louise to the bed and sat down beside her while Bobby stood nearby.

"We wanted to tell you first," Annie said, her eyes dancing with merriment. "I'm about three months pregnant. We're going to have a baby."

Louise couldn't stop the flood of tears. She blinked up at her son, who nodded in confirmation, then threw her arms around Annie. Bobby knelt and put his arms around the two of them.

"I'm so happy," Louise said over and over as she tried unsuccessfully to wipe the moisture from her eyes and cheeks. *Until just now, I didn't know anything could make me this happy.*

"Wait till we tell Daddy," Bobby said. "I'll bet he cries, too."

CHAPTER 71

Annie began to show by early December. She and Louise had gone shopping for maternity wear, and Louise bought almost everything Annie tried on.

"Louise, I really don't need this much. I'll probably only work another three months."

"You never can tell," her mother-in-law said. "It's better to have more than you need than too little."

As Bobby had guessed back in October, Murray seemed as preoccupied with the baby as anyone else in the family, maybe more so. Louise wondered if having a grandchild might finally be the one thing that would encourage her husband to find a job close to home.

Murray had suggested to Louise they consider enclosing the back porch of the house and making it a nursery, and he'd been hinting—but only to her—that Henry's seldom-used radio repair shop would make an excellent playhouse.

"All in good time, Murray," she'd said. "The baby can stay in the room with Bobby and Annie for a while before we have to do major renovations."

Now, on a quiet Sunday after finishing lunch, Louise sat with Murray and her mother in the parlor. After Fannie learned of the pregnancy, she'd taken up knitting and spent most of her time making items for the baby. Boy or girl didn't seem to matter. She had quite a bit of free time, and so knitted duplicates in both pink and blue. And since he or she would be a spring baby, she'd also added pale greens and yellows so as to be commensurate with the season.

As usual, Murray worked on the crossword puzzle while Louise sifted through the newspaper advertisements for more maternity wear.

Henry, who'd been working in the repair shop since finishing lunch, suddenly burst into the parlor. "Turn on the radio! The Japs are bombing Pearl Harbor."

Murray tossed aside his puzzle and snapped the dial on the walnut-finished Truetone floor-model in the corner. They listened intently as the reporter announced at least two waves of Japanese aircraft had bombed and strafed the United States naval base in Hawaii.

Bobby and Annie, out for a walk after lunch, hurried into the house shortly after three, wide-eyed and out of breath.

"Did you hear—?" Bobby stopped short and guided Annie to the sofa beside Fannie.

Fannie reached out and took Annie's hand. "We've been listening. It's awful, just awful."

For the next seven hours, while news accounts of the tragic, unexpected attack unfolded, the whole family sat silently except for an occasional gasp or sob. Annie sat on the sofa with Fannie, Bobby beside her on the floor. Each held one of Annie's hands. Murray, in one of the two upholstered chairs, smoked cigarette after cigarette. Louise would have followed suit, except Henry, who sat cross-legged beside her chair, held her hand so tightly it throbbed.

Darkness had already fallen when, one-by-one, they left the parlor. Fannie offered to cook supper, but no one had any appetite.

Lying beside Murray in their bed, Louise said, "I suppose we'll surely go to war now." She could just see the bottom half of the moon through her bedroom window. It hung suspended in the sky, pale as bone, oblivious to all that transpired below.

Murray turned to look at her. "Yes, I feel sure we will."

"What will happen to us, do you think?"

"To you and me," he said, "probably nothing. Bobby will be drafted, unless he decides to enlist. Then the hard part begins—the waiting."

"Waiting for what?"

"For whatever happens, or doesn't happen, I guess. You live every day waiting for something to happen, but you pray every night nothing does."

"Yes, I remember that from when you went overseas."

Murray rose on one elbow and caressed Louise's cheek. "All the while we were listening to the radio, I couldn't help thinking about Henry being excused from military service. I wondered if—hearing what we heard today—he might feel guilty about not serving. Either that or I'm projecting what I would feel in his place. I wonder how he lives with that, or if he feels it at all. Especially if Bobby is drafted or enlists."

"Henry is sick," Louise said. "That's why they have the examination and testing process before they decide on service ability."

"I know you believe that," Murray said. "Why else would you have done what you did to help him get out of it?"

Later, as Murray snored softly next to her, Louise thought about the differences between Henry and Bobby. She remembered the conversation she and Murray had years ago about how children should be raised—or more accurately—how they should be viewed and treated by their parents. Murray had found an old Chinese proverb that said children were not a vase to be filled, but a fire to be kindled.

She thought she and Murray had done that with Bobby, as best they could. They had facilitated his education, his manners, his creative efforts, and tried to provide whatever he needed to express himself and grow in his abilities.

Henry, on the other hand, had experienced none of that. Fannie believed Henry had been conceived when her father, drunk, forced himself on her mother. Convinced Henry turned out frail and disturbed because of that, Fannie also never forgot the terrible pain she'd experienced with Henry's birth, believing that stemmed from the same encounter.

Louise wasn't convinced, but she imagined stranger things had happened. She thought more than likely Henry had become an emotional cripple due to more reasonable causes. Spurned and ridiculed by his father, threatened with death before he'd learned to put whole sentences together, Henry's mental and emotional problems were the tragic byproduct of a childhood filled with fear and anxiety. The same powerlessness he'd felt as a toddler and young boy had gnawed its way into Henry's psyche, rendering him unable to deal with virtually all life's complexities. Though necessary, the therapy helped only so much. She knew some things could never change—not when it came to Henry.

News accounts on Monday revealed that the Japanese had also attacked the United States-held islands of Guam, the Philippines, and Wake Island. Later that day, the United States declared war on Japan and Germany.

CHAPTER 72

Bobby and Harry enlisted in the Army Air Corps that week. Lines grew long at the recruiting stations as thousands of young men across the country rallied to the nation's defense. Bobby and Harry were sent for training at the Air Corps base near Dyersburg, Tennessee. The whole family saw them off at the Southern Railway Terminal, along with Harry's parents and younger brother.

Louise and Annie cried, and Murray blinked back tears as he hugged his son.

Bobby kissed Annie's eyes, forehead, and lips, and placed his hand on her growing belly.

Louise said, "Promise me you'll be careful."

Her son grinned as he swung up onto the railcar steps. "Don't worry, Momma. I'll fly low and slow." Then the crowd of newly minted recruits swallowed him onto the train. He and many others waved and threw kisses as the engine engaged, the car couplers clanked, and the wheels began to turn.

Louise wondered if and when she'd see him again. She knew Annie and the rest wondered the same. But certain things were just too true to ever say aloud.

In the weeks and months that followed, Louise and the others did as well as they could. Worries of Bobby transferred to fretting over Annie and the baby, and the grocery and cleaners took much of Louise's and Henry's time.

Annie offered to help, but Louise would have none of it. "I won't have you breathing those awful dry cleaning fumes while you're carrying that baby."

See-Boy held a grand opening for his new club two days before Christmas, inviting Louise and Fannie to come celebrate with him like they'd done a few days after he'd "repurposed" his maintenance shed years ago. They declined, and See-Boy told them to extend the invitation to Henry to come anytime.

Henry became interested in the movies and all the fanfare Hollywood had to offer, although he never went to see movies they made about the war and did his best to avoid arriving at the theater in time to view the newsreels. He did write and ask for numerous autographs and pictures from his favorite stars, and sometimes received them.

In February, Louise saw an article in the *Times'* local section regarding the indictment of Parkinson Construction Company owner, Ray Parkinson, who had been accused of accepting kickbacks from subcontracting agencies involved with several strip shopping centers planned and underway within the city. The article also mentioned *questionable relationships* between Parkinson, planning commission chairman, Arlen Brooks, and Houseman Realty Company.

"Mother," Louise said. "Come take a look at this."

Fannie read the article, looked up at Louise, and grinned such a slinky, feline smile Louise half-expected canary feathers to pop out of her mouth. "What is it they say? All that goes around comes around."

Louise grinned, too. *It's not really revenge,* she thought. *I had nothing to do with the investigation or indictment. So call it justice. But you know what? Either way it feels so, so sweet.*

Annie's baby, a little boy they named Charlie, arrived on a Friday in late March of 1942. So glad Murray could be there for the birth, Louise watched as he held the baby—this time he really did cry. Bobby, still in flight training in Dyersburg, got leave to come home for three days. While Louise and Murray stood in the doorway of Bobby and Annie's bedroom, Bobby, resplendent in his uniform, looked down into Charlie's crib and sang, "Danny Boy."

"Why'd you pick that song?" Annie asked.

"I only know the words to two songs, 'Danny Boy' and 'Sentimental Journey.' I just figured it fit better."

Louise invited See-Boy, Pearl, Lawrence, and Frankie to come see the new baby. They showed up soon after Bobby on that beautiful Sunday afternoon. See-Boy had a new Cadillac LaSalle that shined like the sun as he pulled next to the curb.

They all made on over the baby, especially Pearl. See-Boy had brought along a Kodak camera, and he and Frankie had their photograph made with Bobby in his uniform. Then another that Henry took of everyone together.

Louise wanted to cry again when she thought about it. For the first time she could remember, she had her family—all her family—together again. But she managed not to spoil the festivities, instead inviting everyone into the kitchen for lemon pound cake and iced tea.

Henry took See-Boy up on his offer to stop by the new club, and was so impressed he started frequenting the place on weekends when the band played. They had a new drummer, of course, and had hired a new female singer. She looked nothing like Lawanda, and he found that a relief.

Sometimes, Abernathy asked Henry to come up onstage and sit in with them for old times' sake. When he did, the number always contained a drum solo, which Henry—despite his lack of practice—carried out to near perfection.

Many patrons remembered Henry from days gone by. Others, under See-Boy's tutelage, grew to accept him and enjoy the times he played.

"I'll tell you what, See-Boy," said one the club's long-time customers. "That white boy can play every bit as good as that Gene Krupa fellow. I do believe he must have been born with drumsticks in his hands. The way he pounds them drums, it's like he's fightin' off the devil himself."

See-Boy reached behind the bar for a bottle and poured the man a whiskey. "He's good, all right. For sure, he's the best to ever play my club."

The man polished off the whiskey, licked his lips, and set his glass back on the bar. "It's kind of peculiar, though, you know? That boy never seems to smile."

See-Boy nodded. Like he didn't know anything more than what he'd just heard. Of course, he did. Henry was family, after all.